This was going to be a lot harder than he thought.

Why did she have to have eyes that penetrated the very depths of his soul, connecting with that spot he had purposely kept shut off for years?

He broke eye contact. He didn't want her or anyone else invading that private place. Nor did he want her coming home with him.

Think, Haydon! Maybe he could buy her a one-way ticket home and set her up here in a Prosperity Mountain hotel until the next stagecoach.

He scanned the mining town. Several men stood in front of the saloon with their arms crossed and their legs spread, gawking at Miss Devonwood as if they hadn't eaten in days and she were a fresh piece of meat.

His brother should be dealing with this. But with Jess injured, it was up to Haydon to do what he had to do to keep this woman safe.

No gentleman would do anything less. And if Haydon was anything, he prided himself in being a gentleman.

Most of the tim

DEBRA ULLRICK

is an award-winning author who is happily married to her husband of thirty-six years. For more than twenty-five years, she and her husband and their only daughter lived and worked on cattle ranches in the Colorado Mountains. The last ranch Debra lived on, a famous movie star and her screenwriter husband purchased property there. She now lives in the flatlands where she's dealing with cultural whiplash. Debra loves animals, classic cars, mud-bog racing and monster trucks. When she's not writing, she's reading, drawing Western art, feeding wild birds, watching Jane Austen movies, *COPS*, or *Castle*.

Debra loves hearing from her readers. You can contact her through her website at www.DebraUllrick.com.

The Unexpected Bride

DEBRA ULLRICK

Love Inspired

Recycling programs for this product may not exist in your area.

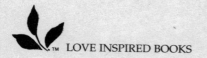

TM LOVE INSPIRED BOOKS

ISBN-13: 978-0-373-82870-8

THE UNEXPECTED BRIDE

Copyright © 2011 by Debra Ullrick

www.LoveInspiredBooks.com

Printed in U.S.A.

Blessed is the man who trusts in the Lord,
and whose hope is the Lord.
—*Jeremiah* 17:7

A ginormous thanks to my dear friends,
Staci Stallings, Dennis Bates, Michelle Sutton,
Rose McCauley and Jeanie Smith Cash.
Your endless hours and invaluable input has
taught me so much and helped make this book
so much better. To my wonderful agent
Tamela Hancock Murray and my fabulous editor
Emily Rodmell, thank you for believing in me.
To the friendly people in Moscow, Idaho,
who helped with my research, thank you so much.

And a humungous thanks to my husband, Rick.
Thank you for always being there for me.
You truly are my hero, and I love you very much.

Last, but definitely not least, to my Lord and Savior
Jesus, thank you. You rock!

Chapter One

Paradise Haven, Idaho Territory
1874

If Rainelle Devonwood's mother knew what she was about to do, she would roll over in her grave.

Grave.

That one word ripped at Rainee's heart, but she refused to cry in the presence of the strangers surrounding her. She lowered her head and pressed her fingers over her eyelids in hopes of holding back the flood of tears.

Oh, Mother, you would be astonished to know what I have done. But even you would understand why I did it. If only you and Father were still alive. Then I would still be at home, living without pain and suffering. But, Mother. I had to leave. I just had to.

In the small confines of the dusty stagecoach, only one thing gave Rainee a measure of peace about her drastic decision—her betrothed had assured her he loved the Lord. Otherwise she would have never gone through with her plans to marry a complete stranger.

The uncertainty of what was about to take place, and

the constant cigar smoke from the gentleman sitting across from her, caused her stomach to become unwell. Rainee pressed her hand over her mouth and leaned her head out the window, silently praying the Lord would help her stomach's contents to settle and help to divert her attention elsewhere.

Dust crowded into her nose. *That is not quite what I had in mind, Lord.* She covered her mouth and sneezed. Her eyes started watering from all the dirt particles, but with her stomach still threatening to purge itself, she decided to deal with the discomfort a few moments longer. She blinked away the particles of debris from her eyes as she studied her surroundings.

Rolling green meadows disappeared into the forest at the base of the mountains. Blue skies stretched before her. Several yards away, a rabbit leapt high in the air and landed in the tall bunchgrass. It did the same thing three times. And each time Rainee giggled at its silly antics.

When her stomach stopped churning, she settled back into her seat.

The stagecoach hit a rut, yanking her body sideways and slamming her shoulder into the lady next to her. "I am so sorry, ma'am."

Sleepy eyes glanced at Rainee before sliding shut. How could the woman slumber through so much jostling? Rainee envied her.

Days and days of being jostled about, first on the train when she left Little Rock, Arkansas, and now even more so on the stagecoach heading to the Idaho Territory, were taking its toll on her overtaxed body. Rainee rolled her head from side to side, pressed her palm against her aching side, and shifted in the seat for the twentieth time in the past few minutes.

Horses' pounding hooves, jingling tack and squeaking leather were the only sounds she had heard for miles upon miles until Daniel, the stagecoach assistant, leaned his blond head near the window. "Only a few more minutes, folks, before we arrive at our destination."

A destination Rainee wanted to avoid but knew she could not because her very life and sanity depended on it.

Within minutes, she would soon meet her betrothed.

Her betrothed.

She still could not believe she was about to be married.

To a complete stranger.

But then again, if Haydon Bowen turned out to be even half as nice as his letters had made him sound, with the help of God's grace and a passel of mercy, her life might not end up so dreadful after all. Anything had to be better than her current situation.

Or was it?

A horrid thought fluttered through her mind. What if the man she was about to wed was not the gentleman he had portrayed himself to be?

Merciful heavens, what had she done?

You ordered what?

Haydon Bowen's own words rang through his brain like the continual clang of a church bell. How could Jesse, his own brother, do this to him, knowing he never wanted to marry again? Knowing marriage to his deceased wife had been a disaster. The hour-and-a-half ride from his family's ranch in Paradise Haven to the stagecoach stop in Prosperity Mountain had done little to abate his frustration. Anger over Jesse's latest outlandish scheme clung to him like trail dirt on a sweaty body.

After reining his draft horses to a stop, Haydon pressed his booted foot on the wagon brake. He sat stone still, dreading the task before him, wishing he could forget this whole thing and hightail it back to the ranch. But wishing wasn't going to change a thing. He raised his hat and wiped the sweat off his forehead with his shirt sleeve.

Knowing he couldn't put off the unpleasant mission any longer, he hopped down from the buckboard. As he went to wrap the reins around the brake handle he heard the stern sound of a woman's voice coming from the direction of the stagecoach platform. "Unhand me this instant."

"Aw, I jist wanna little bitty kiss." The man's barely intelligible words slurred together.

Haydon tied off the reins and headed around the corner of the depot to see what was going on. He rounded it just in time to see a petite lady in a frilly lavender dress kick some shoddy-looking man in the shin with the toe of her laced-up boot. It took Haydon so by surprise that he had to stifle a laugh.

"Ouch! Why you little—" Filthy words poured from the scruffy man's mouth. He yanked the woman close to his sweaty, grime-stained body, his face a mere inch from hers.

The woman managed to jerk back and swing her un-opened parasol in a wide arc, striking the man's head. That only served to anger him more, and he yanked her close again.

He'd seen enough. Haydon leapt up the wooden step, took five steps to cross it, grabbed the man by the back of his shirt and shoved him away. "You heard the lady. Unhand her. Now!"

The man landed in a crumpled heap, but quicker than the snap of a whip, he darted back and rammed his head into Haydon's gut. All air fled from his lungs. He doubled over and struggled to pull in a breath. His hat slid from his head and onto the ground.

The man punched Haydon's face, causing him to stumble backward. Sharp pain pulled through his nose, and his eyes watered.

His attacker lunged toward him, but Haydon sidestepped him.

The man slammed against the wooden planks facefirst.

Haydon jumped on him, yanked his arms behind his back, and pressed his knee between the man's shoulders.

Squirming, the man tried to break free, but Haydon held him in a tight grip.

"Ben! Pack your things and get out of town now!"

Haydon's gaze jumped up to a tall man with a shiny badge splayed against a black leather vest.

"I warned you if you caused any more trouble, I'd run you out of town. I mean to keep my promise. Now get out of here and don't ever show your face around here again."

Haydon stood and hauled the man the sheriff called Ben to his feet. When he released him, the only way to describe what he saw in his beady eyes was evil intent. It tried to curl its way around Haydon, but he shook it off like he would a snake crawling on his hand.

"This won't be the last you'll hear from me," Ben hissed. He scooped up his sweat-stained hat and slammed it on his greasy head. "You an' yore lady friend'll be sorry you ever messed with me!"

"That's enough!" The sheriff aimed his pistol at Ben's heart and cocked it. "Whether you go peacefully or draped over a saddle makes no difference to me. The choice is yours." Wrinkles gathered around the lawman's narrowed eyes, and his burly mustache buried his lips.

Haydon swung his gaze between the sheriff and Ben, not at all sure that he and the lady weren't about to witness a deadly showdown at point-blank range.

"I'm goin', I'm goin'," Ben spat as he lifted his hands in the air.

The lawman gave a quick jerk of his head and gun, motioning Ben forward. The two of them headed down the boardwalk. Their boots clunked against the wooden planks, and neither of them looked back.

Haydon relaxed his shoulders for a full two seconds, until he remembered the lady. He let out a quick breath and turned toward her. Seeing her stooped over, he snatched up his hat and hurried over to her. "Are you all right, Miss?"

Like a well-trained woman of society, she rose gracefully and faced him. Having grown up with the socially elite, he recognized one when he saw one. And she was definitely one.

"Yes, sir, I am." Her lavender plumed hat tilted back, and she looked up at him. "Thank you for rescuing me."

Haydon's pulse throbbed in his ears and his breath hitched. Staring up at him were the most beautiful brown eyes he had ever seen, soft as a doe's hide. The color reminded Haydon of a whitetail fawn, complete with white specks. Thick but not overly long lashes spread across her eyelids. And that Southern accent. It skipped across his heart before drilling right down into him.

"Merciful heavens. Your nose is bleeding." She opened the little beaded bag hanging from her wrist, pulled out a lace hanky and raised it toward his nose.

He yanked his head back. "Don't soil your hanky." He reached into his inside vest pocket and removed his handkerchief, then pressed it against his nostrils, ignoring the pain the gesture produced. Confident he'd gotten all the blood, he folded his handkerchief and shoved it back into his vest.

"I am so sorry, sir, you were injured on account of me."

"Don't worry about it. I'll be fine."

She studied him for a moment, and he squirmed under her scrutiny. "Would you happen to be Mr. Bowen?" Her drawn out words, mixed with a tremor, snapped Haydon back to reality. No matter how beautiful she was, she was still a woman. The last time he had fallen for a beautiful woman, not only had he ruined her life, but also his.

He slammed his hat onto his head and stepped back. "Yes, ma'am. I'm Haydon Bowen."

She daintily clasped her skirt and curtsied. "It is a pleasure to meet you, sir. I am Rainelle Victoria Devonwood. But please call me Rainee."

He knew his eyes had to be popping out of their sockets, but he couldn't help himself. *This* little beauty placed an advertisement for a husband? Someone who looked like her and bled confidence? His eyes narrowed. What was wrong with her that no one had claimed her for his own? *She's a woman, Haydon. That's reason enough.*

Slanting her pretty little head, she blinked several times before her eyes snapped onto his. Innocence clothed her face, making her even more of a threat.

This was going to be a lot harder than he thought. Why did she have to have eyes that penetrated the very depths of his soul, connecting with that spot he had purposely kept shut off for years?

He broke eye contact with her. He didn't want her or anyone else invading that private place. Nor did he want her coming home with him. *Think, Haydon, think fast.* Maybe he could buy her a one-way ticket home and set her up in a hotel here in Prosperity Mountain until the next stagecoach came around.

He scanned the mining town. Several men stood in front of the saloon with their arms crossed and their legs spread, gawking at Miss Devonwood as if they hadn't eaten in days and she was a fresh piece of meat. Prosperity Mountain was definitely no place to leave a lady without an escort. Women were scarce around these parts, and too many men were less than honorable. From what he had experienced, the place overflowed with raucous silver miners and thieves who wouldn't hesitate to steal a person's silver or something even more valuable—a woman's virtue.

With a sideways glance, he battled with what to do. Frustration toward Jesse for putting him in this mess seeped through his mind again like a deadly poison. His brother should be dealing with this. Not him. But that wasn't going to happen. The sight of Jess unconscious on the floor of the barn slashed through Haydon, and he detested Jess all the more for making him so angry he had lost his composure, and flanked his horse. Haydon knew better than to touch a horse's flank; spurring that tender spot between a horse's ribs and hips was bad enough, and yet he had not only kicked it without meaning to, he had also hit it hard enough that it caused Rebel to rear and knock Jesse unconscious. Haydon still felt badly about that.

With Jess injured, it was now up to Haydon to do what he had to do to keep this woman safe. No gentleman would do anything less. And if Haydon was anything, he prided himself on being a gentleman. Most of the time anyway.

His chest heaved at the idea of being in such close proximity to the flaxen-haired beauty on the long ride back to the ranch. It was the last place he wanted to be. But he would not leave her here, not even to save himself the trouble.

Rainee locked her knees to keep them from giving out. What kind of ruffians filled this desolate land anyway? Why, if Mr. Bowen had not come along when he had, she did not know what might have happened to her. Just thinking about it made her shudder.

As he stared forward, Rainee took the opportunity to study him. Her gaze landed on his arms.

Arms that had easily plucked away her attacker.

Mountainous arms that drew her attention and admiration.

Rainee knew she should look away, knowing if her mother were here, she would reprimand her for her blatant impropriety. But she found she could not help herself. Nor did she want to. The bulges beneath his pale blue shirtsleeves captivated her attention as did the width of his broad shoulders and chest.

Her eyes moved to his firm jaw, and she watched in fascination as the muscle in his jaw worked back and forth. Something about the strength of it set her heart all aflutter.

"Do you need anything before we go, Miss Devonwood?"

She whipped her gaze up to his eyes. Warmth rushed to her cheeks. From the icy tone of his voice, he must have seen her gawking at him.

Perhaps he was agitated because of her blunder in telling him to call her by her Christian name. That was far too forward of her, even if this man was to be her husband. Would she ever learn?

How she despised all those ridiculous rules of etiquette and propriety. Aristocratic rules her British father insisted they follow and her Southern mother had taken pride in enforcing. But, she refused to distress herself further about her social blunder because there was nothing she could do about it now anyway.

"It's a good hour and a half before we get to Paradise Haven. Would you like to get something to eat before we head out?"

Rainee loved the deep sound of his voice. Even though his mannerisms at present were somewhat aloof, some of her doubts about coming here eased. After all, Mr. Bowen had rescued her from that vile man with the overpowering stench and yellow teeth. Not to mention his looks were far superior to those of any man she had ever encountered. Granted, she knew from experience looks could be deceiving, but still, his sapphire eyes and blond hair were quite pleasing to her eyes. In fact, the color reminded her of her father's eyes. Immediately Rainee regretted the comparison. Her heart yearned for her father—to be held in his arms again and to feel the security his protection and love provided.

The back of her eyes stung, but she plucked up her courage, knowing crying would solve nothing.

She forced herself to focus on the gentleman in front of her. "Thank you, but no. I am fine, sir." Even if she had need of anything, it would be far too humiliating to inform him she was penniless because some scoundrel at the last stagecoach stop had stolen her money. Good thing she had already purchased her ticket for the last trek of her journey. Otherwise she shuddered to think what might have become of her.

For the millionth time, Rainee wished she had secured her funds underneath her skirt. Her personal maid and dear friend Jenetta had advised her to do so, but once again Rainee's stubbornness had overruled any such logic.

Many times her father had warned her that her stubbornness would get her into trouble one day. He feared he would not be able to secure a husband for her because of her flawed temperament. Inwardly Rainee sighed. So far, Father was right. Well, that was not entirely accurate. Many a man had pursued her. Not because of any burst of feeling toward her but because of her father's money. Except one man. And she would rather go live with savage Indians than marry him.

Mr. Bowen cleared his throat. She looked up at him.

"That your trunk?"

"Yes." Rainee glanced at the medium-size chest containing everything she owned. With a weighty sigh, she decided to not think about what and whom she had been forced to leave behind. It was all too vexing. And so was this man's aloofness toward her. Gone was the warmness his letters contained. Perhaps his journey had tired him. That she understood. Tiredness had seeped into her bones until every part of her ached with fatigue.

She watched him lift the trunk as if it weighed no more than one of the plumes on her hat. He stepped off the platform and headed around the corner of the stage-coach stop. Rainee followed him, careful to keep her eyes anywhere but on his retreating form. One glimpse of his leg muscles had been enough to make her chastise herself for acting like a wanton woman instead of the lady she had been brought up to be.

Once her belongings were secured on the wagon, he headed to the front of the buckboard where she stood, and he extended his hand.

Rainee glanced at his large palm, admiring the strength of it, then looked up at him. Impatience covered his face. She quickly placed her satchel and parasol on the wagon seat, then settled her hand in his, allowing him to help her onto the wagon. She arranged the bustle of her dress and sat, then snatched her satchel and parasol off of the seat and placed them in her lap. "Thank you, sir."

He responded with a curt nod.

Turning her head away from him, she suppressed the urge to roll her eyes and whistle away the awkwardness. She knew their meeting would be uncomfortable, but she had not anticipated it being quite this bad. Then again, what did she expect? That the moment he laid eyes on her, he would declare his undying love and sweep her off her feet, and they would live happily ever after?

Hah. In a pig's eye. She shuttered at the expression. It must be the length of the trip or the hot sun or the man readying the horses and the wagon—something—because every thought she had was taking her places she did not want to go.

Besides, those kinds of things only happened in the dime novels she and her best friend used to sneak into her room and read. Until the day her mother had discovered them. After a long lecture, she forced Rainee to toss them into the fire. It broke her heart watching the edges curl into black ashes. They were her only reprieve from the stuffy social world she lived in, a world overrun with rules of proper etiquette, rules she had a hard time obeying because they all seemed so meaningless and empty.

The wagon seat dipped, jolting Rainee's mind from past shadows. She looped the handle of her satchel over her wrist and opened her parasol, careful to keep it out of Mr. Bowen's way. Careful to keep herself out of his way as well.

His arm brushed against hers, and his broad shoulders took up a goodly portion of the now cramped seat.

Leather, trail dust, and a scent that reminded her of her father after he had shaved drifted up her nostrils. More reminders of home. A home that no longer existed.

Once again, she could not believe she was about to marry a complete stranger. One *she* had placed an advertisement for. That act alone was scandalous. Claws of dread pierced her insides as she realized once again what she had done. The need for air threatened to swallow her up, but she sat up straighter and fought for every breath. No fainting spell would overtake her. Not this time. Though they had been a problem in the past, she vowed as of this moment she would fight them with all her might.

Mr. Bowen snapped the reins. The wagon lurched forward and Rainee clutched the side of the seat to keep from jostling into him, but her shoulder collided with his anyway, and their eyes connected and held for the briefest of moments.

Long after he turned away, however, the memory of his eyes the color of sparkling sapphires stayed with her. Eyes that were handsome but held no warmth. Only a sort of detachment and something else she could not identify. This was going to be a very long ride indeed.

Haydon couldn't wait to deliver the woman to his brother. This well-bred, beautiful woman sitting next to him was the kind he now avoided like poison ivy because they were shallow and cared about nothing but fancy balls and frippery. Appearance and financial status were everything to them. And he'd had his fill of that type of woman.

"Mr. Bowen."

He wanted to ignore her but his conscience and upbringing wouldn't allow him to be rude. "Yes?" Haydon gave her a quick glance.

"You said in one of your letters you lived in Paradise Haven with your family."

His body tensed. He didn't write those letters, so he had no idea of their contents. No knowledge about what her response had been. What her advertisement was about. Haydon shifted his weight and ran his thumbs over the leather reins.

He looked toward the mountain dotted with several clapboard buildings and mining shafts as he struggled with what to say or do, wishing he could flee into one of those mines and hide out until this whole mess was over and done with.

"Would you mind telling me about them?" Her soft voice was a tad shaky, but her asking spoke of a confidence he couldn't deny.

He let out a breath of relief. At least that he could answer. "My brother Jesse is twenty." He glanced at her, then back at the dirt road. "His wife's name is Hannah. They're expecting their first child in a few months. They have their own place on the ranch. My brother Michael is sixteen. My sister Leah is thirteen and Abby is five. They live in the big house with my mother."

"What about you? Where do you live?" Words poured from her mouth like thick honey. Sweetness and innocence surrounded this woman. This woman he wanted to get away from as quickly as possible, he reminded himself. Even though she seemed harmless enough, he knew just how deceiving appearances could be. His former wife Melanie had taught him that. The dread of going through something like that again twisted his gut tighter than a three-stranded rope.

"I have my own place on the ranch." Concerned she would start asking him more questions, he decided to ask her about her home life instead. He only prayed it wasn't something she had already shared in the letters or her advertisement because then he would have to inform her that he wasn't the one who had sent for her. And he wasn't going to do that. That was Jesse's job. "What part of the South are you from?" he asked, keeping his eyes forward.

Talons of fear scraped up and down Rainee's body. How did he know she was from the South? She had not told him that in her letters or her advertisement. She had even gone so far as to have one of her friends post her letters and advertisement in Chicago.

What should she tell him? Not one to tell falsehoods, she would have to choose her words carefully. She gathered her courage and forced herself to look at him.

"I'm sorry. Perhaps you aren't from the South. I just assumed with your accent that you were. But then again—" he rubbed his chin "—your mannerisms remind me of some of our neighbors back East. They were British."

Rainee's muscles relaxed.

"My Father was raised in England, and my mother was raised in the South." Before he could ask her any further questions, she plucked up her courage to say what she had wanted to say back at Prosperity Mountain. "Mr. Bowen, I know you must think it quite strange for a woman to post an advertisement in search of a husband. But please believe me when I say I had no other choice."

Her brother had seen to that.

Chapter Two

"Mr. Bowen? I am sorry to disturb you, but could I trouble you to stop? I am in need of a break."

He looked at her flushed face and the damp tendrils of hair clinging to her cheeks. "I'm sorry. I wasn't thinking straight. I should have let you rest a while before we left Prosperity." Remorse for his ungentleman-like manner and his inconsideration doused him with shame.

With her head tilted off to the side, questioning eyes peered out from under the brim of her hat. Sensing it took a lot for her to ask, he wanted to put her at ease. "I could use a break myself. Whoa, Lulu. Whoa, Sally." He pulled on the horses' reins. The tack jingled and the wagon creaked as it came to a stop.

He hopped down and set the brake, then wrapped the reins around it.

The woman beside him rose and closed her parasol, leaving it and her handbag on the seat before moving toward him.

He reached up toward her. When she placed her hands on his shoulders and he sprawled his hands around her small waist, feelings long buried deep inside him poked through the protective wall he'd built around his heart.

He hurried to set her down and once he knew she was stable on her feet, he extradited himself from her as fast as possible.

"Thank you." Her gaze trailed toward a small creek. "Please excuse me."

As much as his gut wanted him to, he couldn't leave her to traverse the rocky ground by herself. Thin rock and rough terrain wouldn't bode well with her fancy dress. Haydon retrieved two canteens from the back of the wagon. "Allow me to help you." Even though he didn't want to touch her again, he slung aside the turbulent feelings raging inside him and clutched her elbow to steady her.

When they reached level ground, ground devoid of rock, he released her elbow. The cluster of pine trees brought a welcoming reprieve from the hot sun.

He filled their canteens with river water and handed her one. She twisted the lid and tilted it up, taking a long drink. His gaze landed on her sleek, graceful neck. She leaned over and refilled her canteen, then dipped her hanky into the tepid water and daintily blotted her face and neck.

What a vision she was. A lady of poise and grace. The epitome of femininity.

Quicker than a flash, an image of Melanie invaded his mind, bringing with it all the bad memories. Memories he'd rather forget.

That Jess, he groaned inwardly. *It's all his fault I'm even thinking about Melanie again. Well, buddy boy, nothing will induce me to get involved with a woman again. Nothing.*

The sooner he got this task over with the better.

When he got back to the ranch, he'd hand her over to Jesse to deal with.

To distract himself, he unscrewed the lid on his canteen and pulled in a long drink.

Minutes later, after they'd finished taking their break, he steadied her again until they reached the wagon.

She pointed toward the hillside and asked, "Would you mind if I pick some of those red and yellow flowers to take to your mother?"

Did she have to be so sweet on top of being beautiful? That combination was the worst kind to lure a man in. But he couldn't turn her down. His mother loved flowers and thoughtful gestures like that.

"Sure." He took her canteen and put both of them back into the wagon.

Making sure she didn't slip on the small pile of thin rocks, he held her hand until she stepped over them.

She leaned over and broke the long stem off at the bottom and studied the bloom before she placed the flower under her nose and smiled. "These are quite lovely. What are they?"

"Red columbines. My mother's favorite."

She darted her gaze up at him and her face beamed, even though he had seen her fatigue just moments before.

She started gathering more and stopped only to dab the sweat off her forehead.

Haydon couldn't bear to watch her suffer, so he jumped in and helped her. When they had a nice bouquet, they headed back to the wagon.

He grabbed his canteen and opened it, then retrieved his handkerchief from his pocket and saturated it with water. "Hand me the flowers."

She gave them to him, and he wrapped the soaked

cloth around the stems. "That will help keep them until we get to the ranch."

"Thank you." Her smile lit up her face. She really was sweet.

Not liking that train of thought, he quickly helped her into the wagon, climbed up himself and down the road they went. A road that now seemed longer than it ever had been before. Having her sitting next to him had him squirming like a worm. The sooner he got them to the ranch, the better.

Rainee glanced at the flowers in her lap. It was very thoughtful of him to help her gather them and then help preserve them until she could give them to his mother. Her own mother never tired of getting fresh bouquets of flowers, and Rainee loved seeing her smile. How delightful it was to be able to do something nice for Mr. Bowen's mother, too.

Soon she would be her mother also.

Her heart smiled with joy.

Rainee cut a sideways glance at him. Whatever it took, no matter how uncomfortable or how hard things became, she would make this situation work. Fear would not dissuade her from doing anything less. Besides, she had no other choice.

When the beatings became more severe, life-threatening even, after months of praying, she and Jenetta had concocted this plan of escape. Good thing their strategy had worked. Because the night she had fled she overheard her brother's scheme to sell her to their fifty-eight-year-old neighbor—the repulsive Mr. Alexander, or Mr. Gruff as she called him. They were to wed that next day. Just thinking about it made her tremble. That

man was cruel to his very soul. Just like her brother,
Ferrin.

*Thank You, Lord, for guiding my steps and for deliv-
ering me from Ferrin's wicked plans. Help me to be a
good wife to Mr. Bowen. And if You would be so kind,
would You please delay the wedding ceremony to give
us a little time to get to know each other before we wed?
Thank You.*

Rainee hoped God would especially answer her
prayer about getting to know each other first because
her intended was obviously a man of few words. And
even fewer smiles. What if he was cruel like her brother?
That thought frightened her. God have mercy on her if
she had left one boiling pot for another. Or, she gulped,
something worse.

She blocked out the distressing thoughts from her
mind and took in the view around her. Several head of
magnificent spotted horses grazed in a grassy meadow,
which seemed to go on for miles. A frolicking black
foal with a white spotted rump bucked and kicked and
nuzzled its matching mother. A deep longing to spend
time with her mother and to be a carefree child again
bled deep into her soul, but self-pity would not change
the past. She dragged her slumped shoulders into an upright position, determined to make the best of her new
situation.

Farther up the road, she noticed a herd of pigs. She
closed her eyes and cringed against the thousands of
fingernails scraping their way up her spine. A deathly
fear of the four-legged beasts had always plagued her,
and she loathed the stench that accompanied them. Her
nose wrinkled, and her mouth twitched just thinking
about the offensive odor.

To get her mind off of the wretched creatures, she

turned her attention onto an amazing cluster of lavender blooms covering the wide-open field. Curiosity got the best of her. "Mr. Bowen?"

He glanced at her, then back at the crusted road. "Yes?"

"Those purple flowers over there…" She pointed toward the field overrun with the fragile flowers. "What are they, please?"

"They're Camas plants."

"Camas?" Rainee tilted her head and shifted her parasol so she could look at him.

"Yes."

"Are the pigs eating them?"

"Yes. They love them." He looked out over the fields. "In fact, the hogs love the Camas bulbs so much the people around here actually call this place Hog Heaven." He glanced at her. "Informally, that is." His masculine lips curved into a smile.

And what a beautiful smile it was. She wished she could see more of them. If only she knew how to make that happen. But at present, that seemed improbable.

"What a dreadful waste of such lovely flowers."

"It's not a waste. The Camas bulbs are the only thing that helps the hogs survive the rough winters here in Paradise Haven. They're about the only animal that can survive the winters here. For now anyway." He glanced at her, then back at the herd of swine. "But, I've heard tell the railroad will be coming through here sometime soon. That'll make it easier to get supplies to feed cattle through the winter so they won't starve."

Just how bad did the winters get here anyway? Although she wanted to ask, she also wanted to know more about the fascinating Camas plant. "Are they only edible to hogs?"

"No, humans can eat them, too."

"Are they native to this area?"

"No. Farmers from back East brought them with them when they moved here." The reins jiggled in his hands as he twisted his head toward her. "I'm sure glad they did."

She wondered why he was glad, but nothing more was said. She also wondered how much farther it would be before they would arrive at his place. Her arms ached from holding her parasol upright, but every time she lowered it, the hot sun burned through the fabric of her jacket.

Minutes later, at the base of a mountain, they rounded a clearing in the trees. A very well-kept, large, two-story clapboard house flanked by long windows with white shutters came into view.

Rocking chairs, small tables and a porch swing sat under a covered porch, making it look quite welcoming. Off to the left of the house, a makeshift scarecrow on a stick watched over a large garden.

Nestled up against the trees set two smaller but generous-size clapboard homes. They, too, had covered porches, a swing, rocking chairs and small tables—and were equally adorable as the larger house.

A young girl with blond braids skipped around the corner of the house. As soon as she spotted them, she hastened their direction. "Haydon! You're back," she hollered and slowed her pace when she neared the horses. "Did you brung me anything?"

Haydon laughed.

Rainee liked the deep rumbling sound.

"You're too spoiled for your own good, Squirt. I hate to disappoint you, but I didn't *bring* you anything. I didn't go to town for supplies."

The little girl scrunched her brows and looked up at Rainee. "Who're you?"

"Abigail. Mind your manners." Mr. Bowen stepped on the brake and tied off the reins before jumping down.

"Sorry." She lowered her head, her long braided pigtails reaching down her green cotton dress.

He ruffled the little girl's hair, then turned and extended his arms toward Rainee. Situating her belongings out of the way, she laid her hands on his shoulders and allowed him to help her down.

The instant her feet touched the ground he removed his hands from her waist and stepped back as if she had bitten him.

"Miss Devonwood." Haydon looked at her, then at the small child. "This is my sister Abby. Abby, this is Miss Rainelle Devonwood."

Rainee smiled down at the girl with the blond hair and sapphire eyes so like her brother's. "It is a pleasure to meet you, Abby." She gave a quick curtsy as was customary back home when greeting someone. "But please, call me Rainee."

"Nice ta meet ya, too, Rainee. I like the way you talk."

"I like the way you talk, too. You have a lovely accent."

"I dun't got no assent."

"Accent," Mr. Bowen corrected her again.

"That's what I said. Assent."

Rainee waited to see if he would correct her again, but he shook his head and mussed her hair once more.

"Haydon. You're mussing my hair." She planted her hands on her waist and narrowed her eyes, but even Rainee could see the smile in the young girl's frown.

"Sorry, Squirt."

"Thas okay." Abby smiled at her brother, then glanced over at Rainee. Her brows curled, and her forehead criss-crossed. "Whach you doin' here?"

"Never you mind, Little Miss Nosey." Haydon tapped his little sister on the nose and winked. "Listen, Squirt, would you do me a favor and run over to Jesse's and ask him to come here?"

Abby bobbed her head and darted off toward Jess's house.

Haydon wasn't sure if his brother was able to be up and about yet, but if he was, then he needed to get his sorry backside out here and deal with this awkward mess.

Without looking at Miss Devonwood, he wondered what he should do or say before his brother got there.

"The place is quite lovely." A whisper would have been louder, but the awe in her voice screamed loud and clear.

Haydon scanned the ranch, trying to see the place through her eyes. He always thought this area was some of the most beautiful country he'd ever seen, but for some odd reason it pleased him that she thought so, too. *Oh-h-h no you don't, buddy. Who cares what she thinks? She's not staying.*

"Who lives in that house?"

He followed her finger. "My brother and his wife." *The brother that sent for you. But he can tell you that. Not me.*

"And that place?" She pointed to his house.

"That's mine." *As in mine alone. As in, not yours and mine.*

She faced the main house. "Then this must be your parents' home."

"It's my mother's."

She turned questioning eyes up at him.

Quit looking at me with those beautiful peepers, ma'am. "My father passed away a couple of years ago."

Sympathy passed through her gaze, and he forced himself to look away. "Oh, my. I am so sorry." She laid her hand on his arm. Something about her gentle touch sent warmth spreading through his veins.

He stared at the spot where her hand rested. The gesture touched him, but at the same time it sent warning signals flashing through his brain. Her politeness and sweetness were driving him crazy. He dropped his arm to his side, letting her arm slip from his. He didn't want to feel any kind of a bond to this woman—or any other woman for that matter.

Then he made the mistake of once again looking at her face. Hurt and discomfort gazed back at him. She looked so small and vulnerable. Guilt trailed through him like hungry red ants at a picnic, chewing away at his conscience. His thoughtless gesture had hurt her, and she didn't deserve the treatment he had dealt her. But then again, he had to protect himself. He needed to harden himself against the emotions she seemed to stir up in him so easily. Emotions he wanted no part of. The sooner Jesse dealt with her, the better. *Just keep telling yourself she's not your problem, Haydon, and you just might survive this situation with your sanity and heart still intact.*

He turned toward Jesse's place, wondering where Abby was and what was taking her so long.

"Excuse me, please?"

As much as he didn't want to, Haydon faced her again. "Yes?"

Her eyes locked on his for the briefest of moments before her lids fluttered, and she looked toward Jesse's house. "Is Abby the only one who does not know why I am here?" She turned those wide innocent fawn eyes up at him again, and his heart lurched.

The last time Haydon saw a look like that was on a puppy he'd owned as a child. That puppy had won his heart and had gotten whatever it wanted. Haydon swallowed hard. *Rainee's not a puppy. She's a woman. And not just any woman. She's the most dangerous kind there is. Sweet and innocent-looking, and beautiful.* "Miss Devonwood, I—"

"Haydon!" Abby's voice carried across the yard.

Haydon wanted to hug his sister for saving him. He spun her direction and watched as she ran toward him.

"Jesse got hurted this mornin' and he can't come."

His heart dropped to his boots. He had hoped Jess would at least feel well enough by the time he got back that he could deal with Miss Devonwood. Now what?

"How come I didn't know he got hurted?"

"Hurt, not hurted," Haydon corrected. "Because you, Mother and Leah were gone all day, remember?"

Abby hiked her little shoulder. "I forgetted."

"I *forgot*."

"Did you forgetted too?" Her round eyes smiled up at him.

"No, I didn't forget. You said… Oh, never mind. Why don't you run along and go play now?"

"Okay." She skipped back toward the corner of the house and disappeared.

Haydon turned toward the sound of Miss Devonwood's twitter.

Her gaze lingered in the direction Abby had gone.

"Just what do you find so amusing, Miss Devonwood?"

Rainee reeled toward him and blinked. Amusement, not anger, fluttered across his handsome face. "Abby is lovely." She stared at the spot where the little girl had disappeared. "To think that precious girl is going to be my sister is so—" Rainee's eyes flew open and hot blood rushed into her cheeks. She pressed her fingertips to her mouth to stifle her gasp.

Merciful heavens! What is wrong with you, Rainelle? Since you got here, he has not mentioned the subject of marriage even once, and here you are talking about Abby being your sister. No wonder Mother had to rebuke you so often. Will you ever learn? She gazed longingly at the forest of trees, wishing she could flee into their thickness and hide away forever.

She turned and retrieved her parasol, handbag and the flowers from the bench seat.

"Haydon. Where have you been all day?"

Rainee whirled toward the big two-story house. A tall, lithe woman strolled toward them and stopped directly in front of her.

The handsome blonde lady with powder-blue eyes looked up at Haydon and quirked one delicate eyebrow. "Sorry, I didn't know we had company."

"Mother, this is—"

When he stopped speaking, Rainee looked up at him, wondering why he quit talking. Obviously he was not going to say anything more, so Rainee took matters into her own hands. She turned her attention to his mother. "Good afternoon, ma'am." She curtsied. "I am Rainelle Victoria Devonwood."

"Good afternoon, Miss Devonwood. I'm Katherine, Haydon's mother." Katherine looked perplexed as she glanced from Rainee to Haydon and back again.

"It is a pleasure to meet you, Mrs. Bowen."

"Please call me Katherine. We don't stand on ceremony out here. Feel free to address all of us on a first-name basis."

Rainee looked at Mr. Bowen. Mother had always made it clear a man should never call a woman by her given name unless they had known each other for a long time or were courting. Neither one fit this scenario.

His jaw worked back and forth again, but after a few seconds, he glanced at her. "Mother's right. Call me Haydon."

Relief drizzled over her like a warm summer rain. One more detestable rule of etiquette she would not have to follow out here. Mother and Father would not approve of her choice to call someone by their first name, but Rainee loved it. It was much more personable.

"Thank you, Haydon." Using his Christian name felt quite strange and yet lovely at the same time. "Please call me Rainee. I prefer it over Rainelle."

"Rainee," he acknowledged. "Rainelle is a beautiful name, though. I've never heard it before."

Rainee blushed under Haydon's compliment. "My father was British. It was his mother's name." Her gaze lowered and she noticed the flowers in her hands. She extended the bouquet toward his mother. "These are for you, Mrs. Bowen."

"It's Katherine, remember?"

"Yes, ma'am." It would take Rainee a while to get used to addressing an elder by their given name but the very idea brought a smile to her face.

Katherine took the flowers, and her eyes brightened

as she smelled each one. "Oh, I love flowers. And these are my favorites. How very thoughtful of you to take the time to pick them for me. Thank you, Rainee." Katherine smiled and again her questioning gaze swung between Rainee and her son.

The joy of the moment evaporated as quickly as it had come. A sinking feeling came over Rainee. Had this man not mentioned her to any of his family? What was going on around here?

Rainee's blood flow slowed way down—either from all the heat she had endured the last several days or the realization no one seemed to know anything about her.

"Don't just stand there, Haydon. Can't you see Rainee isn't feeling well? Help her inside and get her a glass of water."

She wanted to protest, to say she was fine, but she never got the chance. Haydon was at her side, escorting her into the house and onto a comfortable sofa.

"You'd be more at ease, Rainee, if you removed your jacket and hat. May I?"

She nodded.

Haydon helped her out of her traveling jacket and set it on a nearby chair.

She removed the pins from her hat, wondering if she looked a fright.

He took her hat and set it with her jacket. "Would you like me to take your gloves too?" He extended his hand toward her.

She clutched her hands together and squeezed them until her fingers throbbed. "No. No, thank you."

A quick nod her direction, and he left the room. Within minutes he returned with a full glass of water. "Here. Drink this. You'll feel much better."

When she reached for the glass, their fingertips over-lapped. A warm tingling sensation started at the tip of her fingers and spread up her arm and into her body, causing her to shiver and very nearly drop the glass.

Haydon yanked his hand back, and she barely kept the glass upright between them. For a brief moment, he stared at her with a look of sheer horror. Then he whirled and disappeared through the doorway as if the house were on fire.

Had he felt what she had? Her heart was still flutter-ing from that one touch.

If he had, was it a bad thing or a good thing? If his reaction was any indication, it must be quite bad.

Too tired to ponder that, she tipped the water glass to her lips. The tepid water tasted almost sweet. She drank the whole glass of liquid within seconds, even though it was a very unladylike thing to do.

"Feel better?"

Rainee looked over at Katherine, who strolled into the living room and sat in a chair across from her.

"Thank you. Yes," she answered even though she really did not feel better, but she hated any displays of weakness. Yet, sitting here on a comfy sofa, out of the hot sun, her eyelids felt heavy with fatigue. She strug-gled to keep her tiredness from showing.

An awkward silence filled the room.

Katherine rose. "Would you please excuse me for a moment? And please make yourself at home."

After the woman left, Rainee folded her hands in her lap, not knowing what to do.

Her gaze roamed the living room. On the left of the fireplace were two wine-and-tan-colored wingback chairs. On the right was a matching high-back settee and a tan rocking chair. The wine-and-tan sofa she sat on faced the fireplace. End tables with doilies and oil lamps graced each side of the sofa. The place reminded her of the spacious living room back home. Except this place had Queen Anne–style furniture, and back home the furniture was Chippendale. Sadness crawled inside her, but she shooed it away like an unwanted bug. Dwelling on home would do her no good. No good at all.

Weeks of traveling and being jostled about and the realization no one seemed to know about her had taxed her greatly. Her eyelids were heavy and her stomach was queasy from a lack of food. She really should have eaten something when Haydon had offered. But knowing she was penniless and seeing all those men in Prosperity Mountain leering at her, she just wanted to get away from them as fast as she could.

Her eyes slid shut, and her head bobbed. She sat up straighter, forcing herself to stay awake, when all she really wanted to do was to succumb to sleep and dream about what could have been. Finally she could fight sleep no longer and everything around her faded as she fell into its waiting arms.

Chapter Three

Haydon couldn't get out of the house fast enough as he battled the feelings warring inside him. When Rainee's fingertips touched his, it was as if a bolt of lightning had struck nearby and he felt the effects of it, shocking every part of him. How could a woman, who he'd barely met, affect him so? Whatever the answer, he didn't care. All he knew was he wouldn't allow her or any other woman to penetrate the wall he'd built around his heart.

He glanced toward the house, wondering what was going on in there. Rainee looked so tired, he actually felt sorry for her. He shouldn't have left his mother alone to deal with her, but he had to get away for the sake of his sanity. Besides, why should he feel bad? This whole unbelievable situation was all Jesse's doing. Haydon had nothing to do with it.

Of all the idiotic things his brother had done, this one bested them all. The more Haydon thought about the situation and the sight of that poor exhausted woman sitting on his mother's couch, the more he thought about confronting his brother. He whirled on his heel and headed toward Jesse's house. The brisk walk across the yard felt good and helped relieve some of his aggravation—but not nearly enough. He leapt onto the porch. "Jesse." He banged on the door.

In seconds, the door slung open, and a very pregnant, very perturbed Hannah quickly stepped outside. She jerked her finger to her lips and shushed him. "Haydon Bowen, what is wrong with you? Jesse's sleeping." She closed the door behind her. "Although I'm surprised he can with all that banging you're doing."

That sent Haydon back a piece. "I'm sorry, but he's just going to have to wake up. There are two ladies over there—" he jerked his thumb toward his mother's house "—who need an explanation."

Hannah planted her hands on her hips and glared up at him. "Listen here, Haydon Bowen. I know what Jesse did was wrong. I told him he should have talked to you before answering that woman's advertisement on your behalf. I'm sorry, but you'll just have to deal with it because right now Jesse needs rest. And not you nor anyone else is going to disrupt that. You hear me?" With those words Hannah opened her door and disappeared inside, closing it on him with the softest bang he'd ever not heard.

Haydon raised his hat and ran his hand through his hair. Never before had he seen Miss Timid Hannah act like that. Seeing no other course of action, he stepped off their porch, mumbling, "Must be something about a pregnant woman that makes them cantankerous. It definitely brings out their protective instincts." Haydon slapped his dusty hat against his leg. "Women," he harrumphed, then plopped his hat on his head and strode toward the main house.

He had just finished unloading the last of Rainee's belongings onto the porch when his mother came out and stepped up next to him. "Haydon. I want to talk to you."

"Not now, Mother." He hoisted his leg up to get into the wagon.

"Oh, no you don't." She grabbed the back of his shirt and tugged him back. "I want to know who that girl is and what she's doing here. And I want to know *now*."

Haydon closed his eyes and blew out a long breath before facing his mother. "You'll have to ask Jesse that question."

"Jesse? What has he got to do with this?"

"Everything," Haydon replied, climbing onto the buckboard. Making sure his mother was at a safe distance, he picked up the reins and tapped the draft horses, Lulu and Sally, on their backs.

By the time he pulled the wagon around to the barn and stepped down, his mother was standing at his side. "Haydon, what's going on?"

He looked down at his mother but offered no answers.

"Where have you been and who is that woman? I will not wait until Jesse gets back from wherever it was he said he had to go today."

"So you don't know about Jesse either?"

"Know what about Jesse?" Her gaze slid toward the direction of Jesse's cabin, then back at him. "I just got home about fifteen minutes before you did and no one was around. Smokey and Michael told me last night they'd be late for dinner. What's going on around here?"

Haydon drew in a long breath. "I'll put the horses up, and then I'll tell you everything, okay?"

"You bet you will. I'll be waiting. Right here." She sat down on one of the wood-slab benches outside the barn door.

As he tended to the horses, Haydon prayed God would give him the grace to tell his mother all he knew. When he finished, he stepped out of the barn and sat down next to her. He leaned his arms on his knees and clasped his hands together. With his head down, he debated on where to start.

"Well, are you just going to sit there, or are you going to tell me what's going on? And why is your nose so red?"

"Some guy in Prosperity Mountain punched me in the nose."

"What! Why'd he do that?"

"Because I stopped him from assaulting Rainee."

"What do you mean?" Shock rippled through her voice and across her face.

"When I arrived, some ruffian was trying to force his attentions on Rainee. We got into a fight and the sheriff hauled him off."

"That poor girl."

"Poor girl is right." Only she wasn't a girl, she was a woman. With curves in all the right places. A beautiful, feisty woman who brought out his protective instincts. The kind of woman he was a sucker for. *Oh, no, Haydon. Not this time. Just shove any notions about Rainee out of your mind. Don't go getting any ideas where she's concerned. Remember what happened with Melanie.* That was all the reminder he needed. Thoughts of Rainee vanished from his mind.

"Now, I want you to tell me why Rainee is here."

So much for knocking her out of his mind. "Mother, you know how Jess is always doing stuff without thinking the whole thing through?"

"Yes, but he always means well."

"That might be true, but some of the ridiculous things

he's done, he shouldn't have. This is one of them. Jesse answered an advertisement he'd seen..." He rubbed his chin. "I don't know where he saw it. In a newspaper, a magazine or what. But Rainee must have placed an advertisement to find a husband."

His mother's brows rose and her chin lowered. "A husband?"

"Jesse answered her ad and encouraged her to come out here to become..." He swallowed hard before continuing, "my wife."

"Oh, no, he didn't."

"Oh, yes. He did. I don't know what was in the letter or her ad or anything. You'll have to ask Jesse. But judging by our conversation on the way back to the ranch, she believes I'm the one who sent for her."

Mother looked toward the house and shook her head. "That poor, poor girl. I can't believe Jesse would do such a thing. What was he thinking?"

"That's what I asked him. I was going to send her back to wherever she came from, but the stagecoach had already left. It'll be three weeks before it comes through again. I just couldn't leave her alone in Prosperity Mountain to fend for herself." He thought about when he had arrived at the stagecoach stop and saw her bopping and kicking that man in the shins. Maybe they needed protection from her. He smiled. Then again, maybe he did, too.

His mother laid her hand on his leg. "You did the right thing, son. But why did you go get her if you didn't send for her? Why didn't Jesse go?"

"Because he's laid up. That's why."

"Laid up? What do you mean?"

"He had an accident this morning."

"An accident? Is he okay? What happened?" Although his mother was used to her menfolk getting hurt, it never stopped her from worrying or fretting over them.

"Smokey said he'll be fine." A fresh wave of shame washed over Haydon, even though he was still agitated with his brother. "It was my fault. I got so angry when I found out what he did that I needed to get as far away from him as possible so I could cool down. I decided to go for a long ride. You know, like Father and I used to do."

"I remember." Sadness shadowed her eyes.

"Jess came into the barn right when I was getting ready to leave. I never flank Rebel, but I did. Rebel was so startled he reared and knocked Jesse out."

Her face paled. "You sure he's going to be all right?"

"I'm sure," he said with more confidence than he felt. "I feel terrible about what happened. But to be honest, Mother, I'm still angry with him. He had no right to do that to me or to Rainee."

His mother shook her head. "You're right, he didn't. But unfortunately he did, and now we have to figure out what to do with her."

"*We?* Oh-h no. Not we. Jesse can figure that one out on his own."

"From what you just told me, Jesse won't be able to do much of anything on his own for a while." She stood, and so did he. "I need to go check on him."

"I wouldn't do that if I were you."

"Why not?"

"Because Hannah said he needed his rest, and she didn't care who it was, she wasn't letting anyone wake him."

"Hannah? Our Hannah said that?"

"Yep. She sure did." They stood there for a second

staring at each other before they both shook their heads, chuckling.

His mother's face turned grim. "What am I going to tell that poor young woman?"

"I don't know."

Rainee's eyes fluttered open. She turned her head and started to raise herself, but her body rebelled with each movement. Not one to allow a few aches and weakness of body to stop her, she forced her creaking body into a sitting position, wondering how long she had been asleep.

A young teenage girl with buttery blond hair and powder-blue eyes came drifting into the room. "Hi, I'm Leah. Mother told me to offer you something to eat and drink when you awakened. Would you like some cookies and tea?"

"Tea and cookies sound heavenly. Thank you." Before Rainee had a chance to introduce herself the girl disappeared. Rainee ran her hands over her wrinkled, dirty clothes, but the stubborn creases and dirt would not budge. She was most certainly a mess and not fit to be seen.

Leah returned and set the tray on the end table next to Rainee. She smiled and two dimples accompanied it. "I hope you like them. I made them myself." Leah's look of accomplishment curled Rainee's lips upward.

"I am sure I shall. Thank you." She picked one up, and when she bit into it, a flavorful blend of cinnamon, clove and apple delighted her taste buds.

Leah sat across from her with an expectant look.

Rainee dabbed at the corners of her mouth with the cloth napkin provided her. "One of the best cookies I

have ever eaten. You must teach me how to make them."
To prove her enjoyment, she devoured another cookie.

"I would love to."

"By the way, I am Rainelle. Rainelle Victoria Devonwood. But please, call me Rainee."

"Nice to meet you, Rainee." Leah chewed on the
corner of her bottom lip. "I hope you don't mind me
asking, but I saw you with my brother." She squirmed
and glanced toward the kitchen. "Are you and he...?
You know?" She spiked her shoulder in a quick upward
motion. "How do you know Haydon?"

"Leah. That is none of your business." Rainee's gaze
swung toward Katherine's voice.

Leah jumped up and lowered her head. "Sorry,
Mother." She glanced over at Rainee. "Sorry, Rainee."

"No harm done." She did her best to send Leah a re-
assuring smile.

The young girl gave a quick nod and then looked at
her mother as if she were seeking approval.

"Leah, go see what your sister is up to."

"Yes, Mother." She gave a shy smile Rainee's direction, then quietly left the room.

Katherine sat in the chair Leah had occupied. "Are
you feeling better now?" Compassion, so like her own
mother's, floated from this woman.

Rainee had to look away. Heartsickness for her
mother consumed her once again. She wondered if she
would ever get used to the fact her mother was never
coming back. That she would never comfort Rainee or
give her words of wisdom again.

She plastered on a smile and faced Katherine. "Yes,
ma'am. I am much better. Thank you."

Katherine fidgeted with her hands and darted her
gaze out the window, onto her lap, back out the window,

until it finally alighted on Rainee. "Rainee, I think there's something you should know."

Rainee braced herself for whatever was coming. From the tone in Katherine's voice, it was not good news.

"Mother, I'll handle this."

Rainee swung her gaze toward Haydon, who stood filling the doorway.

Katherine's chest rose and fell. Her hands quit squirming and finally rested in her lap.

"I'm afraid there's been a huge mistake." Haydon strode over and sat across from her next to Katherine.

"What—what do you mean a mistake?" Rainee felt the blood drain from her face.

"I don't know how to tell you this, so I'm just going to say it. I'm really sorry, but my brother Jesse sent for you, Rainee, not me."

Blinking, Rainee fought not to react. "I—I do not understand." She looked at Katherine, then at Haydon. "You told me Jesse is married."

"He is."

Question after question chased through Rainee's mind about what this all meant. Surely these people were not one of those religious groups who believed it was okay to have several wives. The air in the room thickened. Just what had she gotten herself into? She stared at Haydon, waiting for him to continue, yet dreading it at the same time.

"He sent for you. But not for himself."

Hearing Haydon say that at least put Rainee's fears to rest about the numerous wives, but she still did not have a clue as to what was going on.

"He thought he was doing me a favor. And you." He raked his hand through his hair.

Rainee closed her eyes as disappointment, concern and dread inhabited her body. The cookies in her stomach turned to stone. What would she do now? She did not need him to tell her the rest. She already knew. He did not want her here. Her solution had just evaporated before her very eyes.

Never before had she felt so alone.

Usually when a situation arose, memories of her mother's advice came to her. But not this time. Even her mother's words were as silent as the grave.

Grave. That one word always ripped at Rainee's heart, and this time was no different, but she refused to cry in the presence of these strangers.

"Rainee."

Her eyes drifted toward the woman who emanated compassion.

"Jesse meant well. But my son has a tendency to not think things through before he acts."

"That's for sure." Anger sliced through Haydon's tone. "When he saw your advertisement, he decided to send for you. But unfortunately, he didn't mention it to me or anyone else."

That much was obvious. So now what?

Seeing the lingering question in Katherine's eyes, Rainee plucked up her courage and looked directly at her. "I know you must think it quite strange a woman would advertise for a husband, but please believe me when I tell you I had to." She glanced at Haydon, then back at Katherine. "You see, my parents died and I…" Her courage vanished. Rainee could not bring herself to share the sordid details of her life with these people. "I just had to."

"I'm so sorry for your loss. If I hadn't had my sons to take care of me when my husband passed away, I'd have probably done the same thing. I think what you did took a lot of courage."

Courage was not what propelled her to write the advertisement. Fear had.

Afraid they would see the moisture forming in her eyes and start asking questions, questions she did not want to answer, Rainee stood and forced one shaky leg in front of the other as she walked to the window.

No one could find out she had a brother back in Little Rock. For she could not risk being sent back. Neither could she risk Ferrin finding her. The only thing that could save her now was to get married right away. And based on what she had just heard, there was not going to be a wedding here in Paradise Haven.

Scenario after scenario about what she could do now ran through Rainee's mind. With each one, the air thickened with fear. The idea of going back home to that monster tied her stomach into knots and breathing became difficult.

With her back to them, the question she hated to ask but knew she must slid past her lips in a choppy rasp, "Where—where does that leave me?" Spots danced before her eyes, and her body swayed, then blackness pulled her into its embrace.

Chapter Four

Haydon leapt to his feet but could not make it to the window fast enough to catch Rainee. Her small body slumped to the floor. Her vulnerability tugged at his heart. The anger and frustration he'd had toward Jesse came back full force.

Willing himself to feel nothing, Haydon slipped his arms under her knees and back and hoisted her up. She didn't budge but hung as limp as Abby's rag doll. She looked helpless, alone and frail. He tucked her closer into his chest. Her vulnerability and the feel of her feminine frame and soft hair draping over his arm touched something deep inside him. Something he never wanted to feel again rose in him. He shoveled away the unwelcome feelings and buried them deep in an unmarked grave.

"Oh, Haydon, that poor girl. Wait until I see Jesse. I am going to give that boy a piece of my mind. What was he thinking?"

That's what Haydon had been trying to figure out, too.

"Take her up to Leah's room and lay her on the extra

bed. I'll get a cool cloth and some water." His mother scampered into the kitchen.

On his way up the steps, he noticed the stains of tears on her cheeks. Protective feelings flooded through him like a massive gulley wash, but he refused to let them take possession. *No! I don't want to feel anything.* However, when he lowered her onto the bed, rather than walking away, he gazed down at her, wondering what would become of her once they sorted the whole muddled issue out.

The stairs creaked. He shook out of the thoughts and strode toward the door. He took the water basin from his mother.

Thinking was dangerous. He held the bowl while his mother dipped a cloth into it and laid it on Rainee's forehead.

The young woman stirred and slowly opened her eyes.

Haydon's breath hitched at the sight of those beautiful fawn-colored eyes—eyes he had avoided the whole way home. Eyes a man could get lost in if he wasn't careful.

Dread and confusion emanated from her.

He hated seeing her like that. His arms ached to wrap her in them and comfort her. To tell her everything would be okay. That he would take care of her and protect her.

What was he thinking?

Fear slugged into him like a fist. He jerked his gaze away and quickly set the basin on the nightstand, sloshing a small amount of water over the side. Without bothering to wipe it up, he spun on his heel and called over his shoulder, "If you need me for anything else, just holler." Haydon skipped steps as he barreled down them. Out the front door and into the fresh air he flew. He refused to give heed to the feelings Rainee aroused in him. Feelings that scared him to death. From now on, the farther he stayed away from her, the better.

Rainee sat up. She would love nothing more than to bury herself with the yellow patchwork quilt underneath her, but that would solve nothing. All her well-laid plans were falling apart around her. She had no money and no place to go. And no future husband.

"Rainee?"

Her vision trailed toward Katherine, who smelled of baked bread and wood smoke.

"I am truly sorry, Mrs. Bowen. I am not normally one given to fainting spells. But this news has come as quite a shock to me. I am at a loss as to what to do next. All I know is, I cannot go back. I simply cannot."

"It's Katherine, and please don't apologize for fainting. I certainly understand. I'd probably faint too under the same circumstances." Katherine sat on the bed next to her and took her hand. "I am more sorry than words can say for what my son did. I want you to know you're welcome to stay here as long as you wish."

Once again, questions chased other questions through Rainee's mind. Should she stay? Should she go? Should she take Katherine up on her offer until she had time to figure out what to do? The way she saw it, she really had no other choice.

She searched the woman's eyes, seeking something. Reassurance perhaps? That all would be well? What she saw was a kind woman offering her compassion and a place to stay. Her chest heaved, expelling some of the tension in her body. "Are you sure you do not mind?"

"I'm positive. Now, why don't I have Haydon bring

up your things? I'm sure you'd like to clean up before dinner. I'll heat some water so you can take a bath."

"No, no. Please, do not trouble yourself on my account," Rainee said even though a bath sounded heavenly. She did not want to give this woman any reason to send her back. And while she would not take advantage of Katherine's kind offer and hospitality for long, she was grateful for the time to come up with another plan.

If only her mother's words of wisdom would rise up in her, but they would not because Rainee had never encountered anything like this while her mother was still alive. How could either of them ever have envisioned this? The next-closest thing she had to a mother now was Jenetta. The older woman would know what to do. But she was not here. She was back home in Little Rock with her husband and three children.

Something Jenetta had said popped into her mind. "You hang on to that other Christian gentleman's letter in case thangs don't work out." The other letter. Stems of hope sprouted through the darkness. She did have another option. *Thank You, Lord.*

Having received many responses to her advertisement, she had kept the two most promising letters. One she had responded to, the other, well, his letter was tucked securely in her trunk. Although it saddened her that things did not work out with Haydon, she would write the other man straightaway.

"It's no trouble at all." Katherine's voice snapped her out of her musings. "I'll start heating the water now. As soon as Haydon gets your things up here, you can come down and take a bath." She smiled, stood and turned to leave the room. At the door, she stopped. With her hand still on the knob, she looked back at Rainee. "I really am sorry for what my son did. And I meant what I said about you staying here as long as you like." Katherine's smile seemed to hold a secret. But just what kind of secret Rainee did not know.

"Would you please take Rainee's things up to Leah's room?" Haydon's mother pointed to the trunk he had placed on the porch when they had arrived. "She'll be staying with us."

His eyebrows slammed against the brim of his hat. "What do you mean she's staying with us? For how long?" He could no more hold back the panic from his voice than he could hold back a raging river.

"For as long as she likes."

Haydon recognized that smile. His mother was up to something. Just what, he wasn't sure. But something.

He leaned over and grabbed the handles of Rainee's trunk and hoisted it up. His mother opened the door and motioned him by. "Just what I need," he spoke under his breath as he walked past her.

"She just might be."

Haydon swung around so fast the trunk dropped from his hands and thudded onto his foot. He jerked his foot up, put it down, jerked it up again and put it down, all the while holding back the words he wanted to fling out in anger. Without looking at his mother, he snatched the trunk up again and tromped his way up the stairs.

"Haydon." The sternness in his mother's voice stopped him.

Halfway up the stairs, he balanced the trunk on his knee and turned his head toward his mother.

She shook her finger at him. "You be nice to my guest, and don't you dare make her feel uncomfortable."

Make *her* uncomfortable!

"Yes, ma'am," he said as he turned and trudged up the stairs. This whole stupid mess stuck inside him like an infected splinter.

At Leah's bedroom door, he stopped and called, "Rainee." He made every effort possible to keep the irritation from his voice, when what he really wanted to do was take her and her trunk into town and drop her off at Mrs. Swedberg's boardinghouse. But the older widow woman never had any available rooms. Besides, even if she did, his mother had already made it clear Rainee was her guest now, and that was that.

"Come in," she said in that sweet Southern drawl of hers that drove clean through every part of him.

"I'm here with your trunk." He pushed the door all the way open with his back and turned inside. "Where would you like this?" He refused to look over at her. Refused to let her get under his skin any further.

"Over here, please."

He had no choice but to look now as she pointed to the end of the bed.

His gaze snagged on her hands. She still had on those lacey gloves. Why would she wear such fancy gloves in the house? This wasn't some fancy ball.

Fancy balls.

Melanie.

Thoughts of his wife were always one careless notion away but exactly what he needed to keep from being drawn in by Rainee. For that, he was almost grateful to the memories. As fast as he could, Haydon set her trunk at the foot of the bed and turned to leave.

"Haydon?"

He looked back at her. "Yes, ma'am?"

"Thank you." She put her head down and played with the tips of her fingers. "I want you to know that as soon as I can, I will be leaving. I am truly sorry for what your brother has put you through."

"Put me through?" Haydon was instantly chagrinned at his uncharitable thoughts. Rainee was the real victim here. "What about what he put *you* through? You came all this way for nothing. When I think about what you must be feeling right now..." He shook his head. "I still can't believe it. I'm really sorry, Rainee. Truly." He found he meant it. No one deserved to be treated like that.

"It is okay, Haydon. I have a home for now. And one of the other Christian gentlemen who answered my advertisement offered me a home as well, so I am not completely without options."

One of the other gentlemen? How many men had actually responded to her ad? Were there that many desperate men out there?

"I shall contact him as soon as I can send a post off and see if he still wants me."

Haydon's gut twisted into a hard knot. Who was this guy, and would he be good to her? Haydon gave himself a mental tongue lashing. What did he care what happened to her? He didn't want her. What did it matter to him if someone else did? Then he made the mistake of looking into her eyes again. The vulnerability he saw there touched him deeper than he wanted it to. Although he didn't want her, the truth was he hated the thought of this beautiful young woman, who was clothed with despair and innocence, traipsing all over the country to who knows where and into the arms of who knew what kind of man.

Against all rationale and his better judgment, right there, Haydon made up his mind to not let her go. To protect her from undesirables and to provide for her. "Rainee, I—"

"Rainee." Leah burst into the room. "Oh. Hi, Haydon."

He looked at his sister, then back at Rainee, who was gazing up at him with a tilt of her head as if she were waiting for him to continue. "I'll—I'll talk to you later."

She gave a quick nod. "Thank you again, Haydon, for retrieving my trunk." She offered him a sweet smile and to his utter surprise and horror his heart tipped like a schoolboy with a crush.

Chapter Five

Rainee climbed out of the tub and got dressed. Alone in the house and feeling refreshed, she decided to step outside. The late afternoon air surrounded her with warmth. Over by the corral, she noticed some of the spotted horses she had seen on the way here and decided to take a closer look at them.

She stepped up to the corral, and a reddish-colored horse with brown spots came trotting over to her and leaned its head over the fence. "Well, hello there." She ran her gloves over the horse's nose. The horse pressed into her hand and jerked upward. Rainee giggled. "Not only are you lovely, but you are feisty, too."

"And she'll take a chunk out of you if you're not careful."

Rainee swung her gaze toward the barn. Haydon stepped out of the shadow of the stall and into the sunlight of the corral. He came and stood next to the mare and patted the horse's neck. "You behave yourself, Sköldpadda."

The horse stepped back and turned her head into Haydon. He rubbed her cheek and scratched her behind her ears. "You be nice to this lady or no more treats for you, you hear?" Haydon glanced at Rainee but continued to pet the horse.

"Sköldpadda? I have never heard that name before." Rainee tilted her head.

"It's Swedish for a snapping turtle."

"Why did you name your horse after a snapping turtle?" No sooner had the question left her mouth when the horse scuttled back and lunged toward Haydon with its mouth wide open. "Watch out!" Rainee yelled.

Haydon jerked sideways and Rainee watched as he dealt with the horse in the gentlest of manner.

When the horse calmed, Haydon faced Rainee. "Now you know why. Sköldpadda has a good heart and she's a gentle mare, but for some reason I can't seem to break her of this one bad habit." He turned and put his arm around the horse's neck. "You're a good girl, Sköldpadda," he whispered in the horse's ear, but Rainee heard him and admired the gentleness he displayed with the horse.

He never once lost his temper as her brother had so many a time with their horses.

Thoughts of Ferrin and his cruelty sent spasms of pain throughout Rainee's body. *No! I shall not torment myself with thoughts of my brother.* She forced her attention back onto the horse and onto Haydon.

Sköldpadda walked away and joined the other horses at the food trough. Haydon ambled up to the fence and planted one foot on the bottom rail and his arms over the top one.

"What manner of breed are these horses? They are lovely, and I have never seen any spotted horses like these before."

"They're Palouse ponies."

"Palouse?"

Haydon explained their history with such zeal that Rainee got caught up in his excitement. "They're lofty and really active. Plus, they're great for hunting and their stamina is quite impressive." He suddenly stopped and looked at her. "I'm sorry. I've gotten carried away. It's just that I love these animals. They're unlike any other horse breed I've ever been around. Especially Rebel's offspring. If you think these horses are beautiful, you should see Rebel."

"Rebel?" She tilted her head.

"My horse."

"May I see him?"

"Sure. Meet me inside the barn." Haydon headed through the corral and disappeared into the same stall he had come out of.

On the way to the barn, Rainee marveled at the difference between the stoic man who had picked her up from the stagecoach and this zealous, passionate horseman. The two were as different as a bird and a cat.

Haydon met her at the door. "He's in the back." His face glowed with pride.

They headed through the barn. Dust, hay and horse scent swirled around her, tickling her nose with delight.

Out the back door they headed. Behind the barn was a lone stall with a higher fenced corral.

Several yards from the stall, Haydon expelled two short whistle sounds.

A black horse poked its head out of the stall door.

"How you doing, Rebel Boy?" Haydon walked up to him and rubbed the horse on the nose, then patted his cheek.

Rainee stepped up next to Haydon and looked at the horse's shiny coat. She peered into the stall and noticed white spots all over the horse's rump. "Oh, my. What an exquisite animal. God has really outdone Himself on this one. May I pet him?"

Haydon stepped aside and Rainee ran her hand over Rebel's head. "He seems gentle. Did you break him?"

"Yes."

"Do you break all of your horses?"

"Most of them. Jess helps some." He stopped talking and Rainee peered up at him. A shadow covered his face as he looked away. Rainee wondered what was wrong, then realized he had become still when he had mentioned his brother's name. The very one who had sent for her.

"I'm sorry, but it's getting late and I need to finish my chores now."

Rainee knew she had been dismissed. But she understood. Haydon was having a hard time dealing with what his brother had done, and she did not blame him. This most awkward situation vexed her also. To ease his discomfort, she would try and find a new home as soon as possible.

Rainee forced herself not to fidget at the dining room table. Father always hated that sort of improper display, said it showed a lack of confidence and no Devonwood should ever behave in such an unbecoming manner. Because of their wealth and standing in society, they should hold their heads high and have impeccable manners.

As if any of that mattered to Rainee.

She detested all of the snobbery and insincerity that accompanied most people of high rank.

The kitchen door flung open, and in barreled a young man who resembled Haydon in every way, albeit younger and smaller. He stopped short when he saw her, then he hurried around to the opposite side of the table and sat down. His eyes locked onto her. "Who are you? And what are you doing here?"

"Michael!"

Rainee's gaze flew to Haydon seated at the head of the table.

"I'm sorry. I apologize for my brother's rude behavior, Rainee." Haydon turned his attention to his brother and sent several silent but serious messages his direction.

The poor boy's face matched the color of a scarlet ribbon Rainee once had. She longed to ease the young man's embarrassment, but it would be highly improper for her to interfere.

"Rainee, may I present my brother, Michael. And the gentleman sitting next to him is our dear friend, Smokey."

"Ma'am." The man with the gray hair and gentle brown eyes nodded his head once.

"Pleased to meet you, gentlemen." Rainee presented a polite dip of her head to Smokey, then turned her attention to Michael and offered him the same courtesy.

"And of course you've already met Abigail and Leah. Everyone, this is Rainee."

Questioning stares made her want to shrink under the table and disappear out the door.

"Just so you all know, Jesse invited her out for a visit. I do not want anyone in this family embarrassing Rainee again. Is that understood?" His gaze went around the room, holding a moment on each member until they each nodded their assent.

Rainee wanted to hug the man for sparing her any

further humiliation. Admiration for his sensitivity sent a strange swirling sensation into her heart.

Confused, questioning gazes fluttered her direction from around the table. She waited for one of them to ask her why she was not eating with Haydon's brother and his wife, but not one person spoke even though she could tell they wanted to. They obviously respected Haydon's authority. And him.

"Let's pray." Everyone bowed their heads as Haydon said a prayer over the food.

Dinner consisted of Swedish elk stew and cornbread. Laughter floated around the table and the lively conversation reminded her of family dinners back home. Only the conversations around her parents' table were much more formal.

Much to her horror, a wide yawn attacked her without warning and escaped before she could catch it. She covered her mouth, but it was really no use. "Merciful heavens. Please forgive me. I did not mean to be rude. I fear I am overtired."

"Of course you are. Traveling has a way of doing that to a person. Why don't you head on up to bed?" Katherine's look of understanding warmed her insides.

"If you do not mind, I think I shall." She started to rise and found Haydon behind her, pulling out her chair.

When she stood, she turned to thank him, and their eyes connected.

The sound of Abby's giggle reached her ears.

Haydon broke eye contact with a frown. Then he rushed toward the door, snatched his hat off a wooden peg, and disappeared into the night with only a "I'd better check on Rebel" floating out after him.

* * *

Rainee stretched her arms above her and allowed her eyes to adjust to the daylight beaming through the windows. The lavender curtains waved in the light breeze. She glanced over at Leah's empty side of the bed and wondered what hour of the day it was.

Weeks on a train and stagecoach had taken their toll on her. Last night, after she had written her letter to Mr. Bettes and snuggled into the soft pillow, her eyes closed and she had fallen into a deep sleep.

She slid her legs out from under the quilt and placed her feet on the cool floor. Her gaze searched the room for a water pitcher and basin to wash her face. In that moment, it was as if someone had doused her head with a pitcher of cold water because once again she was forced to face reality.

Never again would there be water ready for her.

No maid to help button her dresses.

No Jenetta.

Rainee was certain she would either be dead or have gone mad by now had it not been for Jenetta and her kindness.

Jenetta had doctored her wounds, prayed with her and had even gone against Ferrin's orders by continuing to fill Rainee's water basin. In return, Rainee helped Jenetta with the extra chores Ferrin had heaped on her already-long list.

Rainee's chest heaved. She needed to accept the fact this was her new home now. At least temporarily anyway. The burden of being unsettled hung over her like an ominous cloud.

Not knowing what her host expected from her, she decided to make haste and get dressed so she could go downstairs and find out.

Rainee walked to the end of the bed, knelt in front of the trunk and opened it. She pulled out her pale blue day dress and shook it out. Alone in the room, she slipped her gloves and nightgown off, thankful she nor anyone else could see the raised stripes across her back. A painful reminder of where she had come from.

Within minutes she had her corset on. She slid into her bustle gown and made her way to the mirror. In front of the looking glass, she studied herself, admiring the light blue dress with dark blue bows and layers of lace on the skirt, collar and sleeves. Although she preferred a lighter, simpler dress, sometimes she missed wearing such gowns. Since her parents' passing, the only time she had been allowed to wear such finery was when company came. One old man in particular. An old man who made her shudder with repulsion. Rainee hastened to rid her mind of the despicable memories.

She glanced back at her reflection in the mirror. Her hair was in complete disarray.

After she secured her hair in a chignon, she grabbed her fingerless gloves and slipped them on. Flipping her hands over and back, she realized how out of place the lacey gloves looked here. But she had no choice but to wear them. They covered up contemptible, embarrassing scars. Scars she did not want anyone inquiring about.

Rainee opened the bedroom door. Coffee and bacon aromas greeted her, making her stomach rumble. She made her way down the stairs. As she neared the kitchen, her gaze found Haydon, seated at the table with Katherine, each holding a coffee cup, and out of reflex, Rainee ducked back so they would not see her.

"I wish Jesse would mind his own business. He should have never sent for her."

"Give her a chance, Haydon. You've got to let the past go."

Indecision gripped her. She did not know whether to continue forward or to turn around and make her way back up the stairs. Eavesdropping was wrong, but she could not get her feet to move.

Haydon said something, but Rainee could not hear him because his voice was too low.

"Yes, you can. You can't give up."

"I haven't given up, Mother. I keep this place running and even manage to turn over a profit."

"That's not what I meant. And yes, you do keep this place running. You've done an excellent job since your father died. I'm so proud of you, son. You pushed past the grief of losing him and took charge. Now you need to do the same with Melanie's death."

Melanie? Who was Melanie? Rainee wanted to ask, but she did not dare as they would know she was eavesdropping. Guilt took a swipe at her. She should move, should go forward or back, but her feet were not cooperating.

"Mother, we've had this conversation a million times already. It's my fault—"

"It's not your fault."

Rainee wanted to know what was not his fault.

"You remind me of Nora's brother, the one who's coming to live with her. Nora said he's still stuck in the past. Still hurting. What a tragedy that is."

What in Haydon's past was he stuck in? And why was he like this Nora woman's brother? Had he been responsible for his father's death? Or what? She strained to listen. She wanted to see if her unheard questions would be answered.

"Mother, I know you mean well, and I know what

you're trying to do, but you know I plan to never marry again."

Rainee stuffed down the hurt his words inflicted. Although she knew he did not want her, it still brought an ache to her soul. One she could not cast off like she could a piece of unwanted clothing.

She glanced behind her, desperately wanting to dart back up the stairs, but she did not want to risk being heard.

What should she do?

Haydon's words just now, and knowing he was not the one who had sent for her made her extremely uncomfortable, and she did not wish to be around him any longer.

With great care, she turned and made it up three steps before she heard, "Good morning, Rainee."

Rainee closed her eyes and drew in a long breath. Forcing a smile onto her face, she turned and made her way to them. "Good morning, Katherine."

She tried to look natural, not guilty of eavesdropping, wondering if they knew she had. If so, neither said a word.

Out of courtesy, she turned to greet Haydon, but the greeting never left her lips. His appearance was that of a person who had not slept for weeks. Her heart broke for him.

"Can I get you some breakfast?"

Rainee diverted her attention to Katherine. "Yes, that would be lovely, thank you."

Rainee did not know if she would offend her host by offering to help. In the society she came from it would be a huge social gaffe to do so because the wealthy had servants to do that. But Rainee preferred helping—it made her feel useful, instead of like some ornament waiting to be handpicked by an acceptable suitor. Another rigid rule she loathed.

Just because her family had money, she did not believe that she or they were above anyone else. If her father knew she felt that way and had ever caught her helping, he would have been appalled. Back home, even though she had failed miserably, she had always tried to behave in a way befitting their social status. But here, she did not know the proper thing to do.

Should she offer to help, or should she sit down and allow her host to wait on her?

And did she really want to sit at the table with Haydon after overhearing the conversation with his mother?

His eyes that spoke of his confusion and discomfort locked onto hers. Rainee could not blame him for being uncomfortable. After all, this most perplexing situation was no fault of his. But then again, it was no fault of hers either. She thought the man who had sent for her wanted her—otherwise she would have never come.

He broke eye contact, rose and came to where she stood. He pulled the chair out and held it as she sat.

Haydon went back, sat in his chair and became engrossed in his untouched food.

Katherine grabbed a covered plate from the oven. She lifted the towel, revealing a mountain of thick bacon slices, scrambled eggs and biscuits and set them on the table, along with an empty cup. She filled Rainee's cup with steaming coffee and sat in the chair next to her. "Go ahead and eat before it gets cold."

"Yes, ma'am." Rainee nodded, then bowed her head and said a silent prayer. When she opened her eyes, Haydon was staring at her as was Katherine.

"You're a Christian?" Katherine's blue eyes beamed,

and wrinkles gathered around her eyes and mouth when she smiled.

"Yes, ma'am. I am."

"Perfect." Katherine clasped her hands.

Perfect for what? Instead of inquiring, she picked up a piece of bacon with her fingers and bit off a piece.

Realizing her gaffe, her gaze flew to Katherine, who appeared as if nothing was amiss. Her mother would have noticed her blunder immediately and given her a lecture on fine table manners. She stopped chewing the piece in her mouth and stared at her plate, missing her mother until her heart bled tears.

"Are you okay?"

Rainee looked over at Haydon. She started to nod her head but then thought better of it when she noticed his genuine concern. "No. Not really. I was thinking about my mother."

"What about your mother?" His gaze never left his plate.

"When I was five, my mother scolded me for eating bacon with my fingers. She insisted I cut it into pieces instead. It took me forever to saw through one of those thick slices. When I had finally managed to do so, my fork slipped across the plate and the bacon went flying. It landed in the flower arrangement in the center of the table."

Haydon and Katherine chuckled. When Rainee looked over at him, his smile dropped with his gaze. Perplexed by his sudden aloofness, Rainee fought to fill the ensuing silence, but she did not know if she should continue. The decision was made for her when Katherine said, "And then what happened?"

"I waited for my mother's rebuke, but it never came. I could tell by her look she wanted to laugh, but with

Father in the room, she dared not. Formality was everything to my father, and such things were not acceptable. That was why Mother was such a strict disciplinarian and followed the rules of etiquette. Father demanded it.

"So, Mother showed me how the British use their butter knives to cut their food and gather it onto their fork. After about four or five tries, I finally succeeded in properly cutting the bacon, and my mother's praise was most generous."

Although that precious memory of her mother brought a smile to Rainee's face, it also quenched her appetite.

"How long have your parents been gone?" Katherine asked.

Rainee glanced at her. "Two years." She looked away and stared at nothing in particular. "I now understand what my mother meant."

"What do you mean, what she meant?" Haydon still did not look at her, but instead drank his coffee.

Surprised by his interest, she decided to continue. "Shortly after my grandmother died, I saw my mother sitting in her chair. I knelt beside her and noticed tears in her eyes. I could not imagine what was wrong, so I asked if she was unwell. She assured me she was not ill, but she had been thinking about her mother, and how much she missed her."

The image of her mother dabbing at her eyes with her hanky distressed Rainee further. Perhaps because she knew only too well the cruel pain her mother had suffered.

She could not look at anyone in the room as she relayed the heartfelt words her mother had spoken. "Mother said, 'You know, Rainelle, if I knew my mother

was at the end of the earth, I would crawl through thistles and thorns to see her again.' As a child I never
really understood because I never really knew my
grandmother. But now," she sniffed, "I understand those
words only too well. I, too, would crawl through thistles
and thorns to see my mother again. I miss her more than
words can say."

Tears slipped over her eyelids, and she quickly
brushed them away before continuing. "Any time I was
sad or hurting, mother would comfort me. We spent
many hours going for long walks. Mother would regale
me with tales of her childhood. She constantly helped
me, protected me and defended me. She always put her
family's needs before her own."

With a clatter of his fork, Haydon rose. "I need to get
my chores done. Thank you for breakfast, Mother." He
gave Rainee a quick nod and headed out the door, and
she immediately felt the loss of his presence.

"Your mother sounds like a wonderful person." Katherine's voice snagged her attention away from Haydon's
retreating form.

Rainee slid her gaze toward Katherine. "Yes, she
was."

"Listen, why don't you eat your breakfast and then
go for a nice long walk? It will do you good."

A long walk did sound good. "Thank you. I would
like that." She picked up her knife, cut a bite-size piece
of bacon and put it in her mouth.

She knew she was about to do something that would
not be deemed acceptable back home, but this was not
home, and she wanted to help. She finished chewing
and swallowed. "Katherine, is there anything you would
like me to help with around here? I would love to help
you and earn my keep until the stagecoach comes back

through." Then what would she do? She had no money in which to purchase a ticket. Those thoughts picked the worst moments to spring their unhappiness on her. She squared her shoulders in the face of them. With God's help, she would figure something out. The Lord did not bring her this far only to abandon her.

"Don't you worry about that. You're my guest."

Her hostess's kind hospitality flooded Rainee. However, she would not trespass on the woman's kindness. When she got back from her walk, she would pitch in and help with chores. "Thank you." Rainee finished her meal, put her plate in the water and headed outside.

Warm sunshine greeted her when she stepped off the porch. She tilted her face toward the sun, relishing the feel of it on her face. For now she was free. And freedom had never felt so good.

Haydon backed Lulu and Sally up to the wagon. He needed to head into town for a few supplies and to think. After hearing Rainee talk about her mother and seeing her tears, he had to get away. He had always been powerless in the face of tears, tears he couldn't dry.

"Mr. Bowen."

He pressed his eyes together before standing and turning around. "Haydon."

She nodded. "Are you going into town, Haydon?"

He went back to strapping the horses. "Yes. Is there something I can get for you?"

"Would you mind if I go along?"

His hands froze mid-air. Yes, he minded. So many emotions were running through his head, he just wanted to get away and think. But seeing her standing there with her hands clutched and her eyes downcast, he knew what how hard it was for her to ask. He would not be

rude, no matter how much she reminded him of Melanie, especially dressed in her fancy attire. "Are you sure
you're up to traveling so soon?"

"Yes. Yes, I am."

"Very well then. Can you be ready to go in a few
minutes? I have a lot to do today."

"Yes. Just let me run in and grab my satchel." She
whirled and scurried to the house.

*Dear God, give me the grace to get through this with
my sanity intact.*

By the time he fastened the last strap, Rainee had
appeared at the wagon holding her satchel and a letter.
He wondered who the letter was to but figured it was
her business, not his.

He helped her into the wagon and they headed down
the road.

The first mile was filled with a much-needed silence,
giving him time to think about his mother's words.

"Haydon."

Holding the reins loosely in his hands, he glanced at
her, then back at the road. "Yes."

"Have you always lived here?"

"No. We moved here about four years ago."

"Where did you move from?" She tilted the parasol
to her right, and he got a full view of her face.

He turned his attention back to the road. "Back
East."

"Where from back East?"

"New York."

"I have never been to New York. They say it is a delight to see. What is it like?"

"Like any other big city."

"Did you enjoy it?"

"Some aspects of it, yes. But mostly no. I like it here much better."

"Why is that?"

"The people here are friendlier, and they're genuine. You can trust them to do what they say they will. It's a nice change from New York."

"Do you regret moving here?"

"Only because I lost my father." An ache for his loss poked into his heart. "I keep thinking if we had not moved to Paradise Haven, he might still be alive. I understand only too well about the thistles and thorns."

She turned almost sideways to look at him, and his heart sped up. "What was your father like?"

Haydon wasn't sure if it was the question, her soft voice or her soft face, but he was having definite problems keeping himself in check. "He was one of the kindest, most generous men you would ever meet. He had a real zest for life and an adventurous spirit. In a lot of ways, I'm just like him." He glanced over at her again. "Well, I used to be anyway."

"It is hard on the oldest son to have a father die. That is for certain."

Haydon yanked his gaze her way, but she had her face forward.

"Back home, there is a young man whose parents passed away. At four and twenty, James knew it was up to him to be strong and to keep his family together. To provide for them. To be their protector. It was quite vexing for James to watch his mother and siblings suffer. His burden was great. And he, too, changed after his father's death. It was as if the real James had been buried with his father."

Rainee's words of understanding tunneled through Haydon with a gentleness he couldn't ignore. No one had ever seemed to understand what he had gone through—and still went through. As the oldest, everything fell on his shoulders. And yet he wasn't complaining. He couldn't. He loved his family. But he could also relate to this James fellow. "I can relate," he whispered, then looked at her.

The softness in her eyes and the compassion on her face encouraged him to continue.

"The first year was the hardest. My heart bled every time I watched or heard my family crying. I wanted to take their pain so they wouldn't have to suffer. But there was no way to do that. And it tore me up inside."

She laid her hand on his arm, and he glanced down at it, feeling it clear to the inner depths of his soul. "Your family seems very well cared for and happy. You have obviously done a splendid job."

Her words were like a healing salve, as was her touch, and he desperately needed them both. "Thank you."

They both fell silent the rest of the way. When they arrived in town, people stared, but no one asked any questions. He helped her down from the wagon and into the general store.

He watched as Rainee headed over to the post office section. She removed a letter from her satchel, handed it to the postmaster along with a coin, then turned and walked over to where he stood. "Well, you will not have to trouble yourself with me for much longer. I sent my post to Mr. Bettes, one of the other gentlemen who answered my advertisement. Soon, I will be gone, and that will be one less burden for you to bear." She smiled at him, but no smile reached his lips.

"Rainee, I—"

"You do not have to say a word, Haydon." She

interrupted him, but there was no animosity in her tone. "I want you to know I understand the position you and I have been placed in. You need not feel badly. God will take care of me, of that I am certain."

He nodded through the lump in his throat and pulled his gaze away from her. After he loaded the wagon, they headed out of town.

All the way back to the ranch his heart played tug of war with his mind. He wanted to reassure Rainee she wasn't a burden, but he didn't want to give her the wrong impression. No matter how easy she was to talk to or how sweet she seemed, she was a woman. Personal experience had taught him women caused nothing but heartache. Heartache he could do without.

Back at the ranch, Rainee deposited her satchel in the house. All alone with two hours to go before the noon meal, she decided to take a walk. Her legs were in need of a good stretching.

Her mind replayed the conversations with Haydon on their way to town and back. Haydon was a man who loved his family and would do anything for them. A very tenderhearted man, whose eyes had glistened with unshed tears when he spoke of his father.

It touched her deeply. He was a man who truly cared about people. Here he was, forced into a rather precarious situation with her, and yet he treated her with the utmost kindness and courtesy and protected her despite their highly unusual circumstances.

Haydon was what Ferrin should have been to her.

A guardian. A protector. A provider.

But Ferrin was quite the opposite. Under his care, she struggled daily with hunger, and most of her clothes had become threadbare, except for the few she had hidden away in a trunk. And instead of protecting her, Ferrin had caused her bodily harm many times. That was why she had to flee her once-love-filled home. Homesickness sprinkled over her, but she washed it away. Instead, she determined to enjoy the rest of her day.

On her way to the meadow, she neared one of the smaller houses. A very pregnant woman was standing on the porch, leaning over the railing, shaking out a rug. Or rather the rug was shaking her.

Rainee hiked up her skirt and scurried toward her. "Would you like some help with that?"

The woman stopped and looked at her. "No, but thank you very kindly." She tossed the rug over the porch rail and faced her. "My name is Hannah. Hannah Bowen." She stepped off the porch and extended her hand toward Rainee. "And you're Rainelle."

"Yes, ma'am. I am Rainelle Victoria Devonwood." She returned her handshake, then curtsied. "But please call me Rainee."

Hannah looped her arm through Rainee's and flashed her a mischievous smile. "I have someone who wants to meet you."

Stunned by the woman's fast speech and take-charge manner, all Rainee could do was nod.

Up the steps they went.

They stepped into a very tidy, roomy kitchen. Rainee was surprised to see the cabin was much bigger inside than it looked from the outside. Yellow curtains covered the long windows. A yellow cloth graced the table, and a bowl of fresh fruit had been set in the center of it.

Rainee tried to take in more of the room but was hurried into a bedroom off of the kitchen.

A man with a bandage wrapped around his head lay there with his eyes closed.

Not knowing what to do or say, Rainee waited near the foot of the bed.

"Sweetheart." Hannah touched his arm. "Rainelle is here."

The man bobbled his eyes open. "Rainelle." He started to rise, but pain shrouded his face, and he immediately lay back down. "I'm Jesse." His smile was wobbly and sheepish.

Hannah stepped off to the side of him, and Rainee stepped closer.

"I'm the one who sent for you." He spoke as if every word pained him.

"Yes, I know." She smiled shyly and did a quick curtsy.

"I want to apologize to you for bringing you out here under false pretenses. But to be perfectly honest with you, when I saw your ad, I prayed long and hard about it." He rolled onto his side and strained toward the glass of water sitting on the nightstand. Hannah snatched it up and held the glass while he took several sips. "Thank you, sweetheart." His eyes and smile spoke of the intense love he had for the woman.

Rainee envied Hannah. What she would give for a man to smile at her like that. To marry a man who truly loved her. She pushed those gloomy thoughts away.

"I would have never sent for you if I hadn't had this peace inside of me." He laid his hand on his chest. "I'm sorry." His Adam's apple slid up and down. "I must have missed God."

Rainee desired to ease his mind straightaway. "There is no need for you to apologize. I prayed about my decision to come here as well. And I, too, had peace. At first I must say I was shocked to discover the truth. But even so, I still believe that God, for whatever reason, led me here."

The wrinkles around his eyes disappeared and his body relaxed. "Thank you, Rainee, for saying that. Now if only Haydon would forgive me," he whispered and then his eyes drifted shut.

Hannah motioned for them to leave the room. "Would you like a cup of tea?"

"That would be lovely. But, please, allow me to get it."

"Don't be silly. I can do it."

Rainee politely led the woman with her bulging stomach over to a chair and after finding all the ingredients, she fixed the tea.

An hour later, after Rainee shook out the remaining pile of rugs Hannah had by the front door, she headed toward the field, wondering what had happened to Jesse's head.

Ever since the ride into town, Haydon felt scattered. He tried not to think of her, but every step brought a reminder of the situation, which inevitably yanked thoughts of her right back into his mind. Worse, every time he got things in his life and around the ranch under control, Jess and his willfulness did something to throw a kick into the works.

This morning he'd been so frazzled and frustrated when Michael told him Jess wasn't coming out because he still wasn't feeling well, in his haste to get the extra chores done so he could get to town, Haydon had left the corral gate open and the horses had gotten out. Gathering them by himself had cut mightily into his already-long day.

And now Kitty was missing.

If only he hadn't been so thickheaded and allowed his anger at his brother to get the best of him, then Jess wouldn't be laid up and he wouldn't be dealing with Rainee. There she was again, invading his thoughts. He pressed his hand down his face. It was driving him to distraction seeing what Jess's latest antics were costing that poor woman. And himself. Having Rainee around was wreaking havoc in his life. He had enough pressures to deal with—he didn't need to add a woman on top of everything else. "That Jess," he grumbled.

No more dwelling on it, Haydon. You have work to do.

"Here, Kitty." Haydon swung his leg over the saddle and dismounted. "Come here, Kitty." He scanned the trees and field in front of him looking for her, wondering where she was. Usually when he called her she came right away.

"Good afternoon, Haydon."

Haydon spun toward the voice. It was just as he feared. Her. Again. "What are you doing here?" Guilt snapped into him at his lack of keeping the impatience he felt at seeing her from his tone. But he couldn't help himself. He didn't want to be around this woman who stirred his heart and bombarded his thoughts any longer. She was making him senseless.

One look at the hurt expression on her face, and he pushed aside the unwelcome feelings of attraction she aroused in him. Besides, that was no way to treat another human being. His mother's tongue lashing before Rainee had shown up this morning had reminded him of that fact.

Mother said he needed to let go of the past. But he didn't know how to stop blaming himself for Melanie's death.

He sent Rainee what he hoped was his best welcoming smile. "It sure is a nice day for a walk." He hoped his words would put her at ease. Haydon dropped Rebel's reins, knowing the horse would stand there.

"Yes, it is."

"Whatever you do, try to stick to the baseline of the trees. If you do decide to go up into the woods, make sure at all times you can still see the meadow. That way you won't travel so deep you get lost."

"Thank you, Haydon. I shall do that." She looked around as if searching for something. "Yes, well, I will be on my way now. I am quite sorry to have bothered you again. I would not have, but I heard you calling for a kitty." She shrugged. "Well, I had hoped to see it. I love cats."

Before he could correct her, her eyes widened, her face paled and she let out a scream so loud he thought his eardrums had certainly burst.

Chapter Six

Rainee's scream pierced Haydon's eardrums, making him cringe. He whirled to see what had scared ten years off of not only Rainee's life, but his, too. He didn't see anything but his fun-loving pet trotting toward him with her ears flapping and her belly jiggling.

Having thought something or someone might have killed her, relief trotted through him. "Kitty, girl, you're okay."

Kitty leaned into his leg, and Haydon started rubbing her behind the ears.

Movement behind him hooked his attention. He turned just in time to see Rainee slump to the ground.

"Rainee!" He knelt down on one knee next to her collapsed body. "Rainee," he repeated while tilting her face away from the dirt. Kitty sniffed her with her big nose. Haydon placed his hand on her snout and gently pushed her away. "Not now, girl." Kitty pushed back, shoving her way toward the woman's face. Again Haydon forced her back. Kitty placed her head against his hand and moved her backside around in a half circle. Butting her head, she yanked Haydon's hand off of her nose. Her snout was inches away from Rainee's face.

The woman opened her eyes, and abject horror was the only way to describe what Haydon saw there. She opened her mouth wide, filling her lungs with enough air to be heard clear into Paradise Haven. Haydon braced himself for the piercing scream, but no sound came. Instead her eyes rolled closed, and her head fell limp to the side.

Haydon placed himself between her and Kitty. He scooped Rainee up into his arms and held her, debating whether to take her back to the house or to the river. The river won. It was closer.

Kitty followed closely behind him, oinking the whole way. If Rainee woke up, he didn't want her screaming or fainting again, so as much as Haydon hated doing it, he bent his knee and gave a swift kick to Kitty's rump. The pig squealed, more from shock than pain. She whirled and trotted toward the thick brush. Haydon felt like pond scum for doing that to Kitty, but he had no choice.

He laid Rainee on the grass near the river's edge. He pulled his eyes away from her soft womanly curves, grabbed the clean handkerchief from his pocket and dipped it into the river. He knelt beside her and blotted her forehead. Seeing her so helpless, he fought the emotions rising in him. Haydon had always been a sucker for a woman who needed him to be strong.

Her head swayed from side to side, and her eyes slowly opened.

She bolted upright, clipping his chin with her head in the process.

"What are you doing, woman?" He rubbed his throbbing chin.

"Where is it?" Her wild eyes and hands darted about. Shifting on her rump, using her feet, she scurried to her left, then to her right, before making a complete circle, apparently looking for an unseen threat. "That—that thing."

"What thing?"

"That—that *pig!*" she all but shouted.

"That *pig* has a name. Her name is Kitty."

She blinked and stared at him as if he had lost his mind. Well, one of them had but it wasn't him. "Kitty is a—a pig?"

"Last time I checked she was," he answered with a slow chuckle.

Rainee's eyes narrowed, and she pursed her lips. She shifted her legs off to the side, pushed herself onto one knee and, using her hands for balance, she started to stand.

Haydon leapt up and placed his hand under her elbow to brace her. Touching her was not a good thing. Well, it was, but it wasn't. It made his blood pump faster. But he had no choice. He couldn't very well let her fall again.

"You named your pig Kitty?" She blinked up at him.

"No."

"No? What do you mean 'no'?"

"No. Abby named her Kitty." He moved his gaze away from her, not able to handle how her eyes always seemed to pierce through him. After making sure she was stable, he released her arm to rid himself of the tingling sensation she aroused in him. He could feel her eyes on him even as she brushed the dirt off of her arms and skirt.

"Is there just the one..." she gulped "...pig?" She said the word "pig" the same way Abby said the word "ghost" when she was scared.

The protective side of him wanted to wrap her in his

arms and comfort her like he did Abby, but the way his insides were shaking, his urge to protect her would not be a good thing. "No. Actually, we have fifty sows and three boars."

"Fif— Fifty!" The whites of her eyes were no longer hidden. "But—but why?"

Did the woman have a stuttering problem or what? "Because," he drew out, "we raise them. That's why. Didn't Jesse tell you?"

Merciful heavens, what had she gotten herself into? "No, Haydon. Jesse did not mention that bit of news. I assure you if he had, I would have never come here. I am terrified of pigs."

"Why?"

"Why? Because when I was a young girl, I was attacked by one. That is why." The memory made Rainee's knees feel as flimsy as a hair ribbon. She searched for something to sit on and noticed a felled log. On shaky legs she took the few steps toward it, tucked her skirt under and lowered herself onto the piece of wood.

Haydon placed his bulky frame next to her. His hard features were softer now.

"What happened?" he asked, sounding like he actually wanted to know.

She brushed the fallen hair from her face. "My parents owned a few head of swine. An acquaintance of mine and I wanted to see the newborn babies up close." Careful to not mention her brother's name for fear Haydon would ask where Ferrin was, she chose her words wisely, "I was told by someone it would be fine to pet them, that the sow would not hurt us."

One of Haydon's eyebrows spiked.

"My friend Tamsey and I opened the gate and headed

toward the mama sow. The other pigs came toward us and surrounded us. One of them pushed me. When I screamed, they started acting fidgety. We were so frightened. We did not know what to do.

"Everything happened so fast after that, I am not sure what happened next. All I know is the mama sow was charging toward us. We ran toward the gate. Tamsey made it out, and I almost did except I slipped and fell."

"Were you hurt very badly?"

She stared at the crystal-clear water that washed over the rocks and disappeared down the creek. "Yes. The sow kept snapping at my legs, and when I fell trying to get away, she tromped on my hip and thighs until her sharp hooves ripped through my clothing and skin. When I was finally able to roll over, she came after me again, heading right for my face with her mouth wide open. I raised my arms to defend myself, and when I did, my arm brushed against a piece of broken board, so I grabbed it and shoved it into the swine's mouth." Rainee pinched her eyes shut and shuddered at the memory.

When she turned her attention back to Haydon, she squirmed under his intense scrutiny, especially when his gaze landed on her hands. Knowing she could not tell Haydon about her brother and that it was Ferrin who had inflicted the scars on her hands and back and not the pig, and that the only scars the sow had caused were the ones on the back of her legs and hip, her mouth turned dry and swallowing became difficult.

Having secrets was a heavy burden to carry.

In an attempt to stop him from asking questions about her hands, she looked away and quickly added, "My father snatched me out of the pen before that wretched thing inflicted any more harm on me."

And afterward her father had given Ferrin a beating for telling her it was okay.

Rainee never understood her brother's hatred toward her, although she had felt it often even before her parents' deaths. Many times she thought it was because Father doted on her, but there had to be more to it because their father had spent many hours with Ferrin, spoiling him, too.

"Rainee."

Rainee's gaze collided with his. "Yes?"

"I hate for you to think all pigs are mean. Granted, they can be when they're trying to protect their young, but most of the time they're very loving animals."

"A pig? A loving animal?" Rainee scrunched her nose. "What a ludicrous notion. Just thinking about them makes me cringe. I have no desire to be anywhere near the little beasts. Ever."

"Well then, ma'am—" he stood and offered her his hand "—I suggest you stand behind me."

"Why?" She laid her hand in his abundant one and allowed him to help her up.

"Because." His chin jerked upward once. "Here comes Abby, and Kitty is hot on her heels."

Rainee whirled. To her utter horror, that four-legged thing was heading her way. Fear dropped into her stomach like a heavy crumpet. She wanted to flee, but her feet were as transfixed as her mind. Worse, there was nowhere to go.

The closer the curly-tailed beast got to her, the weaker her knees became. "Help me, Jesus," she whispered, gulping down the fear attacking her from all sides.

Haydon stepped between her and the pink animal he

called Kitty. "Hi, Abby." He tugged on one of his little sister's pigtails. "What are you up to, Squirt?"

"Just playin' with Kitty."

"So I see." He knelt down. "Hey, Kitty girl."

The pig trotted toward him with her ears flapping like an upset hen. She leaned into his legs. He stumbled but caught himself before the swine toppled him over.

Rainee moved her tongue around to moisten her mouth, but it did no good. Dampness covered the palms of her hands. And air was sorely lacking.

"Hi, Rainee." Abby's sweet voice pulled her gaze away from the frightening creature. One look at her and the little girl's smile vanished. "Hey, you don't look none too good." Abby's eyes narrowed. "You okay?"

"I—I…" She tried to breathe but her tight corset prevented it. The bright outdoors turned into a cloud of hazy black. The only other time she remembered fainting this much was during one of Ferrin's vicious beatings because the pain had become so unbearable her body had succumbed to it with blessed blackness. And that blackness descended upon her now.

Her legs gave way.

In slow motion, she felt herself slipping to the ground, but instead of hitting the rough terrain, her body connected with solid arms before blackness engulfed her in its embrace.

Haydon carried Rainee's limp form back to the house. This was becoming a habit. One he wanted to break. Holding her in his arms affected his heart in a way he didn't need nor want. "Abby, open the door, please."

Abby raced ahead of him and held the door open. The wooden planks creaked as he climbed up the steps and onto the porch. "Mother," he hollered, stepping inside. "Mother!"

His mother bustled into the living room carrying a load of sheets in her arms. One look at Rainee and she thrust the sheets onto the chair and rushed toward the sofa where she propped up a pillow.

Once again, he laid Rainee's small frame on the sofa.

Mother sat next to her and removed her jacket. "What happened?"

"Kitty happened."

Mother's gaze darted up at him. "What do you mean 'Kitty happened'? Did she attack her?" Anger and concern flowed from her voice and eyes.

"No. All it took was one look at Kitty, and she fainted. Twice."

"Twice?" Mother's eyes widened, then narrowed. She looked at Abby, standing beside him. "Abby, grab me a wet cloth." She glanced at Haydon. "I'll call you if I need you."

That was his mother's way of dismissing him.

Even though Haydon saw Rainee as another weak city female, it bothered him she lay there unconscious… again. He hated to leave without knowing if she was all right or not, but he did as his mother bade. With a quick spin on his boot heel, he headed outside. He'd check in on her later.

Leah met him coming in with an empty clothes basket. "Hi, Haydon. What are you doing here? I thought you were checking on the pigs."

"I was. Rainee—" he gave a quick nod of his neck toward the inside of the house "—fainted again."

Leah dropped the basket on the porch, brushed past him and rushed inside. "Mother," she hollered.

"In here."

"Is she okay?" Leah's voice clouded with concern.

"She'll be fine."

Although he was relieved to hear she was fine, he wondered if he ever would be again. How had the little filly gotten under his skin so quickly? And more important, what was he going to do about it?

Chapter Seven

Rainee rolled her head to the side.

"Rainee?"

Hearing Katherine's voice as if she were in a tunnel, Rainee opened her eyes. "What happened?"

"Haydon said you fainted. Don't you remember?"

A floppy-eared, curly-tailed, big-snouted image jumped into her mind. She cringed. "Yes. I remember. How did I get here?" She pressed her fingers to her temples.

"Haydon brung you," Abby piped in.

"Brought you," Katherine corrected.

"That's what I said. Can I go out and play now?"

"May I?"

Abby let out a huff and rolled her eyes. "May I?"

"Yes, you may."

Abby skipped out of the living room and disappeared. What Rainee would give to be carefree like that again. To sit with her mother on the front-porch swing back home and listen while her mother regaled Rainee with stories about her childhood.

"Leah, would you please fix us some tea and bring it in here? And grab some syltkakor cookies, too."

Syltkakor cookies?

"Yes, Mother." She turned but looked back at Rainee. "I'm glad you're okay." Leah smiled and then left the room.

Rainee rose into a sitting position. Her head throbbed.

"The tea will help with your headache." Katherine smiled, but there was uncertainty in it. She stood and moved one of the wingback chairs until it faced Rainee. "Rainee?"

"Yes, ma'am."

"I know this is rather personal, but may I ask you something?"

The thought of Katherine asking a question Rainee had no desire to answer caused her stomach to twist into knots. But if she said no, it would be rude. "Yes, you may." She braced herself for the question.

"Are you wearing a corset?"

The woman was not kidding when she said it was personal. Heat filled Rainee's cheeks.

"I'm sorry if I embarrassed you. Haydon said you fainted because of Kitty, but I also wonder if that corset has something to do with it. They definitely restrict your air flow. This is the country, Rainee. Not the city. Out here, you don't have to wear one if you don't want to. Back home I was always fainting because of mine. Shortly after I moved here and noticed none of the other women wore them, I got rid of mine. The only time I wear one now is when I go to the city. I can't stand the confining things."

Rainee wanted to hug the woman for saying that. Because of Katherine's easy ways and her honesty concerning something as personal as undergarments, Rainee felt at ease to openly share her thoughts. "I, too, cannot stand the vile contraptions. I find them too confining. But my mother always made me wear one.

"I remember on my fourteenth birthday I decided to go without one to see if my mother would even notice." She looked at Katherine and smiled. "She did. And no matter how much I pleaded with her to not make me wear it on my birthday, she would not relent. Told me that properly bred young ladies do not go anywhere without a corset. So even though I despise the wretched things, I wear them out of respect for my mother and her wishes."

"My mother told me the same thing, so I know how you feel. But things are much different out here than they are in the city. It's up to you whether you want to wear one or not. But I must warn you…" Her eyes crinkled with mirth. "There are no fainting couches here."

They shared a laugh.

Every room in Rainee's house back home had a fainting couch. It infuriated her that women were forced to stuff themselves into those things until their bodies actually became deformed and their lungs were deprived of air and proper blood supply, which caused them to faint often.

Rainee thought the person who had come up with all those ridiculous rules of etiquette should have found something better to do with their time. Well, Rainee did. She wanted to walk without being short of breath. And she was tired of almost fainting every time she removed her corset and the blood traveled back into her head. Rainee despised fainting. To her it was a sign of weakness. What must these people think of her for fainting like she had?

If only she had been born a male, then she could wear

trousers instead of layers of clothing. And no one would think anything of it if she climbed trees, got dirty, ran up the stairs or fished. Rainee loved to fish.

She placed her hands in her lap, torn between doing what her mother had taught her and the desire to rid herself of the encumbering contraption. She really did not have much of a choice. None of her clothes would fit without the corset.

"If you're worried about your dresses not fitting, Leah and I can help you let them out."

Had the woman read her mind? From the moment Rainee had met her, Rainee felt an immediate kinship with Katherine.

Leah walked into the room with a tray laden with cookies and tea. She set it on the end table, poured three cups of tea and filled three small plates with sandwich-type cookies. The filling reminded Rainee of the jar of red currant she saw sitting on the table. After Leah served her mother and Rainee, she sat on the opposite end of the sofa.

Memories of sharing tea and cake in the parlor with her mother and best friend Tamsey flashed through her mind. But she refused to allow herself to dwell on that memory, knowing it would cause her nothing but great sadness. "Thank you, Leah."

"You're welcome." Leah smiled that beautiful smile of hers, and her eyes sparkled like crystallized ice.

Rainee took a long sip of her drink and daintily set it down before looking toward Katherine. "I am not sure what to do, Katherine. In less than three weeks I will be leaving here. And if I go to the city, it would be improper for me not to wear a corset."

"You're not leaving us, are you, Rainee?" Leah looked horrified, which warmed Rainee's heart even more. Everyone had been so kind to her, making her feel truly welcome.

Too bad Haydon had not been the one to send for her. She would have so loved to be a part of this family, and even more so, Haydon's wife, for there was a gentleness about him she could not deny, in spite of his on-again-off-again aloofness.

And as for them raising pigs, well surely she could help around the house and not be subjected to the curly-tailed terrors. Especially the one Haydon called Kitty. Her body quivered just thinking about the vile creature.

"Are you cold?" Katherine sat her teacup on the saucer.

Rainee shook her head. "No. I was just thinking about—" her nose wrinkled "—Kitty." Her gaze landed on the ceiling, and she blew out a very unladylike breath. "What a name for a pig."

"Abby named her," Leah piped in.

She vaguely remembered Haydon telling her that. Seeing Haydon's strong attachment to his sisters, Rainee understood why he would go along with naming a pig Kitty. She giggled.

"What's so funny?" Katherine asked.

Rainee took another sip of her tea and placed it back on the saucer with a tinkling sound. Mother would have reprimanded her for that one. "When I went for a walk, I heard Haydon saying, 'Here, Kitty.' I went over to where he was and looked around for the cat. Instead I saw a pig charging our direction and screamed." She snickered again. "I am surprised y'all did not hear me."

She looked down at her chest as she fought again to gather in enough air. "You are right, Katherine. This corset has to go." It was clear to her now that being frightened along with not getting enough air had caused her to faint.

Rainee took another sip of her tea. Only this time she gently set the cup down with no tinkling noise. "Perhaps it would be okay to let out a couple of my dresses so I have something comfortable to wear while I am here. But I cannot let them all out as I do not have many dresses anymore. I will need to save some so that I have something presentable to wear when I leave for the city."

"Rainee, you don't have to leave. You're welcome to stay here as long as you like."

Rainee looked at Katherine. "I appreciate your kind offer, but I cannot do that to Haydon. It is obvious he does not want me here. I cannot impose upon your hospitality forever."

Katherine looked her straight in the eyes. "Having you here is no imposition whatsoever. Besides, you never know what God will do. I've seen the way Haydon looks at you. He's scared of you, Rainee. That means he feels something."

Rainee's insides skipped with a flicker of hope.

"I've prayed about it and prayed about it. And I believe God brought you here."

"But you do not even know me."

"That's true. But God does. And I know my Savior's voice." The wrinkles around Katherine's eyes and lips curled. Her look held a secret, but just what kind of secret, Rainee did not know.

Haydon tried not to think about Rainee, but his worry for her wouldn't leave. He headed up to the house and yelled through the screen door. "Is it okay to come in?"

"It's okay. Come on in," his mother hollered back.

Haydon stepped inside and headed into the living room. His gaze went straight to Rainee, who was sitting up. Relief expanded his chest. "I came to see if you were okay."

But when he got closer to Rainee, he noticed her face was still a bit too pale.

He glanced at his mother and Leah, pointedly feeling the number of people in the room.

His mother glanced around and the opportunity of the situation crossed her face. Haydon knew what was coming next even as his mother stood.

"I think I have some of my old dresses in the attic. Leah, come help me find them."

Haydon gave her a look meant to say he knew exactly what she was doing, and she smiled sweetly back. He watched as they left the room. He turned his attention back to Rainee. A few moments of awkward silence and the room suddenly seemed to be getting smaller.

Not knowing what else to do, he sat across from her and tried not to stare as he assessed for himself that she really was all right.

She cleared her throat. "Would—would you like a cookie? Or some tea perhaps. I—I could get you some." She started to stand but reached for the side of the sofa with a bit of sway to her movement.

Haydon jumped up and steadied her. His whole attention riveted to only her. He helped her onto the sofa and sat down with her. "Rainee, I don't want any cookies. I came to see if you were all right."

She stopped and for one second her eyes met his, pulling him into their depths. He found he was unable to move away and that scared him. Yanking reality back to himself, he stood so fast the blood rushed to his head. "Now that I see you're okay, I need to get back to my chores." He said the words so fast they almost tripped over each other.

Rainee looked up at him with a slight smirk on her face. "Thank you for checking on me. I am fine, albeit quite embarrassed for my lack of strength."

"Lack of strength?" The words knocked him over like a team of runaway horses. "Why would you be embarrassed? All of us have weaknesses."

"Yes, but weakness is all you have seen of me."

"Nope—that's not all I've seen."

She quirked her head to the side, the smirk not fully gone. "Really? Well, let us see. First, you had to rescue me from the guy at the stage stop. Then, I nearly fainted when we arrived and you had to help me in. And now, I have fainted again. Not once, but twice. No, make that three times if you count fainting twice within minutes."

He glanced at her for a moment, trying not to laugh. "Well, I guess you have a point." For one moment he couldn't believe he said that until she started laughing and his laughter blended with hers. "But I still don't see you as weak. It took a lot of courage to travel to a strange place."

He noticed the appreciative smile in her eyes. "Well, I'd better get back to work. I'm glad you're feeling better."

She started to rise, but he motioned for her to remain seated.

He headed for the door and just as he got there, she said, "Be careful of those curly-tailed beasts."

Her laughter followed him out the door.

Rainee was still laughing when Katherine and Leah came into the living room empty-handed.

"It's nice to see you feeling better." Katherine looked lighter and maybe even happier than before. "Now, let's go get you out of that thing and into something more practical and comfortable."

Rainee followed them up the stairs with a lighter, more joyful step than she had felt in two years. Perhaps God was in this after all. That thought brought joy singing through her heart.

Inside Leah's bedroom, without thinking, Rainee removed her gloves.

Leah glanced down and gasped. "What happened to your hands?"

Rainee's gaze flew to Leah. The poor girl stood there staring in utter horror at her hands.

Katherine came from behind Leah, and she too stared at them.

Shame flooded Rainee. She buried them behind her back.

Katherine and Leah's questioning eyes bore through her. She knew she could not hide her hands forever. With a flushed face and trembling insides, she inched them upward for their inspection, trying to feel nothing as the two of them looked on with shock and horror.

Katherine gently took one of Rainee's hands in hers and studied the raised scars. She looked at Rainee with eyes of compassion. "Who did this to you?"

She wanted to tell them they were from the pig attack, but that was an untruth. The pig had not touched her hands, only the back of her leg and her hips. With a heavy sigh, she answered, "My brother—"

"I didn't know you had a brother," Leah blurted.

Rainee looked at her and nodded. "I do."

"Is he—"

"Leah, enough!" Katherine reprimanded her daughter. "Mind your manners."

"Sorry." Leah lowered her head.

Katherine's words reminded her of her own mother. That would have been something Mother would have said. She envied Leah that she still had her mother to correct and love her. Rainee wished her mother were still alive. Homesickness feathered over her as it did so very often.

"Please, go on."

Rainee lowered her eyes. In a nervous circular motion, she rubbed her fingertips over the welts near her wrists. Rainee looked up at them. "Please, I do not wish to talk about this for it is too painful. And if you would both be so kind, would you please not mention my hands to anyone?"

She looked back and forth between Katherine and Leah, allowing her eyes to plead with them for their total secrecy.

"There is no need for anything we've seen or talked about today to leave this room," Katherine said, more to Leah than anyone else.

"I won't say a word, Mother." Leah looked Rainee directly in the eye. "You have my word, Rainee. I promise I won't say a thing to anyone."

"And neither will I." Katherine's chest heaved. "Now I understand why such a sweet beautiful woman such as yourself ran away."

Ran away? Oh, no. Her insides flushed with terror. Now that they knew she had run away, would they send her back, regardless of what her brother had done to her? Would they betray her like her Aunt Lena had?

Chapter Eight

The ache in Rainee's stomach disappeared when nothing more was said about her running away. Too bad that had not been the case with her father's sister, Aunt Lena. Before she ran away to Aunt Lena's, she had asked Mr. Pennay, her father's lawyer, if anything was written in the will about Ferrin being her legal guardian, and he had assured her nothing had been.

When Ferrin came for Rainee at Aunt Lena's house, even after she had shown the strict socially proper woman the welts on her back and hands, her aunt still forced her to go back with Ferrin when he lied and said he was indeed her legal guardian. Aunt Lena said it was not proper for her or anyone else to go against a father's wishes, and if he said he was her legal guardian, then he was—pure and simple.

It never ceased to amaze Rainee that, even when a person's life was at risk, people still maintained the rules of propriety. That was just one more reason why she detested those rules.

Today, she had broken two of those rules, and it felt delightful.

After Rainee, Leah and Katherine let out three of

Rainee's dresses, they started preparing the evening meal. While Katherine worked on the Lefsa, a traditional Swedish flatbread made from potatoes, Leah helped gather ingredients, peel potatoes and fry the Korv. Korv, Rainee learned, was Swedish for sausage. Rainee baked the pies and made the soup, enjoying every moment of being helpful.

Rainee opened the oven door to remove the pies. Heat drove into her, but with a lighter dress on and no restricting corset, the heat did not bother her like it had back home.

After her parents had died, during the hottest part of the summer, Ferrin had forced her to wear heavy garments with layers upon layers of undergarments. He also had limited her water and food supply to one serving a day, all because he said it gave him great pleasure watching her suffer. Why? She did not know. But suffer she had.

Often, her stomach cramped until she doubled over. Her skin prickled like someone was stabbing it with needles, and her head swam with dizziness.

For fear of getting another beating, she had to force her fatigued body to move.

If it had not been for Jenetta coming to Rainee's aid repeatedly, she would probably be dead by now. But Jenetta had sewn two large pockets into one of her undergarments, big enough to hold a jar of water and some cheese or fruit.

Jenetta's husband, Abram, left a covered bucket of water inside the woodshed, along with a few vegetables he had picked fresh from the garden and managed to sneak inside the shed.

Rainee closed the oven door. The scent of fresh, warm pie crust and sweet huckleberries satiated her nose. With any kind of luck, she would never go hungry or ever endure another vicious beating again—even if she had to move again to Mr. Bettes's.

Katherine hung up her dish towel. "Leah, will you please ring the dinner bell?"

"I will get it." Rainee wiped her hands on her apron and stepped outside.

The breeze penetrated her wine-colored dress, kissing her flesh with its coolness. She patted her damp face with her apron and took a brief moment to enjoy the sensation of freedom the lightweight dress and breezy outdoors created. It was heaven on earth.

She reached up and gave the rope several tugs and winced at the loud clanging noise. Hurrying back inside, she helped put the food onto the table.

The door creaked.

Rainee turned, only to find Haydon standing inside the door, gawking at her.

Her gaze dropped to the floor. After setting down the tray of food, she hugged her waist. All those years of wearing a corset, and she suddenly felt naked without it. Mother's words started to run through her mind as they so often did, but this time she squelched them. Instead she dared a glance at Haydon. Was that approval she saw in his eyes?

Before she had a chance to figure it out, Abby came barreling through the door followed by Michael and Smokey.

Rainee waited for Katherine to reprimand Abby for charging into the house, but the scolding never came. Mother would have made Rainee go back outside and come back in like a suitable young lady, and then she would sit her down to a long lecture on how proper young

ladies should act, followed by a tender hug that left no
doubt in Rainee's mind about her mother's love.

Everyone sat down at the table and bowed their
heads.

"Heavenly Father." Haydon's reverent voice filled the
room. "Thank You for what You're doing in our lives
and for Your healing power that is at work in Jesse. We
thank You for this food and for Your bountiful provi-
sion. And, Lord, help us to be a blessing to Rainee."

Rainee kept one eye closed, but the other one snuck
a peek at Haydon. Never had she heard such humility
or kindness in his voice, especially where she was concerned. In the quietness of her mind, she offered up
her own gratitude as everyone said amen. She moved
her bowl in front of her. "How is your brother doing,
Haydon?"

Sapphire eyes settled on hers. "I don't know. I haven't
seen him."

He made a quick glance around the table and then
looked down at his soup. Rainee wondered what the
sudden change in his disposition was about. Was he
still upset with Jesse for bringing her here, or was something else bothering him? She kept her wonderings to
herself.

She picked up her spoon, dipped it in her bowl and
brought it to her mouth. The thick split-pea and ham
soup tasted heavenly. A nice change from the beans and
rice Ferrin fed her once a day. If she was lucky.

Smokey cleared his throat. "Jesse's doing a little
better today."

"You mean Hannah let you see him?" Leah asked
with raised brows. "She wouldn't let me. She said he
was sleeping and she would not disturb him. She sure

has changed." She laughed. "Hannah's like a protective mama bear watching over her cubs."

Smokey nodded. "Must have something to do with her being in the family way. I pert-near had to beg her to let me check him. And even then she made me promise I'd only stay a minute."

Everyone but Haydon laughed.

Rainee watched as he picked up his spoon and dipped it into the split-pea soup.

"Who knew Hannah could be so feisty?" Smokey commented with a deep rumble in his chest. "Since Jesse's accident, her shyness seems to have fled."

"What happened to Jesse anyway?" Rainee asked.

With a pained expression, Haydon looked at her, then at the rest of his family, then down at his soup. His jaw muscles worked back and forth. Without saying a word, he spooned his soup and ate.

The air thickened with silence.

Rainee scanned the table. Everyone seemed engrossed in the food on their plates. Everyone except Abby. Her bright blue eyes gazed around the table. It was as if she were waiting for someone to say something.

When no one else spoke, Abby did. "Haydon's horse reared and hurted him."

Rainee watched with interest as Haydon's scowling gaze swung toward Abby.

The little girl blinked. Then as fast as she could she wrapped her potato bread around her sausage and took a big bite. Her cheeks bulged like a chipmunk, and she nervously glanced up and down and around the room.

"I think Jesse's just wanting to get out of clipping the newborn piglet's teeth," Leah piped in.

All eyes swerved toward Leah, but no one said anything.

Curiosity and horror got the best of Rainee. "You clip the baby pigs' teeth?"

"Yes." Her gaze transferred to Haydon. "If we don't, when they grow, they can be very dangerous."

"Dangerous." She gulped and worked her tongue around to moisten her suddenly parched mouth. "How dangerous?" She picked up her water glass and took a drink, then rested her hands in her lap and fidgeted with her gloves.

Haydon set the glass he was holding down and locked gazes with her. "Don't worry, Rainee. I won't let anything happen to you."

Haydon broke eye contact and shoved a bite of Korv and Lefsa into his mouth. What he really wanted to do was to remove his boot and give himself a good swift kick in the behind. The last thing he wanted was for her and his family to get the notion he was interested in her.

Their eyes connected for a brief moment before he asked Michael. "Did you get that halter fixed?" He dipped his wrap into his soup and took a bite. When Michael didn't answer, he looked over at him.

Like a lovelorn pup, his brother was staring across the table at Rainee. "Michael!"

His brother jerked his head in his direction, blinking. "What?"

Abby giggled. "Michael's sweet on Rainee. Michael's sweet on Rainee," she singsonged.

Michael's cheeks flamed like a bad sunburn. He dropped his chin.

"Abigail! Stop that!" His mother's stern voice rescued poor Michael.

Haydon watched Rainee's cheeks and neck turn crimson.

"Apologize this instant, Abby," Mother demanded.

"But it's true. Last night I seeded Michael staring at her the whole time we eated. And today, when Rainee was walking, I seeded him hiding in the bushes watching her."

"I was not hiding in the bushes. I heard a scream and went to check it out. When I saw Haydon had it under control and that she was all right, I went back to gathering wood." Michael glared at his sister with narrowed eyes.

"You always stare at her. And I hearded you tell Smokey you thought she was bootiful." She tipped her head, pinched her lips and squinted her eyes. Haydon had seen that look before. Abby was daring Michael to challenge her.

Rainee's cheeks brightened to an even deeper shade of red. Her eyes were downcast, and she shifted in her chair.

"Enough, you two!" Haydon barked.

Abby jumped, and Michael had the decency to look ashamed.

"Can't you see you've made Rainee uncomfortable? You both need to apologize to her this instant."

Abby's lips puckered and tears welled in her in eyes. She dropped her gaze to her lap and sniffled. "Sorry, Rainee."

Haydon glanced at Rainee in time to see her look over at Abby and nod. He glanced at Michael.

"I'm sorry I made you uncomfortable, Rainee." Michael's sheepish grin showed his remorse. "But—" he pressed his shoulders back and puffed his chest out "—I'm not sorry for saying you're beautiful. Because you are." Michael sent Rainee a flirtatious smile and then he shot his older brother a look of direct challenge before his gaze dropped to his soup.

So much for Michael having the decency to be ashamed.

At a complete loss for words, Haydon looked to his mother, who seemed to share his bewilderment.

To take the focus off of Rainee and this whole awkward situation, Haydon shifted his attention toward his sister. "Leah, is that your famous blue-ribbon apple pie I smell?"

"No." She swallowed. "Rainee made it. And it's not apple, it's huckleberry."

So much for getting the focus off of Rainee. His gaze slid her direction.

Her cheeks were as pink as a warm-weather sunset, giving her a wholesome, fresh look. His heart noticed it all.

"You made it?" He didn't mean for his shock to leak through his voice but it did.

"Yes, I did," she answered softly.

Taken aback, Haydon mentally shook his head. At the stagecoach stop when he first laid eyes on Rainee, wearing all the rich city-girl frippery, he instantly thought of Melanie, who thought cooking and cleaning were beneath her. He just assumed the same about Rainee. Had he misjudged her?

Don't let that summer dress and great-smelling pie fool you, Haydon. The Idaho Territory isn't any place for a woman like her. You learned that the hard way.

His gaze slid in his mother's direction. Back home in New York, Mother had been a leader in society. So when Father decided to move out West, Haydon had waited for his mother to protest, but instead, she had readily agreed.

It hadn't taken long for her to adapt to her new surroundings. She was a brave woman with a strong constitution who had survived several harsh winters. Respect and pride for her swelled his chest. He snuck a glance at their guest. Aside from her fainting spells, which he knew happened to the strongest of women, could Rainee be a stronger woman than he gave her credit for?

Not liking where his thoughts were leading, he picked up his spoon and filled his mouth with more of the delicious dinner. "You've outdone yourself on the soup, Mother. This is your best batch ever."

"Mother didn't make it. Rainee did," Leah informed him.

He snapped his head in her direction. "You made this?"

Rainee sat up straight and jutted her chin. "Yes. Yes, I did."

"Rainee can do lots of things," his mother stated, sending Haydon a silent message.

His gaze veered toward Michael, whose admiring gaze clung to Rainee.

Haydon rubbed his neck in frustration. The whole world seemed to have gone crazy with her arrival. What to do about his mother and her not-so-subtle hints was bad enough, but Michael was even worse.

What was he going to do about his little brother and his infatuation with Rainee? As the oldest, Father had left Haydon in charge, so it was up to him to come up with a plan of action to stop his sixteen-year-old brother's boyish passion. And he needed to do it quickly. Not just for Michael's sake. But for hers, and maybe even his.

When Rainee finished helping with the dishes, the Bowens invited her to join in on their family Bible reading.

They all retired into the living room and sat near the fireplace. After Haydon finished reading and praying, Rainee excused herself and stepped outside and off of the porch. The cool air had a penetrating, earthy freshness to it. She headed toward the barn but stopped several yards away from the door and gazed up at the sky. Stars sparkled like sequins on the ballroom gown she had worn at her coming-out party. Just like that dress, they were too numerous to even try to count. But count she would. "One," she whispered. "Two. Three. Four."

"Forget it."

She whirled at the sound of Haydon's voice.

He stood behind her, gazing upward, arms crossed. "You'll never count them all. I've already tried." His gaze alighted on hers. Night shadows fell across his face. And what a handsome face it was.

"There's a bit of nip in the air. I thought you might need this." He draped her wrap securely around her shoulders.

What a sweet man he was to think of her comfort.

A tug on each end of her shawl, and she managed to pull it closer to her. She had not noticed the chill until his warm hands had touched her. "Thank you." Her heart melted at his thoughtfulness.

"You're welcome."

Rainee waited for him to leave, but he did not. He stood there, staring up at the stars.

What an enigma this man had turned out to be. There were times when he was kind to her, times when he barely spoke to her, times when his gaze was soft and others when he looked at her as if he were deathly afraid of her or even outright angry with her.

She could not blame him for his actions or even for his behavior. Though they saddened her, she must not allow the sadness to work its way into her heart. She must accept the fact she had to find another suitable husband. That was best for all involved. Still, this moment, standing here under the stars was not to be wasted, even though it could not last. "Is it always this beautiful out here?"

"Nope. Sometimes it's even better."

"Better than this?"

"Doesn't seem possible, does it?"

"No."

A comfortable silence stretched between them as they continued to gaze at the sky. This place might be in the middle of nowhere, but it was truly extraordinary.

"Is it always this peaceful?" She had not experienced this kind of serenity in a very long time.

He looked down at her. Their eyes connected, searching and probing and her heart responded with a flip.

He turned his head upward again. "Most of the time."

Most of the time, as in, before she arrived?

"I never tire of the night sky." Reverence floated through his voice.

"Nor do I."

"I can't believe God took the trouble to place the stars into various shapes. Like the Big Dipper." He pointed to it, and she followed the direction of his finger until it landed on the pattern of those stars.

"And the Little Dipper," she said. "Slaves used the Little Dipper and the Big Dipper to point to the North Star. They even sang a song about them…'Follow the Drinking Gourd.'"

"I've never heard that before. Did your family have slaves?"

Rainee tensed. If only she could avoid answering everyone's questions about her family until she wed, then she would be free from her brother's controlling clutches. "Before the war my parents had slaves, but they did not treat them cruelly. And after the war ended, they gave them the option to leave or to stay on with a small wage and room and board. How about you? Did you have slaves?"

"No, my parents did not believe in slavery. We had hired servants."

"Is it hard not having servants here?"

"No. Not at all."

"Does your mother mind not having servants to help her?"

"Nope. She loves to cook and clean. She said it's better than sitting around all day doing nothing."

Rainee agreed.

"I've offered to hire her some help many times, but she won't hear of it. It really bothers me watching her work as hard as she does. But she keeps telling me she loves it, and says that if she ever feels it's becoming too much for her she'll let me know so I can hire someone to help her. Speaking of help…" He glanced over at Rainee. "I really appreciate you helping my mother with the baking and cooking. Thank you."

"You are most welcome. I was delighted to do it."

Haydon looked away and the only sounds to be heard were a chorus of frogs and insects. Moments later, Haydon heaved a heavy sigh. "Well, it's getting late and I have to get up early. Let me walk you to the house."

They turned and headed back to the main house.

He opened the door for her.

She slipped past him and then turned. "Good night, Haydon."

"Good night, Rainee."

She closed the door and watched his retreating form until he faded into the darkness beyond, like the moon and stars on a cloud-covered evening. Men were complex creatures. And he was the most complex of all. She had no idea what to expect next with him. In a way that was pleasant and in another way, frightening. Too bad she could not stay long enough to sort it all out.

Chapter Nine

"Now, where is he?" Since his father's death, brother problems seemed to follow Haydon around the ranch like persistent yapping dogs. Between Jess and Micheal, Haydon wondered if he would ever have a moment's peace again.

Haydon checked inside the barn and the woodshed. Chickens flapped their wings, squawking and scattering as he trudged his way through the coop. Inside the filthy pen, the stench assaulted his nose. Frustrated and aggravated the hens and rooster hadn't been fed yet and the eggs hadn't been gathered either, he stomped out of the pen and panned the area for Rainee, knowing Michael would most likely be found in close proximity to her.

Since that night under the stars, he had made it a point to be polite to her, but he had also done his best to avoid her whenever possible. Those few moments felt far too good to him. She radiated a quiet softness by starlight that drew him to her.

Haydon continued looking for his brother and Rainee but didn't see either of them anywhere. He jerked his hat off and raked his fingers through his hair, then slammed his hat back in place. Ever since Rainee's arrival three weeks ago, Michael had slacked on his chores, and the animals were suffering because of it.

Haydon's boots collided with the hard-packed ground as he made his way across the yard. Hearing voices, he thundered around the backside of the house.

Just like he knew it would be, there stood Michael, handing clothespins to Rainee as she hung sheets up on the line strung from one tree to another. His brother could help her, but he couldn't manage to get his own chores finished.

"Michael." He didn't care if anger rolled out of him.

Their laughter and chatter stopped.

"What?" Michael turned disgusted eyes onto Haydon.

Rainee yanked her gaze at him and then at Michael. She put her back to Haydon. Dressed in a light blue dress and matching bonnet, she snatched a sheet from the laundry basket, shook it out and tossed it over the clothesline.

"I need to talk to you."

"Anything you say, you can say here." Michael knew Haydon normally dealt with matters privately so as to not embarrass anyone. Only it wasn't embarrassment reddening Michael's cheeks—it was anger. Shock rippled through Haydon. Michael had never rebelled against his orders before. Father informed his family if anything happened to him Haydon was in charge and they were to do whatever he said. And Michael had… until Rainee showed up.

"Did you forget to feed the chickens and gather the eggs again?"

"Why do I have to do it? Leah can gather the eggs."

Haydon couldn't believe what he had just heard. *Lord, help me out here.* "Because that's your job."

"Not anymore." Michael puffed his chest out and separated his feet.

Rainee snatched up the empty basket and scurried around them. She fled toward the back door without a backward glance. Haydon didn't blame her. This was about to get ugly. He ground his teeth in frustration. Once again he was left to clean up the aftermath of one of Jesse's schemes.

"When was the last time you cleaned the coop?"

"I cleaned it yesterday."

This whole mess was getting worse by the minute. His brother had never been one to lie before, and here Michael was, doing just that. "That coop hasn't been cleaned for quite some time. You need to go do it, and do it right."

Michael didn't move or say a word. He just stared at Haydon as if he didn't care, daring him to call him on his lie.

Haydon opted to try a different tactic. "Michael, Jesse did not invite Rainee here for you to follow around like a lovesick bull. She is a guest in Mother's house and you need to treat her as such."

"I'm not doing anything wrong. I like Rainee." Michael darted a quick glance at Haydon. "And I think she likes me. Besides, you aren't my father. I don't have to do what you say."

Haydon sighed, and his chest constricted. He had wondered when this day would come. *Dear Lord, I'm in way over my head here. Give me wisdom beyond my understanding in how to deal with this.*

"You're right, Michael. I'm not Father, and I wish he were here to handle this. He would know just what to say to you, and you would do it. But he isn't, and I am." He ran his hand down his face. "I know I can't make you do anything, but I'm asking you to get your chores done to help out around here. I can't run this place without your help. And as for Rainee, you're right. She does like you."

Michael's face brightened.

"But not the way you think. She doesn't look at you the way a woman does when she has romantic feelings for a man."

"What do you mean?"

"Does she look at you with stars in her eyes?"

Michael shook his head.

"Does she touch your arm and smile tenderly at you? Hang on to your every word?"

Michael's gaze dropped to the ground, and he shook his head. "No."

Haydon didn't know what else to say, so he remained quiet.

"Sorry I haven't been doing my chores. I'll go do them now." Michael walked a few steps before he stopped and turned. "Thanks, Haydon. I'm sorry about what I said. You're the closest thing to a father I have. I won't give you a hard time anymore."

"Thanks, Michael. That means a lot to me."

He watched his brother head to the chicken pen. Pride welled in his chest. Today, his brother had taken a step down the path to becoming a man. That thought made him sad and happy at the same time.

Haydon headed toward the barn. Inside, he grabbed the pitchfork and forked hay into the horses' stalls. With each toss, the tension of the morning lifted.

Dust danced at his feet and blades of hay floated like big raindrops from the pitchfork.

One major problem created by Jess's stupidity had been solved. Only one remained—what to do about Rainee. The little woman aroused feelings in him he never wanted to feel again. So before he did anything stupid, like give into those feelings, he wanted her to leave.

But where would she go? Who would take care of her? The guy she had mailed the letter to? Had she heard back from him? Haydon's head started to hurt, and the muscle in his neck ached as the tension returned. None of this was his problem, but he couldn't ignore it. After all, she was a person who needed help. And that he couldn't ignore. He jammed the pitchfork into the hay, trying to take his frustrations out on the dried grass.

"Mornin'."

Haydon's pitchfork hit the top board of the stall with a thud.

"How you doing, Haydon?"

"How do you think I'm doing?" he grunted his reply and stepped over to the next stall. He started tossing hay into it, hoping Jesse would take the hint and leave him alone. But knowing how stubborn his brother could be, he knew that wasn't likely to happen.

"Look. Are you ever going to forgive me? I said I was sorry. What more do you want from me?"

"What more do I want?" Haydon reeled around. "I'll tell you what I want. I want you to take care of the mess your careless thinking created. I want you to get that woman out of here so things can get back to normal. That's what I want."

A loud gasp near the barn door snapped Haydon's attention in that direction.

Rainee stood in the doorway with her hand over her

mouth, blinking wide eyes at him. The moment froze around him, and then she whirled and fled from the barn.

"Feel better now?" Jesse shot a look of disdain at Haydon coupled with a quick shake of his head, then bolted after her. "Rainee, wait!"

Haydon closed his eyes and let his head drop backward. He stared at the ceiling as disgust with himself drizzled over him like the particles of swirling barn dust. *"You're a poor excuse of a man."* Melanie's words pierced his soul for the millionth time since she'd first said them. She was right. He was a poor excuse for a man. No real man treated a woman that way even if he thought she was out of earshot.

But then again, he hadn't done it on purpose. How was he supposed to know she was standing there? He hadn't heard her come in. Still, right was right and wrong was wrong. And he was wrong. Although he would love nothing more than to have Jesse deal with this, he knew he needed to go and apologize to her himself. He had been the one who hurt her.

"I'm so sorry, Rainee. I'm sure Haydon didn't mean it."

Without any resistance, Rainee let Jesse guide her toward his house. Sadness pulled her into its embrace, numbing her mind and heart. To actually hear Haydon say he still did not want her here hurt more than it should have.

Though he had already made that perfectly clear, she had held out hope over the past three weeks, praying that maybe he was starting to change his mind because she had seen the looks he had given her when he thought she was not looking, and she had thought she knew what they meant. Obviously, she was very wrong. It was clear he had not changed his mind about her.

The stairs groaned as they made their way up them. Jesse opened the door for her and she preceded him inside.

Hannah stepped through the bedroom door and her eyes widened. She waddled over to them like a baby duckling hurrying to keep up with her mother. Her gaze slanted between the two of them. "What's the matter?"

"Haydon is what's the matter."

Rainee caught the frustration in Jesse's voice.

"I know he's my brother and all, but sometimes the man needs to think past his own selfishness."

Hannah's forehead wrinkled. "What did he do now?" She placed her arm around Rainee and led her to a simple tan-and-blue Victorian settee.

"I'll get some tea and then leave you two ladies alone."

Rainee did not miss the look of understanding that passed between them.

Hannah reached into the pocket of her dull gray apron and pulled out a clean, folded hanky. She pressed it into Rainee's hand. Rainee wiped her eyes and nose.

"Here you go." Jesse handed them each a cup and saucer filled with a pale yellow brew.

He leaned over and kissed his wife's cheek. When he rose, he looked down at Rainee with compassion. "Don't let what Haydon said get to you, Rainee. I know he didn't mean it. He's not a cruel man. He's just— I'm sorry." He shrugged, then gave a small smile before he stepped outside.

Just what? She wanted to scream at him to complete his sentence. The need to know what Jesse had been about to say pressed in on her, but he obviously did not want to finish whatever it was.

With a weighty sigh of acceptance, she took a sip of the weak tea and set the cup back in the saucer.

"Now tell me, what did Haydon do to upset you?" Hannah's soft brown eyes blinked with concern.

Rainee looked down at her lap and ran her fingers over the hanky, folding and refolding it. "He said he wanted me out of here and for things to be back to normal."

"Well, I never. Wait until I get a hold of that man." Hannah started to rise, but Rainee put her hand on top of her arm.

"Please, Hannah, do not. He is right. I must away. My presence here obviously causes him great distress. And he should not have to feel that way in his own home. Besides, there is another gentleman who answered my advertisement and I—"

Hannah interrupted her. "You're not going anywhere, Rainee. Ever since—" Hannah stopped abruptly. "Never mind that. You can move in here with Jesse and me. If Haydon doesn't like it, well, too bad. This is our ranch, too."

Rainee did not wish to cause any more trouble in this family. She had caused quite enough already.

Her Aunt Lena was right when she did not want to get involved with Rainee's troubles. These people should not have to either. If only she would have thought of that before she had posted the advertisement.

Her heart stung at the thought that she should have just graciously accepted her fate at the hands of her brother and Mr. Alexander. A shudder ran through her spine. At least then, these good people would not be made to suffer as well. "Thank you, Hannah, for your generous offer, but I cannot accept it. I expect a post any day now from Mr. Bettes."

"Mr. Bettes. Who's that?"

"The gentleman I told you about. The other man who responded to my advertisement with whom I felt comfortable contacting. He is a Christian, and he did not sound as terrible as some of them." She shivered at the memory of some of the contemptible letters she had received.

"Rainee, I don't want you to go. I've enjoyed our visits. Besides, I have a feeling about you and Haydon."

The smile came very close to touching her heart. "I, too, have enjoyed our visits, Hannah, but truly, it is clear I must take my leave. I came here to get married. And it is quite obvious that is not going to happen. So I must away as soon as possible. Haydon does not want me here. And I shall not stay where I am not welcome."

Haydon tossed his pitchfork into a pile of loose hay and headed out into the bright sunshine, which was the complete opposite of his mood. He needed to find Rainee and apologize.

When he stepped onto Jesse's porch, through the open window he heard Rainee say she would not stay where she was not welcome. He felt horrible. Without hesitating, he opened the door without knocking. "You don't need to go anywhere, Rainee."

Both of the ladies' attention swiveled to him standing in the doorway.

"Haydon Bowen, how dare you barge in here?" Hannah rose, but he held up his hand to silence her.

"I'm sorry, Hannah. But I—" He glanced over to Rainee, embarrassment shrouded her face.

She immediately looked down at her lap, and remorse for his behavior punched his gut.

"Rainee. Can we talk?"

She raised her head and tilted her chin. "I do not believe there is anything to talk about, sir." She rose with the grace of a queen. "Now, if you will excuse me. I have things I must attend to." She faced Hannah. "Thank you, Hannah, for the tea and for your most gracious offer." Shoulders squared, she glided toward him and brushed his shoulder on the way out the door.

He turned to follow her, but Hannah grabbed the sleeve of his shirt. He looked down at her hand and then at her face.

Fury shot from her big brown eyes. "Don't you dare hurt that woman, Haydon Bowen. You have no idea what she's been through."

He touched the brim of his black hat and slipped out the door and into the fresh air, wondering what Hannah meant by what the woman had been through—cotillions and balls? Yes, they were so very hard on a person.

He spotted Rainee storming her way to his mother's house, and his heart locked on the sight. "Rainee."

She picked up her pace and so did he until he caught up to her. Reaching out, he clutched her by the elbow and turned her, though she spun on her own accord and very nearly took a swing at him in the process.

"Unhand me, please." It was an order—not a suggestion.

"Only if you promise you'll hear me out."

Spunk flashed through her eyes. "There is nothing you could say to me that I would wish to hear. I know how you feel. You have made it perfectly clear, and I am sorry for making your life miserable. You need not trouble yourself anymore about me. I am leaving as soon as I am able to make other arrangements. And the sooner the better. For both of us." With those words, she yanked free of him, hiked up her skirts and closed the distance between her and his mother's house within a matter of seconds.

He should have been happy she was making other arrangements and would be out of their lives soon, but he wasn't. And that bothered him.

Chapter Ten

"Men. Why did You ever create the wretched creatures? What do You have against us women anyway, Lord?" Rainee mumbled as she stomped her way through the kitchen and headed toward the stairway.

"What did you say?"

Rainee stopped and looked over at Katherine sitting in the chair darning a sock.

"Are you all right?" Katherine placed the stocking into the basket at her feet and pointed to the chair near her.

Rainee wanted to keep going, but she refused to be rude to Katherine just because her son was a brute. Plus, she needed to inform Katherine she would be leaving soon. Just how she would finance the trip, she did not know, but she wanted to get as far away from Haydon as possible.

With a heavy sigh, she walked over and sat in the chair next to Katherine. "I want to thank you for everything you have done for me."

"This sounds like goodbye." Worry lines etched Katherine's eyes. "Don't you like it here?"

"I love it here." Rainee nodded and fought back tears.

Being around Katherine had made Rainee less lonely for her mother, and she had come to care dearly for this woman. But the reason she had come no longer existed, and she could no longer pretend that it might, nor would she trespass on Katherine's kindness any further.

"Then, why?" Katherine tilted her head, inspecting Rainee. "Does it have anything to do with why you've been crying?"

"How did you know I had been crying?"

"Because your nose is all red and puffy."

Rainee put her head down, but it was too late. Katherine already knew.

"Now, tell me, what has you so upset?"

Not wanting to cause a rift between Katherine and her son, Rainee decided on another tactic. "It has been three weeks since I arrived, and to be honest, there has been no sign of Haydon wanting to marry me. Quite the opposite, actually. So I think it best that I pack my bags and head back to Prosperity Mountain to catch the next stagecoach. If my calculations are correct, it should be arriving in the next day or two."

"But where would you go? Surely not back home to that—"

Rainee knew the words Katherine chose not to speak. That monster, her brother. She took a breath to settle the horror that thoughts of her brother always provoked.

"Rainee." Katherine grabbed her hands. "Why the sudden change? Did something happen to change your mind?"

Reluctantly, Rainee nodded.

"What?"

"I would rather not say. But please believe me when I say I must go even though I wish to stay. But I simply cannot."

"I won't push you to tell me what has caused you to change your mind, but would you consider staying for my sake?"

"For your sake? I do not understand. How could my staying possibly benefit you?"

"Because, I really enjoy your company, and I've come to love you like one of my own. Besides, I would worry myself to death, wondering if you're okay. Here, I know you will be. Plus, you've been a huge help. But that's not the only reason why I want you to stay," Katherine hastened to add, but Rainee already knew what she had meant. Katherine loved people for who they were, not for what they did for her.

Genuine compassion and love flowed from Katherine to Rainee.

"That is very kind of you, Katherine. I, too, have grown to love all of you. But what about Haydon? I know he does not want me here."

"Did he tell you that?"

Not wanting to be a pot stirrer, Rainee simply said, "Let us just say a woman knows when she is not wanted."

Katherine frowned. "I'm sorry you feel that way. But…" She pressed her finger to her lips. "There are several single men in this county. I'm sure you could have your pick of any one of them. In fact, we're hosting church here tomorrow. You can meet some of them then."

Could this be why God brought her here? Perhaps there would be a kind man among the gentlemen tomorrow who would take her as his bride.

Or perhaps not.

Who would have thought she would have to succumb to marrying a total stranger instead of marrying for love? If only her parents had not died. If only she could wait until she found someone who loved her and she him. But time was not her friend in that regard, so she needed to stop dwelling on the "if onlys" because they did no good whatsoever.

And if Ferrin chose to come after her like he had when she had run away to Aunt Lena's, and if he found her unmarried, he would no doubt use brute force to make her Mr. Alexander's newest wife.

Well, she would do everything in her power to not let that happen and pray that God would give her the strength to do what needed to be done. And He would. After all, God had given her the courage and grace to engage herself to Haydon, who she did not know or love, and she knew He would give her whatever else she needed to survive.

Rainee straightened her slumped shoulders. "I will stay. But only until I find out if another man might consider me or until I hear from Mr. Bettes."

Katherine smiled. "Oh, I'm sure they will." She turned her head toward the living room window. "But I'm even more sure before that happens my son will come to his senses and not let you go to another man."

Rainee was certain she was not meant to hear that last part, but she had. She could only hope and pray Katherine was right and the stubborn man in question would indeed come to his senses.

Later on, before the sun had settled in for the evening, after the dishes were finished and put away, Rainee slipped outside into the warm air. The need to be alone and to think weighed heavily on her because she could not shake Haydon's words from her mind. What had happened to him to make him dislike her so?

* * *

"Hello, Rebel."

Inside the barn, Haydon turned his ear toward the sound of Rainee's voice.

"How are you this evening?" she asked his horse.

"I'm fine," Haydon answered.

Rainee whirled in Haydon's direction as he stepped up beside her. Her body stiffened and she turned to leave.

"Don't go, Rainee."

She kept walking.

"Please."

She stopped.

"I'd really like a chance to apologize for my rude behavior and to talk to you."

She faced him. "You do not owe me an apology or anything else, Mr. Bowen. As you are not the one who sent for me, and you have made it perfectly clear you do not want me, I will take my leave as soon as other arrangements can be made. I am not one to burden myself onto another, and it is I who needs to apologize for what my presence here is putting you through."

"Rainee, I can't have you thinking my attitude has anything to do with you. It doesn't. It has everything to do with me. I want you to know you are more than welcome to live here with my family for as long as you like."

She tilted her head in a way he'd come to recognize, questioning him to see if he really meant what he said.

He could only hope he wasn't making a huge mistake with his offer, but right was right and wrong was wrong. And he'd been wrong in his treatment of her—especially these last weeks as he tried to keep his distance. Besides, her staying with them didn't mean he had to marry her.

"Thank you, Haydon."

Hearing her address him as Haydon instead of Mr. Bowen was a good sign, and he felt the relief of it all the way from his head to his toes.

"I appreciate your kind offer. But I have already sent my post to Mr. Bettes, and if he still wants me, I will accept his offer of marriage."

With those words, she headed toward the house. "Good night, Haydon," she tossed over her shoulder.

Sunday morning, Rainee stood at the bedroom window with her hands on the sill and her forehead pressed against the glass. She gazed up at the bright July sun. Today looked to be another scorcher.

Down below she noticed Michael setting up tables. He picked up one end of the long table, and Smokey lifted the other. Michael, such a sweet, sensitive boy, would someday make some woman a fine husband. Just not for her, for he was much too young.

Rainee knew Michael had set his cap for her, but since their encounter with Haydon at the clothesline, she had tried to avoid the boy as much as possible because he was shirking his duties to be in her presence. Still, he seemed to find her wherever she went, and she refused to be rude to him. Guarded, yes. Rude, no. In fact, whenever she was around him, she made sure nothing in her countenance showed anything other than friendship.

It seemed to be working to some degree because Michael's visits had become less frequent and he no longer caressed her with his eyes as he once had. It was if he understood there would never be anything between them.

Haydon stepped into view.

Rainee moved to the side of the window where he could not see her and watched as he hoisted the benches and placed them neatly in rows. How she wished things would work out between them.

He was a gentle man with a caring heart.

A man who loved his family and treated them with the utmost respect.

A man who under unusual circumstances had been polite and courteous to her.

Last night at the dinner table, he had tried to include her in the conversation, but after she had overheard him telling Jesse he wanted her to leave, she had no desire to talk to him. It was such a strange place to be—wanting him to fall in love with her, yet guarding her heart because she knew it would never happen.

So rather than talk to him, she had diverted her attention onto Abby. She loved that little girl as if she were her own sister. Rainee had always wanted a little sister. And if things would have worked out between her and Haydon, she would have had two.

As she continued looking out the window at the handsome man who caused her chest to rise and fall, she whispered, "Lord, Thy will be done." She pushed away from the wall and headed toward the mirror.

Still dressed in her robe, Rainee stood in front of the looking glass contemplating what to do. Since wearing the lightweight dresses without the restricting corset, she never wanted to don that wretched contraption again.

What she did want to do, however, was to take her corset and wrap it around the person's scrawny little neck who had invented it. Did they not know or care how suffocating and stifling the corset and all those layers of clothing were in the scorching heat? And for what? Appearance's sake?

Appearances be hanged. Rainee was sick to death of the whole thing.

Though she loved her father dearly, that was one thing that had always disturbed her about him. Born a British gentleman, position, appearance, and wealth meant everything to him. Since moving to America, however, Mother said he had relaxed some of the stricter parts of his upbringing, but propriety was not one of them.

Rainee scrutinized the articles of clothing she had to choose from. Once again she was faced with the dilemma of what to wear. Her mere wardrobe consisted of four silk gowns and the three dresses Katherine and Leah had helped her let out.

Her mother's words about dressing properly so she did not embarrass her father skimmed through her mind. She did not wish to embarrass the Bowens either, but she did not know what would be considered proper attire for an outdoor church gathering.

Rainee let out a very unladylike snort. She hated having to concern herself with such trivial matters. Sometimes she just wanted to run away and live in the wilds where no one cared about what she wore or how she looked.

A smile graced her lips. The Idaho Territory appeared quite wild to her. And she had run away to it.

She giggled, picturing herself running around in a pair of men's trousers, an oversize shirt and a cowboy hat and boots. She rather liked the visual. It represented a freedom she craved but was likely to never have. In fact, she wondered if she would ever be free from the strict proper upbringing that seemed to haunt her like a ghost no matter where she went.

Unfortunately, clothes were not the only problem

weighing heavily on her right now. Today, the Bowen's neighbors would arrive. Just how would they explain her presence at their ranch? How would they introduce her? And what would she say? Her stomach crinkled just thinking about it.

"Rainee." Katherine's voice sounded from the other side of the bedroom door. "May I come in?"

Rainee pulled her robe shut. "Yes."

The door opened and in walked Katherine wearing a pink cotton dress. No ruffles, no frills, no silk and no layers of hot clothing. Just a simple, lightweight garment. The burden of the morning lifted, and the tight scrunches in her stomach relaxed. Perhaps the freedom she craved was within her reach after all.

"I was wondering if you would like me to braid your hair."

Would she ever. "That would be lovely. Thank you."

Katherine's kindness and thoughtfulness never ceased to astonish Rainee.

She grabbed her clothes and slipped behind the makeshift partition. Within minutes she was dressed and feeling carefree and lighter than she had in years. She all but skipped to the dresser and sat down.

Katherine picked up the brush and pulled it gently through Rainee's long hair. Rainee closed her eyes and relished the rare treat of someone else brushing her hair.

Growing up, servants had always styled her hair. And on rare occasions, her mother had. But all that had changed when her parents died and Ferrin had taken over her life. Some of those servants had moved on, and some of them had stayed for Rainee's sake. With her no longer living at her parents' plantation, she wondered if even more of the servants had moved on and what they were doing. Especially Jenetta.

"You have such beautiful hair."

"My mother used to say the same thing every time she brushed my hair, and she would share something with me from her childhood."

"Like what?" The brush stopped mid-air.

"Well, when she was little, Mother had a horse named Beauty whose mane and tail were the same color and thickness as my hair. She loved horses. So did my grandfather. He had taught her everything she knew about them.

"But she had confessed the real reason she loved spending so much time with the horses was because during those times her father would tell her stories about his many business travels. She cherished those times she had been fortunate enough to spend with him. Just like she treasured the time she spent with me, brushing my hair and talking." Rainee could still see her mother's smile as if she were standing here in the room with her. And what a beautiful smile it was.

A smile she would never see again.

"You must miss her terribly."

"Yes. I miss her so much sometimes the pain becomes almost unbearable."

"Oh, Rainee, I shouldn't have asked you to share with me. I can see how much it disturbed you to talk about her."

"Please, do not apologize. While it is difficult to remember those precious times with my mother, for that brief moment it also brings her back to me. So thank you for asking." Rainee looked at Katherine's reflection in the mirror and smiled.

"You're welcome. Any time you want to talk about your mother, I'd love to hear it."

Rainee just might take her up on that offer.

"There. I'm finished." Katherine set the brush down on the vanity.

"Thank you so very much, Katherine. It has been a long time since anyone has brushed my hair for me." She smiled her gratitude.

Katherine lovingly patted her shoulder. "Well, any-time you want it done, you just ask. I love doing it." She moved her hand from Rainee's shoulder. "Shall we go downstairs?" Katherine turned to leave.

Rainee twisted in her chair. "Katherine?"

"Yes?" She stopped.

"I just wondered…" Rainee's gaze dropped.

"Wondered what?"

"People are going to wonder who I am and what I am doing here. And…" She shrugged and glanced up at Katherine.

"You're wondering what we're going to tell them," Katherine finished for her.

"Yes, ma'am. I am." There. She had said it.

Katherine took her hand and pulled her up. She looped her arm through Rainee's and smiled. "We'll tell them the truth."

Rainee's heart dropped clear to her button-up boots. "The truth?" she squeaked as panic settled inside her. When she had written the advertisement in search of a husband, she had not planned that far ahead. She never thought about what she would say to people when they met her.

Tears battled in the back of her eyes, begging for re-lease for the unfortunate situation she now found her-self in. If only her mother and father had not died. Then she would not have to concern herself with such dreadful things. No longer able to hold back her tears, they slipped out and onto her gloved hands.

"Rainee, look at me."

She sniffled, pressed her fist against her mouth and then looked at Katherine.

"The truth we'll be sharing with them is…" Katherine smiled. "That you are my guest."

Rainee let out a short breath.

"No one needs to know otherwise because it isn't anyone else's business why or how you got here. Haydon and I have already discussed it, and we agreed everyone would announce you as my guest. After all, it's the truth. You're my guest for as long as you like." She smiled.

"But what if they ask how you know me?"

Katherine's brows furrowed. She released Rainee's arm and turned puzzled eyes at her. "I'm not sure. Let's go downstairs and see what Haydon thinks."

"But Haydon does not like me. And I know he does not want to be burdened with me."

Katherine laughed.

Rainee did not see anything so funny in what she had just said.

"He likes you, Rainee. He just doesn't want to admit he does. Come here." Again she looped elbows with Rainee and led her over to her bed. Katherine sat down and patted the spot next to her. Rainee sat and faced Katherine.

"I want to tell you something about Haydon and then perhaps you will understand why he acts the way he does. But first, I want you to know why I'm telling you this. For more than a year now I've prayed for God to send Haydon a wife. And then you came along."

Rainee's mouth opened in a very unladylike manner.

"So, we'll just wait and see what God wants on that point."

Not knowing what else to do, Rainee nodded.

"One thing I do know about my son is that he may rebel against something and even refuse to do it, but he's learned the hard way about going against God's will and following his own desires. Now he only wants what God wants for him."

Those words caressed Rainee's heart. She, too, only wanted what God wanted for her. In fact, before she had made her decision to move out here, she had sought the Lord and He had given His approval. Solutions to the obstacles she now faced, therefore, were best left in His hands.

"Haydon would be furious if he knew I was sharing this with you, but I believe it's the right thing to do." Katherine tucked a wayward strand of hair back into place. "Before Haydon moved out West with us, he made sure his wife Melanie approved. She agreed even after he told her they would be moving to a ranch far from town and how harsh it would be. She assured him it would be fine. Melanie loved adventure. Even a dangerous one. That was one of the things that had attracted Haydon to her.

"Anyway, Melanie had this romantic notion about the West. And she wasn't the only one. Many people romanticize it. Haydon warned Melanie a lot of people had lost their lives and their children's lives because of the harshness of this land." Katherine got a faraway look on her face.

Is that what had happened to Katherine's husband?

Shimmering eyes looked back at Rainee. Rainee

wanted to wrap her arms around the woman and comfort her. She knew only too well the devastation of losing a loved one.

"Haydon doesn't know I'm aware of how miserable Melanie made him, but I noticed it shortly after they arrived here. Melanie hated living here. She had a hard time dealing with the harsh reality of this place. She despised it even more when she realized she wouldn't be attending any more fancy parties. That there was no place to show off her expensive silk gowns. No more servants to tend to her every whim. And no more extravagant shopping sprees. Haydon had warned her about that, too. But the poor thing just couldn't cope.

"Many times I heard her screaming at Haydon, telling him what a horrible failure he was as a husband and as a man. She would say cruel and hateful things to him. Things a mother couldn't bear to listen to. She told him he was worthless and it was all his fault she was so miserable. Said she would never forgive him for the anguish he was putting her through." Disbelief and heartbreak flittered across Katherine's face.

Horrified, Rainee covered her mouth. How could anyone say such cruel things to another human being? Let alone their own husband?

"Finally, Melanie told Haydon if he really loved her, he would move them back to New York. Haydon promised her he would, but they had to wait until spring because travel was much too dangerous in the winter. But she had no desire to wait. She snuck out during the night, and the next morning Haydon found her battered body at the bottom of a steep hill not too far from here. She had slipped on the rocks and fallen to her death."

Rainee gasped. "Merciful heavens. How dreadful. Poor Haydon."

"He hasn't been the same since. He still blames himself for Melanie's death, and he's built a stronghold around that soft heart of his to keep himself from feeling that hurt again."

Rainee's heart broke for what Haydon had endured. Everything made sense to her now. She even understood why Jesse had sent for her. He just wanted his brother to be happy again. Rainee wanted that, too. Perhaps she could make him happy. After all, not all women were like Melanie.

Rainee was not. She loved helping people, not being helped. Fancy balls and extravagant gowns meant nothing to her. She loved the outdoors and the wide-open spaces. The only thing she did not love was pigs.

Chapter Eleven

Rainee stepped into the living room, and Haydon did his best not to stare at the beautiful woman. He expected to see her dressed in her fancy frippery, but her attire surprised him. The simple yellow dress she wore brought out the gold in her hair and eyes, and her overall appearance was wholesome and not that of a rich socialite.

Something about the way she looked at him caused his breath to hitch. He couldn't say what the look conveyed exactly, but something was definitely different.

"Are we all set up outside?" his mother asked.

He pulled his gaze away from Rainee and looked at her. "Yes. I was just coming to get you two. Shall we?" He offered each of them an arm and tried to ignore the tingling sensation Rainee's touch created.

His mind froze, and the silence in his brain was deafening.

He needed to quit feeling like this, no matter how remarkable Rainee was. But every time he saw her, he liked what he saw more and more, not her outward beauty but her inward beauty. And when she touched him, even as innocent as this was, his feelings became stronger.

His hand itched with the temptation to yank Rainee's arm from his and to flee far away from her while he still could. But he feared it might be too late already and besides, his manners wouldn't allow him to. He corralled his emotions and did what needed to be done—and found he enjoyed doing it far too much.

Outside, under the clear blue sky and warm morning sun, he escorted his mother and Rainee to the rows of flat log benches situated under the morning shade on the east side of the house.

He noticed a small huddle of people off to the side. Jesse and Hannah were among the group, talking to the neighbors. Haydon turned his back on his brother. The last thing he wanted to do was talk to Jess before a church service.

He'd tried to forgive his brother, but every time he got around Rainee, he was reminded again what Jesse had done not only to her but also to him and anger over the situation would settle on him again.

His gaze touched on his mother's for a brief moment. She wasn't pleased or fooled by his actions, but he needed to stay away from his brother for a little while longer. Otherwise he might say or do something he would regret. And he had enough regrets to last him two lifetimes.

Rainee gazed up at him. Her countenance appeared sweeter than it had last night. He couldn't quite read the look in her eyes—nor did he want to—so he broke contact and looked in front of him to where all the neighbors were seated. He was met with glances and stares of curiosity, gaping mouths and whispering.

He glimpsed Rainee's flushed face and wondered

again what would drive a beautiful, kind woman to do what she had done. Desperation? Lack of money? What? The more he pondered her reasons for leaving her home and how hard it had to have been for her to place an advertisement, the more his heart softened toward her. It took a brave woman to do what she had done. He admired her for that. She deserved a suitable husband.

Not liking where his thoughts were leading him, he gave himself a mental shake and looked for an empty seat.

Leah and Abby sat with the neighbor's daughters, who were close to their own ages. Michael and Smokey sat at the far end of the back row. Haydon followed Michael's trail of vision to a young blonde beauty talking with Mrs. Swedberg. The girl appeared to be close to Michael's age. Haydon smiled, relieved that his brother had taken their talk to heart and given up his infatuation with Rainee.

He led his mother and Rainee to the only available bench. He stepped back and motioned Rainee forward, but his mother stepped ahead of her and sat down, forcing him to sit beside Rainee. His gut twisted, knowing his mother had done it on purpose.

He sat down on the cramped seat. His leg brushed against Rainee's, and warmth spread down his leg. With one jerk, he moved his leg over as far as he could.

Reverend James walked in front of the makeshift podium and removed his hat. The sunshine blazing down on his head brought out the orange highlights in his copper hair. His green eyes connected with each person. "Thank you all for coming. I look forward to our time together." He smiled. "Today I feel led to teach about the importance of seeking God's will for our lives.

Have we become so independent and self-sufficient that we think we don't need our Heavenly Father or His direction? If so, where has that attitude gotten you?"

A deceased wife and nothing but misery. It would have been nice to be able to get clear of those thoughts, but they were chained to Haydon's spirit as surely as if they were physical.

"Whose will do you want in your life—God's or your own?"

Haydon's shoulders dropped. At one time he had longed to do God's will and sought it out on a daily basis. But not once had he sought God's will concerning Melanie.

He had loved Melanie and wanted to marry her, despite the many warnings he'd received from his friends, his father and, if he could bear to admit it, from his Heavenly Father.

He thought back to all the warning signs. Signs he had chosen to ignore. He'd been deceived not only by his own willful stubbornness, but also by his wife and her many charms.

Back East Melanie had attended church regularly. She said and did all the right things. But after they'd married and moved out West, she refused to attend their local meetings. Instead she holed up in their cabin until everyone went home because she refused to socialize with these "backwoods lowlifes," as she called them.

And it had only gotten worse over their short time here. In one of Melanie's fits of displeasure, she mockingly confessed the only reason she had attended church in the first place was to show off her new dresses and to impress everyone with her high social standing. He should have seen that, but he'd been too blinded by what he wanted to see, by what he wanted to be real.

The ultimate blow came when she told him she wasn't a Christian and she didn't believe in God or Christ. She'd faked faith because she knew Haydon wouldn't marry her otherwise.

Haydon's heart ached afresh, knowing Melanie had possibly died not knowing Jesus. He could only hope before she'd drawn her last breath, she had asked Christ into her heart. After all, Melanie had heard the salvation message plenty of times.

The sound of people singing splintered his mind from its painful memories.

Haydon closed his eyes and sang the words that meant so much to him. A few choruses later, his concentration switched to the sweet but slightly out-of-tune voice next to him. Only it wasn't Rainee's off-key singing that had hooked his attention, it was the conviction in her tone. She sang as if the words meant something to her.

He stole a sideways glance, and what he saw mesmerized him—Rainee's face raised toward heaven, shiny drops sliding down her sun-bronzed cheeks and glowing face. Gone was the snobbish image he had engraved in his mind from their first encounter.

Reverend James said the closing prayer. The women excused themselves and started setting out the generous fare.

Haydon stood back and watched Rainee as she jumped right in and helped. She draped tablecloths over the makeshift tables and made several trips to the well, filling bucket after bucket with water and carrying them to the table. She made numerous trips in and out of the house, her arms loaded with homemade desserts.

Melanie would have never done any of that. In fact,

Melanie did nothing but read her dime novels, sit in front of a mirror or bark orders at his sisters. When he had found out she had been ordering them about, he had immediately put a stop to it.

Abby's cry snapped his attention in that direction. His little sister was sitting on the ground, looking at her knee, crying loud enough to alert everyone within a 30-mile radius to her plight. He started toward her but stopped when he saw Rainee hurrying toward Abby. Haydon watched as she dropped to her knees in front of the child, never once giving heed to what the dirt was doing to her dress.

"What happened, Abby?" The kindness and genuine compassion in her voice touched a chord deep inside him. A chord he would rather not have strummed.

"I hurted my knee," Abby cried.

"Oh, sweetie. I am so sorry. Come. We will make it feel all better." She scooped Abby up and carried her into the house.

Minutes later, they stepped outside together. Abby held Rainee's hand, smiling and skipping happily at her side.

Haydon picked up another bench and carried it over to one of the tables, eyeing his neighbors as they too watched Rainee's every move. They had to be wondering who this woman was. So far, his mother had offered no other information other than her name. It wouldn't be long, though, before someone asked how she came to be here.

From yards away, Haydon's gaze zoned in on nineteen-year-old Jake Lure strutting up to Rainee like a bull on the hunt. Haydon dropped one end of the bench. It thudded as it hit the ground.

Abby pulled away and ran toward her friends.

Jake cocked his shoulders back and tipped his nose up higher than normal. He reached for Rainee's hand and kissed it.

Her cheeks suddenly reddened. To make things worse, within seconds, forty-five-year-old Norwegian widower Tom Elder, seventeen-year-old John Smitty, and twenty-three-year-old Peter James, Reverend James' brother, each took turns introducing themselves and kissing her hand. Each tried to outdo the other. They reminded Haydon of a bunch of young bucks trying to claim their territory. It would have been funny if he could have allowed himself to laugh about it, but his protective side had already kicked in.

He wanted to forget moving benches and go stand next to Rainee's side to keep the predators away.

But what gave him the right to do so?

Her new admirers were only doing what he refused to do.

Rainee looked around until her gaze touched his.

His heart did an upward kick like a frisky colt on a brisk spring day. The quiet desperation in her fawn-colored eyes pled with him to rescue her. And rescue her he would. After all, a promise was a promise, and he had promised the Lord and himself that he would watch over her today. Even so, he would have done it without a promise, knowing how desperate men out West were for womenfolk.

Haydon finished setting the bench down and strode over to where she stood. He extended a hand to each of the men. "Hello, gentlemen." They each shook his hand but never took their eyes off of Rainee. He couldn't really blame them. She was a very beautiful woman.

A woman who was under his care for the time being. "The ladies have the food ready now if you'd like to grab yourselves a plate."

"Miss Devonwood, would you do me the honor of joining me?" Tom bent his elbow and offered her his arm.

John stepped in front of Tom. "I'd be mighty honored iffen you'd join me, Miss Devonwood."

"She's eating with me." Jake grabbed Rainee's arm and yanked her to his side.

This whole thing was getting out of hand. He needed to do something and fast. Haydon stepped up along the other side of her. "Sorry, gentlemen." He eyed each one with a warning glance. "Rainelle is with me." The second those words left his mouth, his gut cringed. Where did that come from? Couldn't he have said something else?

She looked up at him. Her smile of approval warmed his soul. Even though it felt hypocritical, he knew he had done the right thing. He tucked her hand through his arm, and the sudden fluttering of his heart made him even more confused about what the right thing was.

As he led her to the food tables, the men's stares bore through him like railroad spikes. No doubt, the men believed he was staking his claim on her. Well, let them think what they wanted. His only intention was to watch over her while she was a guest in his mother's home. *Just keep telling yourself that, Haydon, and you just might believe it yourself pretty soon.*

Then, a few steps forward, he realized his mistake. The perfect resolution to the mess Jess had gotten him into might very well be standing in the food line. If she married one of his neighbors, he would be free of his burden.

Burden.

But was she really a burden? Or was he scared to death she wasn't?

Since her arrival, she had helped his mother and sister prepare meals, bake bread and desserts, weed the garden, scrub the kitchen floor, clean the house, wash clothes and do any other chore that needed done.

He liked that about her. She was at home being one of them. More important, when he was honest with himself, he realized he liked her. He always had. In fact, the word like was starting to feel too tame.

Reverend James's message trailed through his mind. The point here wasn't whether or not she was a burden. But what did God want him to do? Determination rose in Haydon. He needed to find out just what God's will was in this situation. This time he needed to know before he let his feelings take over.

While Rainee gathered a small amount of food onto her plate, Haydon filled his with fried fish, quail, a thick slice of ham, morel mushrooms, potatoes boiled with dill, a slab of butter to eat with his potatoes and Lefsa.

She grabbed two tin cups and dipped them into one of the buckets of water and handed one to him.

"Thank you."

"You are welcome." There was that smile again. The one that could turn a man's head and heart into mush, including his. He mentally shook himself.

Drinks and plates in hand, he led her to an empty table. At least it was empty—until Rainee sat. Then her group of admirerers barreled to their table and sat across from her.

Guess they didn't think he was staking his claim on her after all. Haydon sighed inwardly and lowered himself next to her. His shoulder brushed hers. Their gazes connected. Her eyes sparkled and she smiled that sweet smile of hers. Haydon's heart melted like sugar in a cup of soothing hot tea, and his lips curled upward.

She looked away, and he heard her suck in a sharp breath.

Wondering what was the matter, he followed her gaze. Locked in one of the pens, Kitty's little beady eyes looked directly at them through the slats in the fence. The sow dropped her nose to the ground and started scooping up the dirt under the bottom fence rail. After several scoops, she looked through the slats again. Then repeated the process.

He laid his hand on Rainee's arm and leaned over to whisper in her ear. "Kitty can't get out. I promise."

She looked at him, unconvinced. "Why—why is she penned up so close to the house?"

Kitty wasn't all that close, but he'd let that part of the question go. To Rainee, having the pig anywhere within eyesight would be too close. Once again he whispered in her ear to protect her from any kind of embarrassment she might encounter in front of his neighbors. "If I didn't pen her, she would be joining us in the yard like she often does. I locked her up this morning because I didn't want her frightening you again."

"That is so sweet of you, Haydon. Thank you. You will never know how truly grateful I am for your thoughtfulness." She glanced toward the pen again and back at him. "Are—are you sure she cannot get out?"

"I'm sure. Don't let her digging get to you. She'd have to dig a huge hole before she could slide her fat belly under the fence. You're perfectly safe. Trust me."

Could she? Could she trust him when he didn't even trust himself anymore?

She nodded and then picked up her drinking cup.

"So, tell me, miss." Tom shoved a huge chunk of ham into his mouth. "How do you know the Bowens?"

Haydon's insides stilled and his smile vanished.

Chapter Twelve

Sunday evening, after everyone had gone to bed, Rainee draped her shawl around her shoulders and headed downstairs. She stepped out onto the porch to think things through and to pray for guidance about her situation. She tucked her robe around her and lowered herself onto the porch swing. Using the balls of her feet, she put the front porch swing in motion.

Stars glistened like precious gems in the endless inky sky, and a chorus of frogs filled the silence. Rainee leaned back in the swing and closed her eyes, sighing, relieved this day was over.

Sitting at the table with all those men at lunch asking her how she knew the Bowens had been quite daunting. She had been prepared to answer anyone if they asked why she was there but not how she knew them. Why, if Haydon had not spoken up when he had, diverting their attention away from the topic, Rainee shuddered to think what would have transpired.

Because of her love for the Bowens, she had prayed fervently the night before the church service that God would work everything out and spare them any humiliation her being there might cause.

God, in His tender mercy, had once again answered her prayers. Even when Katherine had introduced Rainee to her neighbors as her guest, the questions lingered in their eyes, but none put a voice to their curiosity, much to Rainee's relief.

Rainee smiled as contentment wrapped itself around her. Though she had only been here a few weeks, she felt at home because of the kindness of these people. Especially Haydon, who kept her in a constant state of confusion. He wanted her to leave, then he protected her from the onslaught of male neighbors. Somehow he had even managed to keep the conversation off of her and onto other things.

Against her better judgment, she admired everything about him. How he protected and took care of not just his family, but her, too.

His obvious love for the Lord.

His kindness and compassion toward his neighbors.

His deep love for his family. Well, except Jesse, perhaps. She noticed he avoided him.

She also admired his physical attributes.

Eyes the color of sapphire gems.

Teeth as white as freshly fallen snow.

Hair the color of winter wheat.

Strength in his masculine jaw.

And muscular arms Rainee longed to feel, to see if they were as solid as they appeared.

Rainee's cheeks heated at that thought. If Mother knew she was thinking about a man's muscles, she would surely give Rainee a tongue lashing. Before her mother's words had a chance to formulate in her mind, Rainee blocked them. Proper or not, she found she did not want to stop thinking about him. He represented everything she desired in a man.

Gentle yet strong.

Kind but bold.

Sure and steadfast.

A man who under all that gruff exterior had a heart as big as the Idaho Territory. A man she now greatly esteemed, perhaps even loved.

A conversation she and her mother had shared about that very thing strolled through her mind.

"Mother, how will I know when I am in love?" Rainee had asked.

Her mother had stopped working on her tapestry and gazed at Rainee. She wove her needle through the fabric and rested her hands in her lap. "Trust me, Rainelle, you will know."

"But how?"

Mother rang the bell and asked for tea. "The day I met your father, I knew he was the one for me."

"How did you know?" Rainee had asked again.

With a smile, she looked at Rainee. "The truth is, the moment I laid eyes on him, I knew."

"You knew that fast?" That idea completely astonished Rainee.

"Yes." Her mother straightened and gave Rainee a stern look. "It does not happen that way for everyone," Mother had cautioned her, then relaxed her austere facial expression. "But it did for me."

"Did Father return your affection?"

Mother's sweet laughter had filled the room. "No. He told me he did not even notice me as more than a businessman's daughter until one day when I was gathering roses for the table. I was so engrossed in their beauty and lovely scent I did not hear your father approach.

When he said my name, I whirled so fast, I tripped over my flower basket and landed on my backside. Your father said when he offered me a hand to help me up, the second our hands made contact he felt a strange, unexplainable attachment to me.

"When I stood, he kept hold of my hand. Our eyes connected and held. And it was as if we were the only two people in the world." When she looked at Rainee, her eyes had sparkled with love for her husband. Rainee hoped and prayed she would someday know the special kind of love her parents had for each other.

"Before I knew what was happening, he had taken me in his arms and kissed me. That very same day he asked Daddy if he could marry me." Stars had filled her mother's eyes.

They had silently finished their tea, each lost in their own thoughts. She and her mother shared many precious moments like that. How she longed to hear even just one more tale of her mother's life.

After reliving that memory, Rainee opened her eyes and sucked in a sharp breath. There, standing with his arms and ankles crossed, resting against the porch post was Haydon, staring at her. "When—when did you get here?"

"A few minutes ago. Sorry. I didn't mean to frighten you or disrupt your thoughts. You looked like you were a million miles away." He uncrossed his ankles and arms and walked toward her. "May I?" He pointed at the swing.

Rainee could not find her voice, so she nodded and moved over as close to her side of the swing as possible. But even that was not far enough because his broad shoulders covered a major portion of the swing. Rainee found the open space and endless sky did not appear so vast anymore. In fact, it seemed to be crowding in on her closer and closer.

Soap and peppermint filled her senses.

"Would you like a piece?"

"What?" She blinked. "A piece of what?"

"Of peppermint." He reached inside his leather vest pocket and pulled out a small pouch and opened it.

It had been a long time since Rainee had enjoyed any peppermint. She reached inside the bag and removed one stick. "Thank you." She bit off a piece.

Eyes closed, she savored the feel of the hard candy in her mouth and the clean fresh sensation. She opened her eyes and found Haydon watching her. Embarrassment flooded into her cheeks. "I—I am sorry. It has been years since I have had peppermint. Mother used to buy it all the time."

Haydon broke off a section of candy before he closed the bag and slipped it back into his vest pocket. "Did your mother give you candy often?"

Rainee wrapped her hand around the rope holding the swing. She planted her feet firmly and gave the swing a shove, repeating the process until Haydon finally slowed it down. "Mother always made sure we had special treats. And my father often had candy shipped over from England. He wanted us to know the delicacies and delights of his country, too. I sure miss them."

"I miss my father, too."

Rainee swung her gaze his way. Astonishment trickled through her. She could not believe once again Haydon was opening up to her. She only prayed he would continue.

Haydon stared into the darkness, amazed he was sitting out here on the porch with Rainee. For a man who was trying to avoid her, he wasn't doing a very good job of it.

"Tell me about your father. What was he like?"

He barely heard her request. He glanced over at her silhouette. She wasn't looking at him but straight ahead. An air of serenity radiated from her, a serenity he had never felt around a woman before.

"My father was a kind, caring, generous man. He loved us all so much. It was my father's dream to move out West. He said he might have been born a city boy, but he belonged out here. I feel the same way. He was never comfortable with city life, and neither was I.

"My father detested all the hypocrisy of his acquaintances and how they flaunted their wealth with extravagant parties instead of helping those less fortunate. Out here, he loved the freedom to be himself. Loved the outdoors.

"He and I used to go for long rides and talk about what we could do to build up the ranch. To make it a better place to raise a family. This place has so much lumber, and the volcanic ash soil is so rich you can grow just about anything.

"He had such great plans for this place, but he didn't get to enjoy it for very long. Two and a half years after we moved here, a tree fell on him and crushed his chest." Haydon pressed his eyes shut to blot out the horrific memory.

"I am so sorry." She gently laid her hand on his arm.

He glanced down where her gloved hand rested, then up at her.

She plucked her hand from his arm, and he immediately felt a sense of loss.

"Thank you," Haydon whispered.

Rainee nodded. From what little he could see in the dark, compassion was the only thing he noticed on her sweet face.

"How did your parents die?"

In the shadow he saw her chest rise and fall. "My family and I attended a neighborhood ball. Mother, Father and a few other guests were standing under a second-story balcony. No one knew it would not hold the weight of so many guests." Her voice hitched. "It collapsed, killing six people, including my parents."

Losing a parent was a terrible thing to endure. And she had lost both of hers at the same time. In that instant, his heart softened toward her another notch. "I'm sorry for your loss, Rainee."

Though darkness surrounded them, he saw the stars reflecting from her glistening eyes. He couldn't turn away from them, and as he looked into those eyes, he didn't want to. Rainee surrendered all fears in a soft gentle glance that begged him to do the same thing. For one tingly moment, he did, and they shared a breath. He broke eye contact, blinked to regain control and asked, "Do you have any other family?"

Rainee stopped rocking. She knew she could not avoid his questions forever, but she could control what information he did receive. "Yes."

"And they wouldn't let you stay with them?"

"My aunt Lena died three months back."

"I see. I'm sorry, Rainee."

She picked her gaze up and studied his profile. Boldness overtook her. It was not her place, but she wanted to know just the same. "Jesse sure looked miserable today. He and Hannah went home early."

Haydon pushed with his feet, setting the swing into

a rocking motion. "Well, that's not my problem. He should've left well enough alone."

"With me." Her gaze slipped out into the darkness. His silence gave her the answer she already knew. "I understand how you feel, but Jesse meant well even if he did not go about it the right way."

"I don't recall asking for your opinion." At his bluntness, she whirled her head toward him and squared her shoulders.

"No, you did not, but I am going to give it anyway. Family is extremely important. And even when they do vexing things to us, things that are hard to forgive, refusing to forgive hurts not just them, but us also. I am truly sorry my being here has caused a rift between you two," she said with a softer tone. Their eyes, shadowed by the darkness, locked. "Will you at least consider forgiving Jesse?"

"You don't give up easily, do you?"

"No. I do not."

When he nodded, there was almost a laugh attached to it. "I'll think about it."

For a long moment, that seemed to be the end of the conversation, and Rainee would not have been surprised to see him stand up and leave.

"Rainee?"

She swallowed back the apprehension that rose in her throat at the soft hopefulness in his voice. "Yes?"

"Would you like to go for a horseback ride tomorrow and see the rest of the ranch?"

Rainee's mouth fell open. It was a very unladylike thing to do, but she could not help it. Of all the things she thought he might ask, that was not one of them.

Through the darkness, she tilted her head and tried to

study his face but could not see it well enough to judge his expression.

Why would a man who made it clear he wanted her to go back home protect her from his neighbors, sit and visit with her and then invite her to go for a ride? Whatever his reasons were, they did not matter. She wanted to spend more time with him, to get to know him better. And this was her chance to do so. "I would love to."

Haydon rose and faced her. "I'll have Mother pack us a picnic lunch then."

"No need to bother her. I can do that." She stood. "When would you like to leave?"

"After I finish my chores."

Rainee tilted her head and placed her finger against her lips, then smiled sassily. "Kitty will not be there, will she?"

Haydon laughed. Rainee loved the deep rumbling sound.

"Only if you want her to be." The teasing in his voice caused Rainee's lips to tip upward.

He walked down the porch steps. "See you tomorrow, Rainee. Good night." Off into the darkness he went, heading toward his house.

In the secret garden of her soul, hope sent up a new shoot. She could scarcely contain her excitement at the idea of spending more time with Haydon. Tomorrow seemed as far away as the stars.

Chapter Thirteen

No matter how hard Rainee tried, sleep eluded her. Thoughts of spending the day with Haydon kept her tossing and turning. Finally, she gave up, got dressed and went downstairs.

She grabbed a couple of oil lanterns and lit them and then put on a pot of coffee. She could do this. Katherine had taught her well. "Let me see. Katherine said she wanted to have ham steaks, fried potatoes and Swedish pancakes. I think she called them plättar or something like that," she whispered to the empty room.

Arranging wood and kindling into the stove, she got the fire started and decided she would make the pancakes first.

She grabbed a bowl, the lingonberry sauce and several of the ingredients she needed from off the shelf. She cracked three eggs into the bowl and whipped them until they were nice and thick. Just like Katherine had shown her. Next, she stirred in the milk, flour, sugar and salt, and mixed until it was smooth before covering the bowl with a towel.

Humming while she added a small amount of batter onto the hot buttered pan, she spread the batter until it was thin. When it turned a light brown on the bottom, she turned it over. Moisture beaded her forehead, so she used her apron to blot it away.

She retrieved a baking sheet and placed a clean towel on it, then added the finished plättar on top of the towel. She repeated this process until the batter disappeared. The last one, however, did not make it onto the towel or into the oven to stay warm.

Rainee looked around, smiling, feeling like a child sneaking a licorice stick. She laid it on a plate, spooned melted butter over it, sprinkled it with sugar and rolled it up. Then she added a dollop of lingonberry sauce on the side, dipped the pancake into the sauce and bit into the thin, sweet pastry. The first bite melted in her mouth. Sugar and butter ran down her chin. The texture of the treat reminded her of the crepes their French cook used to make back home.

"Couldn't wait, huh?"

Rainee whirled at the sound of Haydon's humor-filled voice.

Her cheeks, already hot from the stove, heated even more. She swallowed the last bite. It was so large she had a hard time getting it to go down. "What are you doing here so early?"

"I could ask you the same thing." He walked over to where she stood by the stove.

Rainee put her head down. "I could not sleep." She looked up at him. "You?"

He shrugged. "I have a lot of chores to do before our ride, so I thought I'd get an early start."

Rainee tilted her head. "So what are you doing here?"

"I came to see if there was anything to eat before heading down to the barn."

"I just finished a batch of crepes. Well, Frenchie, our cook called them crepes anyway." Realizing the blunder she made about mentioning her life back home, she rushed on, "Katherine says y'all call them 'plättar.' She taught me how to make them, so I thought I would get an early start on breakfast."

She pivoted her back on him and reached for a coffee cup before filling him a cup of the hot brew and handing it to him. "Would you like some crepes? I mean, plättars?"

"Looks like you've already had some." He pointed to her mouth and humor curled his lips and sniggered through his words.

At this rate, if her cheeks got any hotter, they were certain to burst into flames. "I did." A twitter of a giggle followed. She sighed and wiped her mouth off with her apron. "Caught in the act again. I never was very good at being sneaky." She turned and retrieved a cup of coffee for herself. "I always told on myself when I did something wrong. Well, most of the time anyway. Mother called it 'bearing harmful witness.'"

"What do you mean, 'most of the time'?"

"On occasion I opted not to tell Mother."

"Why's that?"

Merciful heavens, the man has beautiful eyes. "Because I knew if I did, a certain hour-long lecture would follow." Rainee took a sip of her coffee. The bitter taste slid down her throat. Truth be known, she preferred tea, even at breakfast.

"Ah, I see. I know that only too well. At one time, my father was a stickler like that also. I sat down to many a lecture when I was younger. I used to dread them. And now, I would give anything to hear one of them." Sadness crossed his face.

"I, too, would give anything to hear one. To hear my mother's voice again. To see her face just one more time." Not liking the uncomfortable gloominess that had rested upon them, she wanted to lighten the mood. "Mother always said she lectured me because she loved me. Said if she did not love me, she would not even bother. I must have been the most loved person in the entire universe."

"Me, too."

They both laughed.

"Now, how about some breakfast?" She set her cup down and reached for the potatoes.

"No time for potatoes. The plättars will do just fine."

"At least allow me to fry you a slice of ham." She motioned for him to be seated before she sliced off two thick chunks of ham and tossed them into the cast-iron skillet. While they cooked, she placed in front of him dishes, silverware, plättars, bread, a small bowl of melted butter and the lingonberry sauce, then added the fried ham onto his mounding plate.

"These are delicious, Rainee," he said around the large bite in his mouth.

Rainee's heart skipped with happiness. She watched as he devoured one crepe after another. If he kept this up, she would have to make another batch, and she would do it with pleasure.

"Aren't you going to have any?" He sliced off a massive chunk of ham and shoved it into his mouth.

Rainee marveled, wondering where he put all of that food. "No. I am going to start tending to the potatoes. It will not be long before everyone else arrives. I want to surprise your mother and have breakfast all ready."

His eyes sparkled as if she had pleased him with

her comment. Rainee turned to the task of peeling and dicing the potatoes. Minutes later, she heard the chair scrape against the floor. She glanced in his direction.

Haydon headed toward her, carrying his empty dishes. She wiped her hands off on the apron and hurried over to him. "Here. Give them to me."

He handed them to her. "Thank you, Rainee, for breakfast."

She glanced up at him. "You are most welcome."

He stood there for a moment, looking as if he wanted to say something, but instead he turned on his heel and headed out the door, taking a portion of Rainee's heart with him. She could hardly wait for their ride.

After everyone had their breakfast and the dishes were finished and put away, Rainee packed a light lunch. The thought of spending more time with Haydon sent excitement coursing through every inch of her. Rainee raised her skirt and ran up the stairs.

She scurried inside Leah's room and donned her brown riding habit. She stepped in front of the looking glass and tucked in the wayward strands of her flaxen hair, grabbed her hat with the feather plume and tied the ribbon under her chin. It would have to do. If she had her way, she would put on a pair of man's breeches and a cowboy hat, but it was not to be.

With a smile on her face and her heart feeling lighter than it had in so very long, she floated down the stairs, grabbed their picnic lunch and headed outside.

Haydon scanned the barnyard and saw Jesse out by the woodshed. Rainee's words about forgiveness swam through his head. He started to head toward his brother, but when he glanced toward his mother's house, he stopped.

The sight of Rainee in her fancy riding habit brought back painful memories of the last time he'd watched Melanie leave on horseback wearing a similar outfit. At the time Haydon didn't know his wife was heading out to meet her lover. When he discovered her affair, the man fled the county. Melanie blamed Haydon for her actions, saying if he wasn't such a horrible husband, she would have never been tempted. Even now his blood boiled thinking about how innocent she had always acted, when all the while she was a vixen.

"Good morning, Haydon." Rainee's gaze traveled upward toward the sky and then back at him. "It looks to be a lovely day." A smile graced her face.

"Is it?"

Her smile vanished. "Is something wrong?" She tilted her head, looking innocent. But Haydon knew better. Women like her were anything but innocent.

Judge not, lest you be judged. The Bible verse poured through his spirit, searing his conscience.

You're right, God. I need to stop judging Rainee and comparing her to Melanie.

"Did you change your mind?" Turbulence filled her eyes and remorse flashed through him like a bolt of lightning.

He wanted to say yes, he had changed his mind, and flee, but his desire to replace the hurt he had caused her with his attitude wouldn't let him. "No. I didn't change my mind." This time he held his frustration back.

He reached for the sack she held. "I'm sorry I haven't gotten the horses saddled yet. I had to finish fixing a few broken boards on the corral." He motioned for her to follow him to the barn.

She stepped up alongside him. The feather in her hat flopped in tune to her steps. "I can saddle my own horse. Just show me which one it is and what saddle you want me to use, and I can take care of it."

"You? You're going to saddle your own horse?"

"Yes, me." She peered sideways and stopped. "I have been doing it for years. And if my mother had known, I would have been sat down to yet another one of her lectures on etiquette. I mean, really..." She huffed and planted her hands on her small waist.

"Young ladies are quite capable of saddling their own horses. But because someone decided it was not proper for a woman to saddle a horse, or to run up the stairs, or to use a fork instead of her fingers or wear those dreaded binding cors—" Her words suddenly stopped, her eyes widened and her mouth plunged open. "Merciful heavens. I—I...." Her hand flew to her mouth, and her eyes blinked rapidly. "I am so sorry," she stammered. Her cheeks dusted scarlet.

Haydon threw back his head and laughed as relief poured over and through him. Never before had he heard a woman speak such things with such passion. Except for his mother. Mother loathed and rebelled against all the rules of society, too. His laughter deepened until his gaze landed on Rainee's scowling face. His laughter evaporated like morning dew kissed by the heat of the sun.

She pierced him with her pursed lips and narrowed eyes. "Are you laughing at me, sir?" Because of her pronounced Southern accent, the word "sir" sounded like more like "sah." The grit in her voice and her feisty attitude fished another chuckle out of him.

Haydon held up his hand in surrender. "I'm sorry, okay?" But he really wasn't. "But look at you." He eyed her up and down before his gaze landed once again on her disapproving face.

She bent over at the waist and scrutinized her body. Narrow eyes and scrunched up lips met him. She stared at him as if he had lost his mind. "There is nothing wrong with my appearance, mister." Again he wanted to chuckle, but this time it was how she said "mister." It sounded more like "mistah." He kind of liked when she got all fiery. He loved her accent and could listen to it for hours.

He corralled the laughter rolling around inside long enough to speak. "You're dressed as if we were going to a social outing and yet you're willing to saddle your own horse. And from what you just told me, you don't much appreciate the rules of etiquette either. You are a mystery, Rainelle Devonwood, that's for sure." He smiled, feeling the happiness clear to his bones. "Come on then. Let's get started." He closed the distance between them, placed his hand at her elbow and led her toward the barn.

"What did you mean I do not appreciate the rules of etiquette *either?* Do you know someone else who feels a strong aversion to them as I do?"

"Yes. My mother."

"Your mother?" Tilting her head back, her wide eyes looked up at him from under the broad brim of her hat.

Again Haydon chuckled. It felt good to laugh again. "Yes." He stopped at the barn door, tugged it open and motioned for her to precede him. They stepped inside and let their eyes adjust to the dim interior before he set the food bag down on a bench inside the door.

Rainee faced him. "Katherine mentioned a couple of social rules that she no longer abided by, but I had no idea she felt as strongly about them as I do. Are you teasing me?" The look she gave him was incredulous and suspicious.

"Nope." He walked past her, grabbed a couple of halters off of a wooden peg from inside the tack room and headed toward the stalls. "She never let on she felt that way until we moved out West."

Rainee stepped up beside him and reached for one of the halters.

Haydon tightened his hold.

"I want to help. Please?" Seeing her sincerity, he handed her a halter.

"You take Raven." He pointed toward the stall that held his most gentle mare.

He watched her open the stall door and shut it behind her. She coaxed the Palouse pony to her. And with expertise she slipped the halter on the black horse with the white spotted rump and led it out of the stall.

Haydon haltered Rebel. When he stepped inside the barn, he saw Miss Piggy heading his way. "Well, hello there, Miss Piggy."

Rainee whirled around and jumped back. Raven balked, but the pint-size woman kept the horse under control. Her eyes darted wildly about the barn. "Where—where is the pig?" She pressed her back against the horse.

Haydon laughed again. "*Miss Piggy* isn't a pig."

Rainee's brows darted heavenward as if being held at gunpoint. "What is it then?"

With his back to Rainee, he squatted down and scratched Miss Piggy behind the ears. He picked up the gray-and-white cat and hugged the feline to his chest. He turned and faced Rainee. "*This* is Miss Piggy."

"*That* is Miss Piggy?" Her eyes danced with surprise.

"You have a cat named Miss Piggy?" Her head weaved back and forth and the feather on her hat waved. "Wait." She stopped shaking her head. "Let me guess? Abby named her, right?"

"Nope. I did."

Her hand shot to the side of her face. "Very strange. Very strange indeed." She stepped in front of him. "May I hold her, please?"

"Sure." He handed the fluffy ball of fur to her.

She held the cat close and stroked its fur. "What a sweet little thing you are." She rubbed her nose against the cat's.

Haydon couldn't believe he was standing there wishing it was him she was lavishing her affection on and rubbing noses with.

After a couple of minutes, Miss Piggy squirmed. "You want down, sweet thing? Okay." She lowered the pet to the ground. Her gaze followed the feline, who was strutting toward the barn door with her tail held high. "Goodbye, Miss Piggy."

Rainee tugged on the horse's lead rope and started walking away. "A cat named Miss Piggy, a pig named Kitty and a horse named after a snapping turtle. I suppose if you had a dog you would name it Fishy, or Moosey or Miss Cowey?" Dust swirled at her feet as she continued walking.

"Actually, we had a dog named Mule, but it died."

Rainee stopped and her spine stiffened, but she did not look back at him. Seconds later, she led Raven toward the tack room. "I had to ask," she muttered, but Haydon heard her.

Again she surprised him by refusing the side saddle and opted for a regular saddle instead. He glanced at her dress. Just how would she accomplish that feat?

From the corner of his eye, he watched with admiration as she brushed and saddled the mare.

A new respect for the tiny woman dusted over him. Maybe God knew what He was doing after all. He chuckled inwardly. Of course God knew exactly what He was doing.

"Do you not just love the smell of horses?" she asked, raising her pert nose in the air and sniffing.

Haydon drew in a long whiff. Horse, hay, dust, leather and a hint of manure filled his nostrils. "Sometimes." He could do without the dung smell. But he wouldn't tell her that. He'd never known a woman to admit liking the scent of horses.

Haydon tied the bag of food onto the back of his saddle, adding some string and a few homemade hooks. "Well, let's go." They headed out of the barn, leading the horses into the warm morning sunshine.

Before he had a chance to help Rainee onto her horse, she placed her left foot into the stirrup and swung her right leg over the saddle. Haydon's eyes all but popped out of their sockets. This woman was something else. *What* yet he didn't rightly know. But he was actually looking forward to finding out.

Atop the horse, Rainee glanced over at Haydon. The whites of his eyes were showing. She followed his gaze to her split skirt. What would Mother do if she could see her now? Rainee abhorred riding sidesaddle and hated straddling a horse in a dress. So, she had asked Jenetta to make this split skirt for her.

The first time she had put it on, her mother had come close to having a fit of apoplexy and made her take it off straightaway. She had not worn the dress since. Until today. She hoped out here it was okay to wear such a garment. Judging from the shock trailing across Haydon's face, perhaps it was not.

"I—I am sorry if my skirt offends you. I shall go and change." She started to dismount.

"No, no. It's fine." He captured her gaze. "You're really something. Ya know that?"

Rainee situated herself back onto the saddle. Was being something good or bad? She dared not ask.

He swung his bulky frame into the saddle and headed around the barn.

Nudging Raven forward, Rainee caught up to him. "Haydon?"

Leather creaked as he shifted in his saddle toward her. "Yes?"

"Are we going to be around any pigs today? I mean, you are not going to introduce me to any more animals with weird names, are you?"

His crooked grin sent a thousand tiny fingers tickling her insides.

"We will have to ride through some in order for you to see the whole ranch. But you'll be on horseback, so don't worry, okay?"

Not okay, but Rainee nodded anyway. She refused to let anything stop her from enjoying this outing or from getting to know him better. Not even the dreaded curly-tailed beasts.

As far as the eye could see, rolling hills of wheat decorated the landscape. They rode their horses up the mountain and wove their way through spruce trees, fir trees and several species of pine trees. But the most fascinating of them all was the huge grove of giant cedar trees. Rainee felt like a speck of volcanic ash next to them.

Along the way, Haydon waited while she stopped to gather wild strawberries to have with their lunch.

They continued riding around and down through the woods. Rainee heard the faint sound of running water.

Within minutes a small river came into view. It was not much of a river compared to those back home, but it mattered not because the surrounding area was exquisite. "Does this river have a name?" Rainee asked.

"The Palouse."

"What an odd name for a river."

"Don't forget the horse you're riding is a Palouse."

Rainee reached down and patted the horse's neck. "She sure is a nice mare. You did an amazing job breaking her. Raven is so calm and easy to handle."

Raven?

"Wait." She reined her horse to a stop, and he stopped alongside her. "I cannot believe it."

"Believe what?"

"Raven is a bird."

"No, she isn't. She's a horse." The smirk on his face had humor written all over it.

"How did I not catch that before?" She shook her head, and he laughed. "I shudder to think what you will name your children." Realizing what she had just said, she nudged her horse forward to hide her embarrassment.

Two hours later, Rainee was ready to take a break and eat their noon meal.

Haydon must have felt the same way because he followed the Palouse River until he came to a nice clearing.

Rainee swung her leg over to dismount, but sturdy hands circled her waist and lowered her to the ground. When Haydon let go, she turned and faced him. "Thank you."

"You're welcome." His gaze traveled over her face for a moment.

Under his intense scrutiny, she held her breath, watching, wondering what he was thinking. His eyes eased toward her mouth and stayed there. Hopes of him kissing her stayed hidden inside her heart.

All of a sudden he whirled and strode toward his horse.

Perhaps she had not hidden her desire so well after all and had frightened him off. With a one-shoulder hike, she hurried to remove her hat. By the time she finished and had it tied to the saddle horn, Haydon had their bag of food.

Rainee made haste toward him. "Here, let me get that."

He glanced at her, then nodded. Gathering their horses' reins, he led them to the river. Both horses dipped their heads and drank.

Rainee removed the tablecloth and spread it out in the shade of a cottonwood tree. She knelt down and placed the ham, rye bread slices, jam-filled shortbread cookies, strawberries and water on the cloth.

Something blue caught her eye. A gorgeous bluebird perched on a low branch descended on an insect, then flew off. Birds were such fascinating creatures. Always happy. Always flitting about. And free. Something she envied. She wondered if she would ever feel truly free as long as the threat of her brother finding her still lingered.

Haydon tied the horses to a tree and came and sat opposite her.

"Did you see that magnificent bird?" Rainee pointed toward the bush it had evacuated.

He followed her gaze. "No."

"It was the prettiest color of blue I have ever seen."

She pointed toward a bush. "That woody-looking plant with the red berries on it, what is it, please?"

"It's a kinnikinnick bush."

"Are the berries edible?"

"They are. Bears love them."

"Bears?" She glanced all around, up into the trees, then back at him. "Do you have bears here?"

Broken shafts of light seeped through the trees and danced across his handsome profile. "Don't worry, they won't bother you."

She took that as a yes and hoped he was right. Seeing a bear did not appeal to her. She placed a thick slice of ham between two slices of buttered rye bread and handed it to him before fixing one for herself.

They bowed their heads.

"Father, thank You for Your bountifulness, and for this beautiful land. Bless this food and bless this time Rainee and I spend together. In Jesus' name. Amen."

"Amen," she echoed.

As they ate their sandwiches, she listened to the water lapping over the rocks and the birds singing in the surrounding trees. Serenity rolled over her like the water rolling over the riverbed rocks. This place was delightful. A place she could stay at forever. *Oh, Lord, let it be so.*

He picked up his canteen of water, unscrewed the lid and took a long drink.

Rainee watched his neck as he swallowed and marveled at the strength it possessed.

She reached for her own canteen and strained to loosen the lid.

"Here, let me get that."

She handed it to him and watched as he opened it with ease before handing it back to her. "Thank you."

"You're welcome." He popped the last of his sandwich into his mouth. "Rainelle is such a beautiful name. I'm curious." He leaned forward. "Why do you prefer Rainee over Rainelle?"

"Because Rainelle sounds too stuffy. Too sophisticated. But Rainelle is better than Sissy."

"Sissy? Who called you Sissy?"

"My brother. He used that name to taunt me. To dare me to do things he knew I was not supposed to do. And because I despised his teasing, I usually gave in to his dares. Which usually led to another lecture," she twittered.

She tilted her canteen up to her lips, took a sip and dabbed her mouth with her riding gloves. Not very ladylike, but she did not care. "Sometimes his challenges were quite dangerous."

"What kinds of dangerous things did he dare you to do?"

Rainee thought about it for a moment. "To ride Maggie, for one. I was not allowed to ride newly purchased horses. Father feared I would get hurt, so he had Jimmy, the stable boy, ride them until they were gentle enough for me to ride. The second day we had Maggie my brother dared me to ride the mare, but he failed to tell me no one had ridden her before and that she was only saddle- and bridle-broke."

"So what happened?" He removed his hat and laid it beside him. His blond hair reminded her of the petals of Arkansas tickseed flowers or the color of the yellow-breasted chat bird she had seen back home. He leaned his back against a tree, crossed his ankles and joined his hands behind his head.

"After he saddled and bridled Maggie, he led her out of the stall and around the barn. My brother was no dunce. That side of the barn was out of my parents' view." She picked up a twig and started snapping it into tiny pieces. "He held the mare while I put my foot in the stirrup and climbed aboard. The horse stayed still. It was when he let go of her that she took off at a dead run, bucking all the way."

He removed his hands from the back of his head and sat up straight. "What did you do?"

"I was able to hang on until we got to the river. As soon as the horse got to the riverbank, she stopped and whirled sideways. I lost my grip and flew face-first into the river. I do not think I have ever seen my father so vexed."

"Did you get hurt?"

"Only my pride." She raised her canteen to her mouth and drank freely.

"How old were you then?"

"Sixteen."

"Where's your brother now?"

To avoid his question, she took another long pull of water and took her time replacing the cap.

Once the lid was secured on her canteen, she set it down and looked around, stalling for time. "I am so glad you found a spot without any pigs." She looked back at him. "Thank you for that."

"You're welcome."

Rainee handed him three cookies. He popped a whole one into his mouth. And what a well-formed mouth it was. Her gaze trailed up his face until it landed on his sapphire-blue eyes. Eyes that were staring at her. Eyes that had caught her studying his lips. She dropped her head and quickly snatched up a cookie and bit off a piece, looking everywhere but at him.

"You never answered me. Where is your brother now? Is he still alive?"

Cookie crumbs sucked down her windpipe. She covered her mouth as she struggled to free her lungs, but it was either cookies in or cookies out, and she was not sure which would be worse.

Haydon flew toward her, patted her back and handed her his open canteen. "Take this." He knelt on one knee beside her.

Rainee put the canteen to her lips and took several sips before handing it back to him. "Thank you, Haydon," she rasped.

She coughed again, her mind a swirling mess about how she would answer his question without giving anything of her past away.

His masculine nearness overpowered her senses. Sensations she never knew existed. Horse, leather, fresh air, male scent emanated from him.

Their eyes collided for the briefest of moments before Haydon turned his gaze away and shifted his body sideways.

"Rainee."

Please do not ask me again about my brother. Please. Her eyes followed him as he stood.

He leaned over, grabbed his hat and set it on his head before looking down at her. "I brought you out here today for a reason." The serious look on his face caused her stomach to churn like a strong undercurrent in a rushing river. Was he going to send her home? She would not go. She would run away first. Her heart stopped beating as she waited for him to speak.

He raised his hat, raked his fingers through his damp hair and rubbed the back of his neck. Playing with the brim of his hat, his gaze shifted from her to the hard ground beneath him.

Whatever he wanted to say was sure giving him a bad case of the nerves. And her, too. She brushed the crumbs off her skirt and stood. "What is it?" She braced herself for the answer.

He stepped closer.

Her breath caught.

"After Reverend James' sermon Sunday, I've been doing some serious praying."

Something moved behind him. She looked beyond him to see what had snagged her attention.

Her eyes widened.

"And I want to—"

"Oh, no. Not again," Rainee screeched.

Chapter Fourteen

Haydon's heart kicked like a bucking horse and his ears ached from Rainee's high-pitched scream. He whirled around to see what had caused her distress and turned her face as pale as his grandmother's dusting powder.

Kitty was trotting toward them. Her pink ears flopped and her belly jiggled as Kitty called with her little throaty grunt.

Before Kitty had a chance to get any closer, Haydon hurried to the pig and stopped her.

Over his shoulder he said, "It's okay, Rainee. Kitty won't hurt you." He knelt by the pig's side. "Kitty, you naughty girl, are you following me?" He looked back at Rainee, who had climbed atop a fallen log and looked ready to bolt through the brush at the slightest move of his beloved pet.

He hated seeing her so frightened. Wanting to ease her fears, and knowing Kitty wouldn't hurt a soul, he rubbed behind the sow's ears with one hand and extended his other toward Rainee. "Come here, Rainee. I want to show you that Kitty won't hurt you."

Her mouth opened, but no words came forth. Her

head jerked back and forth, but her fear-stained eyes never left Kitty. Seeing her frightened face tore at his heartstrings.

Lord, please don't let her faint again. Haydon looked at Kitty, who leaned into him so hard she almost pushed him over. *You're not making this easy, Kitty.* "Trust me, Rainee," he coaxed, trying to keep his balance from the two-hundred-plus-pound pig bearing her full weight against him.

His gaze trailed to Rainee's rigid body and pallid face. Softly and calmly he continued, "I promise you won't get hurt."

For a brief moment her gaze darted to him before landing back on the swine. "I—I cannot." Her voice quavered.

"Yes, you can. I'll help you." He could tell she wanted to, but her fear kept her feet planted yards away from him. Like an infected splinter under the skin, it irritated Haydon what someone had done to her, making her so fearful of these playful creatures. Sure, they could be mean when it came to protecting their babies, but otherwise they were fun-loving animals. He waved her toward him. "C'mon on, Rainee. I know you don't trust Kitty, but you can trust me, can't you?"

Her eyes bounced back and forth between him and the pig. A battle was definitely going on inside that pretty little head of hers.

"I trust you. But I am not sure I trust her." She pointed at Kitty. "Are—are you sure it is safe?"

"I'm sure. I wouldn't ask you to come here otherwise." Haydon shifted his weight onto his other leg and waved her forward.

Her chest expanded. She stepped off the log and took one tiny step forward and stopped.

"It's okay," he encouraged again.

She took another small step forward.

He nodded his approval.

Then another.

"That a girl. You're doing great. Keep coming."

Five more steps and she was standing beside him, on the opposite side of Kitty.

"Squat down here."

She looked back and forth between him and Kitty, shaking her head. "I—I cannot do this."

"Yes, you can. I'll help you. Give me your hand." He used the same gentle voice with her that he used while breaking a young filly. He stood and extended his free hand toward her while keeping his other hand on Kitty.

Inching her hand toward his, she laid her fingers in his palm. He gently tugged her forward, and with his hand on top of hers, he placed her hand behind Kitty's ears.

With a muffled whimper, she jerked back.

Keeping his hand on hers, Haydon patiently and tenderly placed her hand there again and rubbed. Contented, Kitty stood still. After a few moments, Haydon eased his hand from Rainee's and grinned when she continued the rubbing motion, never taking her eyes off of the pig.

Stepping back a foot he watched them.

Kitty sidestepped closer to Rainee and closed her eyes. Soft grunts emerged from the friendly sow. She leaned into Rainee.

Rainee gasped, jerked her hand back and fixed questioning eyes on Haydon.

"It's okay," he whispered. "You're doing great." He stepped next to her.

Her lips quivered as they edged upward in a tremulous smile. She nodded with short jerks. Her chest heaved, and then with trepidation in her eyes she placed her hand back on Kitty.

One minute turned into another, until finally Kitty opened her eyes and straightened.

Rainee's hand fell away.

The pig glanced up at Rainee. Her snout moved in a sniffing motion, almost as if to say thanks. Kitty waddled off to a muddy spot where she scooped at the mud with her round nose before lying down.

"Oh, my."

Haydon glanced toward the sound of Rainee's soft voice. Seeing her wide eyes replaced with wonder caused his chest to swell with pride. She had taken her first step in casting down her fear of pigs. "Now that wasn't so bad, was it?"

Rainee stopped watching Kitty and looked up at him. Gone was the fear, replaced with relief. "No. Not at all. I never knew pigs could be so friendly."

"They can be. I think Kitty is friendlier than most because when she was born we had to bottle-feed her to keep her alive. Abby and I took on that chore together. After Kitty was able to eat on her own, she spent more time with us than with the rest of the herd. That silly little pig followed us everywhere." He chuckled. "Still does. I'm surprised you've only seen her near the house one day since you've been here. Then again, knowing how afraid you are of pigs, maybe God kept her away." He could feel the mirth dancing in his eyes.

Rainee laughed, then headed to the river and stood at the bank.

Haydon grabbed the string and hooks he'd brought with him and stood beside her. She looked so beautiful and serene. His affections toward her were growing, along with the urge to pull her into his arms. It was getting harder and harder to not give into the desire to kiss her. He needed to get his mind off of that before he gave into his yearnings. "Do you mind if I do some fishing while we're here? I'd like to take back a mess for dinner."

"No, not at all." She clasped her hands in front of her and dipped her chin. "Do you mind if I join you?"

One eyebrow hiked upward. The woman fished too? What else did she do?

"I know it is not proper for young ladies to fish, but I do so enjoy it."

Again he wanted to kiss her. Just to be close to her. This woman was lovely inside and out. He realized how wrong he had been to compare her to Melanie. Melanie would have never saddled a horse, gone for a horseback ride, taken a picnic in the wilds as she called it, touched a pig, fished or anything else other than attend parties with high-society folks and complain about everything else.

Feeling lighter than he had in years, Haydon couldn't wait to finish their talk. But right now it would have to wait. If this woman wanted to fish, then fish they would.

"You caught the fish?" The look of incredulity lit up Michael's face as he stared at Rainee in awe. Rainee was glad Michael and she were friends. He had even apologized to her for his earlier behavior.

"She sure did." Haydon's smile contained his promise to her that he wouldn't tell anyone she had taken the fish off the hooks and had cleaned them, too.

A silent thank-you passed between them.

Once again she was thankful her mother had not witnessed her not only going fishing but cleaning them, too. Mother would have fainted straightaway.

Haydon poked a piece of fried trout into his mouth and ate it. "You did an amazing job of frying them, too." Admiration showed in his eyes.

"Thank you," she said, feeling the blush clear to her toes. "But I had help. Leah and—"

"Me," Abby cut in, pointing her thumb at herself.

Rainee shifted in her seat and faced Abby, sitting next to her.

"Me helped, too." The little girl's face beamed with pride as she pointed to herself again.

"I helped," her mother corrected.

"Nuh-uh, Mother," Abby said, shaking her head. "You didn't help. Just me and Leah did."

"I know I didn't help. It isn't 'me helped.' It's 'I helped.'"

"Huh?" Abby wrinkled her little pixie nose. "But you didn't help."

"Oh, never mind." Katherine scooped a spoonful of fried potatoes into her mouth.

Rainee kept her laughter inside. She loved this wonderful family. She cut a glance at Haydon. She loved him, too. That thought scared her half to death.

While he had been very attentive to her today, he still had not given her any indication that his feelings toward her had changed. When she had first arrived at the ranch, she had overheard Katherine telling him to be nice to her. So she was not sure if that was all he was doing or if maybe he had begun to consider her as a bride.

Not liking how the uncertainty made her feel, she focused on Abby and smiled. "I do not know how we would have finished frying all these fish if it were not for you, Abby."

The little girl wiggled in her chair, sitting up taller.

After everyone finished eating, Rainee rose and put water on the stove. While it heated, she shooed everyone away and gathered the dishes from the table.

"I'm not leaving you to do the dishes by yourself." Bags hung under Katherine's eyes. And her face was devoid of its usual color. She was either unwell or in need of rest. Whatever the case, Rainee would not let her help. "I want to do them. Please."

Katherine studied her face. "Are you sure?"

"Yes, I am sure."

"Well, okay. But Leah can stay and help you."

Leah picked up her plate and leaned over to pick up another.

"Leah, you would not be offended if I want to be alone, would you? I love doing dishes."

Leah looked at her as if she had gone daft. Rainee giggled. "I know, I know. I am quite strange. But truly, I enjoy doing them. It gives me time to think."

Leah turned toward Katherine. "Mother?" Her blue eyes lit up with anticipation.

Katherine shrugged. "What can I say? If Rainee wants to do dishes, then we'll let her. Besides, we have a basketful of mending that needs taking care of."

Leah nodded. "I'd rather do mending than dishes any ole day." Smiles flitted through her words. "Thank you, Rainee." Leah's face brightened. Her waist-long blond braid swished like a horse's tail as she sashayed into the living room.

Katherine's steps were slow as she too headed toward the living room. Rainee frowned. She quickly snatched up the dishes from the table. She wanted to hurry and get the dishes done so she could help Katherine with the mending. Katherine's pale face bothered Rainee.

"Lord," Rainee whispered as she picked up a pot holder with her lacey-gloved hand and dumped the water into the sink. "I am worried about Katherine. She seems quite unwell. Either that, or something is really bothering her. Whatever it is, Lord, would you please tend to her needs and heal whatever is ailing her? Thank you, Jesus."

"Amen."

Rainee whirled at the sound of Haydon's voice behind her. When he had walked up, she did not know, but his nearness stole her breath and caused her heart to beat faster.

"That's so sweet of you to pray for my mother."

Her eyes collided with his, and she found she could not pull her gaze away, and it appeared he could not either.

"I've never met a woman like you before, Rainee," he whispered.

His eyelids lowered to her mouth. His lips parted and a cloud of peppermint circled the air.

Neither moved.

Rainee's eyelids lowered. She could feel his presence closing the distance between them.

A warm, calloused finger touched under her chin and tugged it upward. Lips, both soft and slightly dry touched hers.

She locked her knees to keep them from buckling. Delight swept through in shivering waves.

Haydon jerked back. "I'm sorry, Rainee. I—" He took a step back and ran his hand through his thick hair. "I don't know what came over me. Forgive me."

With that he whirled and fled, the screen door shutting behind him.

Rainee reached behind her, feeling and searching for something to grasp on to for support because her knees were too weak to hold her upright. She leaned against the sink. Closing her eyes, she touched her lips where the peppermint still lingered. That man could kiss. Of course, she had nothing to compare it to, but she did not need to or want to either.

"Are you okay?" Katherine asked softly.

Rainee's eyes flew open. She pushed away from the sink, praying her legs would hold her. "I—I am fine."

Katherine looked at her and then at the door Haydon had just exited. A knowing smile graced her lips. "I'm sure you are." A twinkle lit the woman's eyes.

Heat flooded through Rainee and onto her cheeks. She did not want to discuss that kiss with Katherine or anyone else. She just wanted to keep reliving it. Better yet, she wanted Haydon to keep kissing her so she did not have to relive the memory of it alone.

Katherine giggled. "That good, huh?"

What? Rainee could not believe Katherine would comment about the kiss she and Haydon had shared. The woman was the man's mother, after all. Reeling with shock, Rainee needed to distract the attention off of her, so she planted her hands on her hips. "And what pray tell are you doing in here? You are supposed to be sitting down and resting. I mean, mending."

"I just came for a cup of tea. Is there any hot water left?"

Rainee grabbed a cup and saucer off the shelf and started to fix the tea.

"I can do that."

Rainee stopped and faced Katherine. "Please. Let

me." After the tea was fixed, she sat down beside her. "Are you unwell, Katherine?" Rainee searched her eyes.

Katherine drew in a deep breath, glanced into the living room, then back at Rainee. "Just lonely." Katherine picked up her cup and took a sip. "I try not to dwell on it, but since my husband died, the isolation is almost unbearable. While Mr. Bowen was alive, I didn't mind living out here. But now..." She shrugged.

Compassion and empathy for the woman drizzled over Rainee.

Rainee had been under the impression that Katherine was extremely happy living out West. That she loved living where she was free from the strict rules of etiquette and high-society snobbery. She also believed the two of them were a lot alike, but perhaps she had been mistaken because Rainee would rather be lonely and isolated then have to revert back to the rules she abhorred.

"You're probably wondering why I shared this with you."

Rainee nodded.

Katherine laid her hand on top of Rainee's. "You might be young enough to be my daughter, but we share a common bond."

Rainee could not imagine what that was.

"I can never go home again either."

Rainee blinked. "What—what do you mean you can never go home again?" All sorts of scenarios ran through Rainee's mind. But rather than let her thoughts run wild, she patiently waited for Katherine's answer.

Katherine took a long sip of her tea, then set the cup on the table. "At seventeen, I ran away from home and eloped with Haydon's father."

Rainee's mouth formed a wide O.

"My father was a very abusive man, Rainee. Not just physically but mentally as well."

Her heart went out to Katherine. For she knew only too well the cruelty of abuse.

She clasped the woman's hands and cradled them with her own. She wished she could remove her lacy gloves, but she feared someone other than Leah and Katherine would see her scars, so she kept them on.

"To everyone else Father appeared to be a loving husband and father. But to my sisters, my mother and me, he was evil personified. We all have the scars to prove it."

"You have scars, too?" Rainee blurted without thinking. She wanted to scan Katherine's arms, neck and any other skin showing, but she forced her eyes to remain on Katherine so as to not make her uncomfortable.

"Yes, I do."

Rainee wanted to ask where, but she did not, and Katherine did not offer the information.

"Before my father had a chance to follow through with his plan, Sylva, my personal maid, came to us in the middle of the night to tell us she had overheard my father talking to some man in his study. I knew my father was a vicious man, but I never knew the true depth of his maliciousness until that night." She looked at Rainee, then her gaze dropped to her lap. "Father had hired a man to kill my soon-to-be husband and to make it look like an accident."

Rainee tried to stifle a gasp but failed. She squeezed Katherine's hand, and Katherine returned the gesture, holding on so tight Rainee's hand began to tingle.

"He wanted my husband dead so he could take back control of my life. My father was foolish enough to believe I would let him have control of not only my life again, but all my husband's assets as well. That same night we fled to New York. Years later, we moved out here, and I haven't seen any of my family since."

Now it all made sense why God had led her to this particular place and why Katherine had been so kind to her from the very beginning. Katherine understood exactly how she felt.

Rainee hoped and prayed she would never have to leave Haydon or this wonderful family she had grown extremely fond of.

But how could she stay when she needed to get married? Getting married was her ticket out from under Ferrin's care, and Haydon's intentions on that account were confusing at best.

Then she remembered Haydon's kiss. Did his sweet kiss mean he had feelings for her? Hope peaked into her soul, making it soar as high as the night stars.

Chapter Fifteen

Haydon scrambled to the barn, saddled Rebel and raced into the woods. When he reached the river, he dismounted and lowered himself onto a large boulder near the water.

The full moon threaded silver-and-black ripples over the riverbed rocks, and the trees cast their lots over him.

He closed his eyes and allowed the lulling sound of the water to calm his racing heart. How could one barn-raising kiss have such a powerful effect on him? It was wrong of him to kiss her, but when she closed her eyes, it was as if his lips were drawn toward hers beyond all reasoning.

Chills spread through his whole body when their mouths had connected. "Lord, I didn't want to have feelings for her, but I do. Now what?"

What had he been thinking by inviting her to see the ranch, knowing that against his will his affection toward her had already been escalating? He couldn't help but notice her actions over the past few weeks.

Couldn't help but notice *her*.

Her kindness, her willingness to help do anything,

her beauty inside and out and the feisty spirit she displayed so often had knocked a gaping hole in the wall he had built around his heart.

And he didn't want that wall to crumble.

His heart yanked him in several directions.

"Lord, I don't want to love anyone. It hurts too bad. I can't bear the idea of failing again or hurting another human being, including myself. Once was devastating enough. I'm so confused."

Fear wrapped around his heart and squeezed until he could hardly breathe. "I can't handle this. Being with her is out of the question."

"You betcha it is!"

Haydon whirled toward the sound of the voice. His leg slipped on the slick rock. Pain shot through his hands and knees as they collided with the hard ground. He scrambled to stand but froze when the cold barrel of a gun pressed against his right temple.

"Stay right where you are."

That voice. He had heard it somewhere before. From the corner of his eye, he spotted a worn-out boot. If he spun just right, he could knock the man's leg out from underneath him and grab his gun.

The gun cocked.

Haydon froze. He didn't dare move.

While Rainee finished up the morning dishes, she gazed out the kitchen window above the sink, wondering again why Haydon had not come to breakfast.

Michael waved at her from the wagon as he and Smokey wheeled by the house, heading toward town. She raised her wet hand and wiggled her fingers in a wave. Water ran down her arm. She plunged her hands back into the dishwater and glanced out the window again, hoping to get a glimpse of Haydon. She scanned the yard, and her gaze stopped at Jesse's house. Jesse was standing on his porch, with his arms wrapped around Hannah, kissing her. Rainee knew she should look away, but the sweet, tender sight mesmerized her. Envy wrapped around her like a choking vine.

"Well, I'm off to Nora's," Katherine said from behind her.

Rainee whirled with a jump.

"Sorry, I didn't mean to scare you. I'm leaving now. Today's the day I will meet Mr. Svenska." Katherine's eyes sparkled.

"Who is Mr. Svenska?" Rainee dried her bare hands on a towel.

"Nora's brother."

"Oh. And pray tell, how old is this Mr. Svenska?"

"Fifty-three." A knowing smile passed between them before Katherine hugged her.

"Have fun."

"Oh, I will. You, too." Katherine turned and gathered the gift basket she had prepared for Nora from off the kitchen table.

Leah strode into the room and pulled Rainee into a quick hug. It felt good to be hugged by those she cared about. "Seems like we don't ever get to talk much anymore. I'm either at my friends' quilting or helping Mrs. Bengtsson with her twins. They're sure cute. I'm going to hate it when Mrs. Bengtsson gets better and doesn't need me anymore."

"Leah!"

They both jerked their heads that way.

Leah giggled. "I see how that must have sounded, Mother, but that's not what I meant. Of course, I want her to get well, but I just meant I will miss the twins."

The wrinkles around Katherine's eyes relaxed and she nodded in understanding.

"I'll see you later, Rainee." Leah and Rainee smiled at each other before Leah picked up her bundle from off of the table and headed out the door.

Abby darted into the kitchen from outside and barreled into Rainee's leg, knocking her into the sink. Her tiny arms flew around Rainee's hips.

"Abigail!" Katherine shook her head and Abby's wide-eyed gaze darted toward her mother. "I really did raise my children better than this, honest. Sorry, Rainee."

"Do not be sorry, Katherine. You did a fine job of raising your children." *Especially a certain handsome man.*

Abby sent Katherine a smile that said, "See there is nothing wrong with me," then she looked up at Rainee. "See ya later, Rainee. I love you."

Rainee's heart melted. This sweet little girl, who Rainee adored, loved her. "I love you too, Abby." She leaned down and pulled Abby into her arms, careful to keep her scarred hands hidden. When everyone except Katherine and Leah had left the house that morning, Rainee had taken a chance and removed her gloves and laid them next to the sink. She eyed them now, wishing she had them on.

Abby gave her another hard squeeze around the neck and skipped outdoors again before Rainee finished standing.

Katherine studied her. "You sure you don't want to go with us?"

"I am sure. But thank you for asking."

"Oh, and don't worry about Haydon not showing up

for breakfast. With him not working yesterday, he said he had a lot of chores to catch up on."

Rainee nodded even though Katherine's words did nothing to reassure her.

"A lot of times Haydon gets up early and, after he finishes his chores, he'll go for a long ride. Especially if he has a lot on his mind." Katherine sent her a knowing glance. "I'm praying things work out between you and Haydon. After that kiss last night, I'd say it's only a matter of time." With a wink, Katherine flew out the door, chuckling all the way.

Rainee stared after Haydon's mother. If she did not close her mouth soon, a fly would surely land inside it. Rainee clamped her lips together.

She watched as Katherine, Leah and Abby squashed themselves into the buggy to go visit their neighbors as they had done a couple times since she had been there. Rainee thought it sweet of them to invite her along, but she did not feel up to being very social today because she could not shake the uneasiness dwelling inside her. Haydon not showing up for breakfast snatched any hopes she had of staying here.

Had he regretted kissing her?

And had his regret kept him away?

Katherine believed things would work out between them. But she surely must be mistaken.

With a weighty sigh and a heavy heart, Rainee washed the last pan, dried all the dishes and put them away, and tidied up the rest of the kitchen. She stood back and surveyed her work. Seeing the kitchen sparkling clean was so rewarding. She removed her apron and hung it on the hook by the door.

The warm sunshine beckoned her. A walk would do her good and give her a chance to pray.

In case Haydon showed up and wondered where she was, she grabbed Abby's slate and a piece of chalk and scribbled a note indicating she was going for a walk. She tugged her gloves on, placed apples, biscuits, left-over bacon, and a canteen of sweetened tea in a sack and headed outside.

"Good morning, Rainee," Hannah hollered and waved.

She did not feel like talking to anyone, but she would not be rude to her dear friend either, so she walked over to Hannah's house. "Good morning, Hannah." She looked around the area. "Where is Jesse?"

"He's doing his morning chores and Haydon's, too. I sure worry about him sometimes. I know he's doing better and you can't keep a man down, but I sure wish he would have given himself more time to heal. But no, within three days he was outside working again. Of course, I forbid him to do a lot of heavy work. But he never listens to me. You know how men are."

She sure did know how men were. "Wait. Did you say that Jesse was doing *Haydon's* chores?"

"Yes. Why?"

So, Haydon did not stay away from breakfast because of chores. That unsettled feeling she had earlier escalated. She needed someone to talk to about her concerns. A friend she could confide in. And Hannah had turned out to be that person. "Do you mind if I sit down?"

"No, of course not. Would you like some tea?"

"No, thank you." She lowered herself onto the swing, stabilized the food sack on her lap and turned her face toward Hannah.

"What's wrong, Rainee?"

Rainee looked around to make sure they were alone.

Of course they were alone. Everyone had gone except Jesse, and he was away doing chores. "Please keep this between us, okay?"

Hannah nodded. Fine strands of red hair outlined her face, and her brown eyes studied Rainee, waiting.

"Yesterday Haydon and I went for a ride."

"Yes, I know."

"You do?"

Hannah giggled. "I saw you two ride out together."

Rainee smiled. Nothing got past Hannah. She placed her hands on top of the food sack and pulled and tugged at the palm of her lacy glove as she relayed everything that had happened up until the kiss. "And then he kissed me."

"He kissed you?" Hannah's eyes lit up. "Oh, Rainee, I'm so happy for you."

"I would be happy for me too, if after he had kissed me he had not apologized and run off. I have not seen the man since."

"Rainee." Hannah took her hands into hers. "Trust me when I say that Haydon has feelings for you, but he's scared. I can't say anything more than that. It's not my place. But things will work out. Have faith."

It was faith that had brought her to this strange land to marry a perfect stranger. And it was faith that had kept her alive. Hannah was right. She needed to have faith that God would work everything out. No wonder the Bible said to encourage one another daily. Even though she knew God would work things out according to His perfect will and His timing, she still needed to be reminded of it on a daily basis.

"Rainee. Haydon has only kissed two women in his life. And you're one of them. The other—" Hannah stopped and tucked her bottom lip with her teeth.

The other he married, Rainee mentally finished Hannah's sentence for her. She could only dream that he would marry her, too. Their shared kiss had scarce given her hope that perhaps there might be a future for them after all. Time would tell.

"I've said enough already." Hannah let go of Rainee's hands.

Although she was disappointed Hannah had not continued, she felt a measure of relief at Hannah's revelation. That alone reignited the spark of hope she had yesterday. And she could not very well ask Hannah to say more. After all, Hannah was not aware that Rainee knew about Melanie. Katherine had told her about Haydon's wife in the strictest of confidence, and Rainee would not break her word. "Thank you, Hannah."

"You're welcome." A smile of understanding passed between them.

Rainee clutched the sack of food and stood. "I need to go for a walk, to think and to pray. Please, do not get up. I will talk to you later." She headed down the porch steps and turned to wave at Hannah.

Unable to shake the nagging feeling that something was wrong with Haydon, she headed toward the barn to see if he was there. Instead, she found Jesse.

"Good morning."

Jesse turned and a hint of a smile wafted through his eyes. "Morning." He went back to scooping the hay.

"Have you seen Haydon?"

"Um. No. I haven't."

Rainee stared at Jesse for a long moment, sensing something was not quite right. "All right. If you do see him, would you please tell him I am looking for him?"

"Okay."

She turned and had almost reached the outer sunshine when his voice stopped her.

"Rainee."

When she turned, she knew it was serious. He came toward her, head down, boots sliding on the dusty barn floor. Stopping only two feet from her, he removed a crumpled envelope from his pocket and held it out to her.

"I should have given this to you when I picked it up last week." His gaze was only on the letter and never lifted to hers. "I'm sorry."

His hand came up, offering the envelope to her.

Rainee stared at it, perplexed as to its meaning. Then she glimpsed the name on it. Bettes. Her breath caught. With shaking fingers, she took it from him. "Thank you, Jesse."

He nodded. "I better get back to work."

Taking the letter that could change her life, she walked out and into the grassland covered with those beautiful purple flowers Haydon called camas plants.

She should look at it. Yet she could not bring herself to. What did she want it to say? If Mr. Bettes was sending for her, she could easily be gone from here tomorrow. Rainee followed along the edge of the field near the tree line. Seeing the pigs grazing in the distance, her pulse quickened but she kept her wits about her. She increased her pace, keeping her eyes on the swine, hoping and praying that Kitty or any of the other pigs would not spot her and follow her. She may have petted Kitty, but she still was not over her fear.

She spotted the trail Haydon had shown her and tucked the letter into her pocket. It could wait. She headed up into the trees until she reached the Palouse River. Along the way, Rainee stopped to sniff the white blooms on several of the syringa bushes. A divine citrus smell tickled her nose. She watched and listened to the bees buzzing around the flowers, fascinated that they enjoyed the flowers as much as she did.

Rainee followed the riverbank. Water lapped over the smooth rocks on the bottom of the river, and sunlight glinted off the small caps of the water, glimmering like diamonds. She smiled. How could she be so fortunate as to have come to such a beautiful country? And could she now leave it behind if God beckoned her forth from it?

Ahead she saw a thick grove of trees and brush, and for a moment, she wondered how far she had come. Was she even on the Bowen's property anymore? She panned the area in search of something familiar. She smiled when she found it. Twigs snapped under her feet as she hurried toward the special place she and Haydon had shared the picnic together.

Haydon? Why did his name bring such a jangling in her spirit? After all, it was silly of her to worry about him. He was a man who could handle himself, but still, the unsettled feeling in her stomach said all was not right with him. She hoped during her walk she would run into him, but so far she had not seen any sign of him.

Her throat felt scratchy and her mouth was as dry as the hard-crusted ground beneath her. She reached for her canteen and tilted it to pull in a long drink, enjoying the sweet taste and the feel of the liquid as it glided down her throat.

She heard something in the distance and stopped to listen.

A harsh male voice carried its way through the trees, but she could not make out what he was saying. Her skin prickled. Whoever belonged to that ill-tempered voice was not someone Rainee wanted to meet.

She made haste in screwing the lid back on the canteen, shoved it in the food sack and looked around for a place to hide. Trees rustled as she buried herself into their thickness and stopped.

"You'll never get away with it."

That sounded like Haydon talking. She moved closer toward the angry voices.

"That's what you think. I'm here ta do a job and I aim ta do it right."

Raucous laughter followed. She steeled herself. Now was not the time to lose her nerve. Easing her way through the thick brush heading toward a cluster of cottonwood trees, she could hear the voices more clearly.

She froze, knowing if she got any closer they would surely see or hear her. Her gaze trailed up a large cottonwood tree and then down to her skirt. A plan formulated in her mind. If she thought about it, she might talk herself out of the crazy idea, so she started acting on it. Making haste, she pulled the back of her skirt between her legs and tucked it securely into the waistband as she had done long before she became a lady.

Placing her foot carefully and securely, Rainee climbed up the tree, like she had so many times before. Unbeknownst to her mother, when Rainee was a little girl, she had mastered the art of climbing trees in dresses. She could scale them as quietly as a cat sneaking up on its prey. Good thing Mother could not see her now. She would be appalled.

No time to think about or concern herself with propriety now.

Rainee lowered herself onto her stomach, and like a

caterpillar, she inched her way out onto a sturdy limb. She scanned the area until she spotted Haydon propped against a tree in a small clearing near the river. His legs were stretched before him, tied with a rope. And from what Rainee could see, his hands were bound behind his back.

Who would do this to him? And why?

Rainee held her breath as she looked for the person responsible. When he finally came into view, she could not see his face because of his hat.

Something seemed vaguely familiar about the man's stance and clothing.

Her mind scrambled to figure out where she might have seen him before.

She sucked in a breath and quickly pressed her mouth against her arm lest he hear her.

It was that ruffian from the stagecoach stop.

The very one who had accosted her.

The man she had hoped she would never see again. The man the sheriff called Ben. Just the thought of how he treated her sent a wave of shivers throughout her body.

She shifted her head, trying to get a better view of the layout. A flash of silver reflected off the gun in his hand, and that gun was pointed at Haydon.

Her heart slid into her toes. Surely he did not plan on using that thing on Haydon. Then she remembered Ben saying they would be sorry they ever messed with him. She closed her eyes for a brief moment as she realized he had followed through with his threat that it would not be the last they would see of him. She had to do something to keep him from carrying out the rest of his threat.

From the way he had treated her and Haydon at the

stagecoach stop, she knew Haydon's life was in danger. Somehow she needed to come up with a plan to help Haydon escape. But what could she possibly do? Her first thought was to run back to the house and get help, but by the time she made it to Jesse's and back, the man might kill Haydon. That thought brought a rush of boldness descending on her. She would not let that happen.

Chapter Sixteen

Lying motionless on the limb, watching and praying for the right time to make a move, Rainee forced herself to stay calm. With each minute that stretched by, her hope of setting Haydon free slipped further away.

But she was not about to give up. She watched patiently until the man grabbed his canteen and headed toward the water.

Now was her chance.

Careful not to make a sound, Rainee wormed her way back down the limb and tree trunk. Hunched over, she wove her way to the tree where Haydon sat.

Ben turned his head in her direction as if he had heard something.

Rainee dropped to the ground and flattened herself in the tall grasses behind a bush. She could still see him, but she prayed he could not see her. When he turned back around and squatted to fill his drinking vessel, Rainee dug her elbows into the ground and inch by inch she wiggled forward until she came to the base of the tree.

The tall grass concealed her as she peeked around the side of the tree, the side away from the man's view, to make sure the coast was clear. "Psssttt, Haydon," she whispered as loud as she dared, without letting her nerves come out through her voice.

Haydon's shoulders stiffened, but he did not move his head.

She glanced at the river where Haydon's kidnapper was still crouched. It looked like he was having trouble removing the lid from his canteen. Good, she hoped the thing was screwed on tight. "Do not move while I untie your hands," she whispered again. Only this time she was unable to keep the quavering from her voice.

He gave a quick nod.

Rainee tugged and pulled at the knot but it would not budge. Ben had tied it tight. As fast as her fingers would move, she continued working at loosening the knot, while her eyes vacillated between the rope and the gunman.

Ben started to rise just as Rainee freed the last knot. She quickly worked her way back through the brush.

Several yards away, she hid behind a thick bush, keeping her eyes fixed on Haydon.

Ben glanced over his shoulder at Haydon. With his back still facing Haydon, Ben tipped his canteen and took a long drink.

Quietly Haydon hunched over and stretched his arms toward his feet. His large hands tugged at the rope binding his ankles together.

Crouched like a lioness ready to pounce and forcing air in and out of her lungs as quietly as possible, Rainee watched and waited for Haydon to make his move. Her blood pumped through her ears so hard and fast she thought they might burst at any moment now.

Behind her, a twig snapped.

Rainee darted her neck around and frantically searched for the source of the noise.

If she thought her heart was pounding hard before, it was nothing compared to what it was doing now. Her instinct was to flee, but the last thing she wanted was to reveal her whereabouts in case she had to run back to the ranch for help.

She scoured the ground searching for something to use as a weapon. A broken tree branch would work. Quietly she picked out a sturdy one.

Armed and ready, she watched, waiting to see what would emerge.

A pig's head came into view.

A scream hitched into Rainee's throat but it did not escape.

She watched in horror as the pig, which she now recognized as Kitty, trotted toward Haydon grunting, oblivious to the danger that lay ahead.

Ben whirled.

His canteen flew from his hand and hit the ground with a watery tin echo.

He fumbled to free the gun from his holster.

Rainee's hand flew to her mouth, and she bit into her flesh to keep from screaming out.

Quick as a gunfighter's bullet, Haydon leapt up, tackled Ben to the ground, and knocked his gun a good six feet away from them.

Between the leaves of the thick bush, Rainee struggled to see what was going on, but she could no longer see the two men.

Not knowing what was happening, she could no longer stand it. Without thinking things through, she rushed through the bushes.

Branches scraped at her face.

She ignored them and the pain they brought and continued to plunge forward.

Spotting the gun, she kept her gaze locked on it as she rushed to it and snatched it up.

Fists hitting flesh echoed in her ears.

Haydon and Ben rolled over and over.

"Stop! Or I'll shoot!" she yelled with more confidence than she felt. Her knees were seconds away from buckling, though her hand held steady as she aimed the gun at Ben's head.

Ben froze. His sinister dark eyes turned on her, burning right through her. She wanted to toss the gun aside and run, but Haydon's life depended on her remaining brave. That was all it took. Her courage rose to the occasion.

With a quick jerk of the gun to let him know she was in charge and that she meant business, she stared Ben down.

Haydon jumped up, jerked Ben up by his vest and shoved him the opposite direction from Rainee.

Arms thrashing, Ben tumbled backward. He tripped and fell over Kitty.

Kitty squealed and ran toward Haydon, who had moved next to Rainee.

Before Rainee had a chance to react to her fear of the pig, Haydon spoke, "Don't let her frighten you, Rainee. Keep the gun on Ben, while I tie him up."

Rainee pressed her shoulders back and pointed the weapon at Ben. Her hands clutched the gun so tight her fingertips turned white.

Haydon tied Ben up.

"You dirty—" Ben stopped and glared at Haydon. Vile laughter poured from his tobacco-stained mouth.

"Purty bad ya weren't man enough ta save yourself. A woman had ta do it fer ya."

"Shut your mouth," Haydon growled.

"Wassa matter, the truth hurt?" Ben sneered.

Rainee wanted to whack the man over the head with the handle of the gun for talking to Haydon like that. But the risk of Ben possibly taking it from her gave her the ammunition she needed to fight against the urge.

Haydon jerked the rope tight.

Ben flinched. "Watch it, you—" His evil gaze slithered from Haydon to Rainee. "C'mon, sweetheart. Why don't ya rid yerself of this loser?" Ben jerked his head once toward Haydon. "And hook up with a real man." Lust-filled eyes raked over her body.

To stop Ben from leering at her, she wanted to hide behind Haydon, but she refused to give Ben that satisfaction.

"I told you to be quiet," Haydon hissed again.

Along with the cringing going on inside her, the urge to beat him with the butt of the gun grew stronger.

"What'd ya want with a man who cain't even save hisself? He hassa have a woman do it fer him. I'm twice the man he'll ev'r be."

Rainee had heard enough. Beating him with the gun would not be enough to satisfy her anger at him for kidnapping and insulting Haydon. Shooting him, now that just might work. She stepped closer and aimed the gun at Ben's heart. "There is only one *real* man here. And it is not you. Now, silence your mouth, or I will pull this trigger." She cocked the gun.

Hearing the gun cock, Haydon swung his gaze toward Rainee. Fire flashed from her eyes. A jolt of shock rushed through Haydon's body. The woman meant business. Before she did something foolish, Haydon jerked the last knot tight and rose from his squatting position. He laid his hand on top of hers. Resting his finger between the hammer and the cylinder, he took the gun away and pointed it away from them. With his thumb firmly on the hammer, he pulled his finger out and put the hammer back into its resting spot.

He pointed the weapon at Ben, but his eyes strayed to Rainee.

With narrowed eyes and pursed lips, she glared down at Ben.

For a little bitty thing she sure was feisty. Haydon had never met a woman like her: sassy, intelligent, kind, compassionate and brave. Even her deep-seated fear of pigs hadn't stopped her from doing what needed to be done. His deep respect for this woman opened his heart up to feel again.

From the corner of his eyes, Haydon glimpsed movement.

Ben was rocking on his backside, struggling to get lose.

"Sit still!" Haydon ordered. "Or I'll let her have the gun again."

Ben squirmed, and a hint of fear flashed across his face.

Haydon had to keep himself from laughing. He would no more give Rainee the gun back than he would return the weapon to Ben.

"Rainee." Haydon looked at her and stopped. His gaze trailed down her arm. He shook his head and chuckled.

Rainee looked up at him like he had gone plum loco. "What is so funny?"

He gave a quick nod toward her hand.

Rainee followed his gaze, and her hand froze. Kitty was leaning against her leg, an inch away from Rainee's fingers. He waited for Rainee to scream or faint, or both. Instead, she hiked a shoulder, dropped to her knees and threw her arms around the sow's neck. "Good girl, Kitty. Who knows what would have happened to Haydon if you had not shown up," she cooed and gave the swine's ears a good rubdown.

Haydon ran his hand over his whiskered chin. If he himself hadn't witnessed Rainee showing the pig affection, he would have never believed it. Her concern for him had annihilated her fear of pigs. Not only that, with her skirt tucked into her waistband, she had tossed aside all the rules of propriety to save his life. His insides felt as warm as the noonday sun. In that instant, he decided he would not let her leave, and he would do whatever it took to win her heart. She may have come here to marry him out of convenience, but now he hoped she would marry him out of love.

Before he could put his plan into action, however, he needed to take care of the no-good scoundrel on the ground in front of him.

"Rainee, can you untie the horses and bring them here?"

She removed her hand from Kitty. "Sorry, Kitty, I have to stop. Haydon needs me." She stood and started to swipe the dirt from her skirt. Her hands froze midair. She whirled around and when she turned back her cheeks were the color of ripe apples, her skirt no longer tucked in at the waist.

She looked so cute standing there that all he wanted to do was pull her into his arms and give her a big hug and maybe even steal a kiss or two. But now was not the time. He needed to get Ben safely tucked behind bars first. Maybe later. No, *definitely* later.

Haydon smiled and winked at her.

She blinked as if in shock. "I—I will be—" She hiked up her skirt and darted toward the horses, taking his heart with her.

A thousand winking eyelashes fluttered through Rainee's stomach. How could one smile and wink affect her so? For one second she thought she might faint straightaway. Instead, she bolted toward the horses, only slowing when she neared them. While untying them, she drew in a few steadying breaths before she led the animals over to Haydon.

Her gaze caught his. There was something soft and caring in his eyes. Something that hadn't been there before. Gone was the aloofness. And gone was her heart. It now belonged to him.

"Here, hold this, but don't do anything crazy," Haydon said, handing Rainee the gun. Their fingers touched. Warmth spread through her. "Keep it pointed at him."

Rainee said not a word for fear her words would come out raspy. Instead, she gave Haydon a quick nod, took the gun from him and aimed it at Ben.

Haydon led Ben's horse next to him and jerked him up by the ropes. Ben twisted and tossed out obscenities.

Rainee narrowed her eyes and shook the gun at him. "If I were you, sir, I would be still and hush your foul mouth before I decide to pull this trigger."

He stopped fighting and glared at Rainee. "You wouldn't dare."

With Haydon standing behind Ben, a surge of

boldness possessed her. "Try me." She sent him her cold, crazed-woman stare. The one she had practiced in the mirror. The look she had used to run off unwelcome suitors who only wanted her for her father's money.

As she continued giving Ben that cold, hard stare, shaking the gun wildly at him, Ben glanced between her and Haydon, who stared at her as if he too wondered if she would do it.

Ben's shoulders slumped and his steely gaze turned to that of a whipped puppy. She found no pleasure in making a man feel like that, but at the same time, she did find it came in quite handy when a man tended to get rough or forceful with her.

Haydon tied the horse to a tree. He wrapped his arms around Ben's legs, squatted and hoisted him up and over the saddle.

"This saddle horn is killin' my side." Ben kicked and squirmed until his body slipped from the horse and landed on the ground with a thud.

"You should have thought about that before you decided to hold me at gunpoint." Haydon yanked him up and slung him over the saddle again.

Ben's belly slapped against the saddle. "Watch it. You dirty, no-good—" He went on and on, swearing until Rainee could stand it no longer. She wanted desperately to press her hands over her ears.

Haydon walked around to the other side of Ben's horse, shoved his hand inside the man's filthy pocket and pulled out a stained handkerchief. Rainee wrinkled her nose at the disgusting sight. Repulsion wrinkled Haydon's face, too. He tossed the vile thing into the river and pulled a clean bandanna out of his own pocket.

Ben continued his tirade until Haydon shoved the

bandanna in the man's mouth and tied it behind his head. Even gagged Ben continued on, but at least the insulting words were muffled.

Haydon looked as relieved as she felt.

With the same rope Ben had used on him, Haydon tied Ben's hands and legs together under the horse's belly.

Haydon took the gun from her and tucked it into his belt.

After untying Ben's horse, he handed Rainee the reins. He grabbed Rebel's from her and tossed the leather straps over the horse's neck. He swung into the saddle and reached his hand toward her. Rainee handed him the reins to Ben's horse. He kicked his left foot out of the stirrup and with his free hand motioned for her to join him.

She hesitated, wondering how she could manage mounting the horse in her dress with Haydon in the saddle. She looked down at her dress and then up at him.

"Head over to that rock." Haydon jerked his head toward a large stone.

Rainee walked over to the boulder and climbed on it with as much grace as she could muster.

Leading Ben's horse, Haydon maneuvered Rebel as close to the rock as he could.

Rainee yearned to pull her skirt between her legs and tuck it at her waist again, but she did not want to embarrass herself further. Sometimes being a woman living in an age where certain things were forbidden vexed her greatly. But other times, she discovered being a woman held certain advantages.

Haydon cleared his throat.

She swung her leg over Rebel's back. The horse

shifted. Rainee threw her arms around Haydon's waist. He clutched them and secured her behind him.

She glanced at her arms, still clinging to Haydon's waist. She yanked her body away from his, but Haydon's voice stopped her. "Stay." He turned his face toward her. Their gazes collided. "I like having your arms around me." His voice did not sound the same. It had a low, broken timbre to it.

With their searching gazes still joined, Rainee realized that her mother was right when she said Rainee would know when she was in love because true love now kissed Rainee's heart. She smiled shyly at Haydon and wondered if her eyes revealed her true feelings. Did he feel the same way she did, or were the feelings hers alone?

His blue-eyed gaze softened before drifting toward her mouth.

Rainee looked at his.

Haydon leaned his face closer to hers, and his eyes drifted shut, and hers did as well. Their lips met, and a shudder ran through her.

Good thing Ben could not see them.

She lost herself in the exquisiteness of Haydon's tender caresses. His soft lips continued to hold hers captive.

Rainee concentrated on the feel of Haydon's mouth against hers. This kiss was every bit, if not sweeter than, the one they shared in the kitchen. She wanted this moment to last forever, but Haydon pulled back. A sigh of disappointment escaped her.

"Rainee, I—"

Ben's mumbling stopped Haydon's words.

He closed his eyes, and his chest heaved. He shifted in the saddle and reined the horses toward home.

Home. It had a nice ring to it.

She secured her arms around Haydon's waist and pressed her head against his back. Would she finally be able to call this place home?

Chapter Seventeen

"**W**eren't you scared?" Leah's wide eyes followed Rainee's every move as the two of them sat on the bigger house's front porch drinking a spot of tea with Katherine and Hannah.

"Only after I thought about what I had done." She giggled. "The more I think about it, the more I realize it probably was not the wisest thing to do. But at the time my concern was for Haydon."

"I could have never done something that brave." Leah's admiration poured through the tone of her voice.

Rainee caught sight of Abby down the way, carrying a bucket of water and heading toward Kitty. That sweet little beast had followed Rainee and Haydon back to the house. She smiled, then looked back at Leah.

"Ki-i-ty, you gotted me wet. Stop it." Abby stood there with one hand on her hip and shaking a finger at Kitty with her other. "Hold still or I'll shoo you outta here." Abby raised the third pail of water and dumped it over Kitty's head.

Kitty squealed and shook her head.

Rainee actually felt sorry for the little creature as

mud ran down her sides, over her face and into her eyes. Kitty scrubbed her face against Abby's skirt, knocking Abby onto her backside. Abby jumped up and gave the pig another good scolding, while all of them sat laughing until their eyes were damp.

Rainee marveled at how fond she had grown of that curly-tailed animal. Although she was not completely over her fear of pigs, she was getting used to Kitty.

"Well, I need to get back to the house and put my feet up. They're swollen again." Hannah rose, and Rainee noticed her protruding stomach was getting rounder with each passing day.

"Leah, if you're going to the Bengtsson's you'd better leave now so you'll be back before dark."

"Yes, Mother." Leah rose from the swing she and Rainee occupied. She looked down at Rainee. "Thanks for saving my brother today. I don't know what we would do without him." She leaned over and gave Rainee a big hug and a kiss on her cheek before she rushed to the barn to retrieve her saddled horse.

Katherine looked out toward the yard and Rainee's gaze followed her. Kitty waddled next to Abby as the little girl headed into the field covered with camas flowers, and small puffs of dust swirled behind Leah's horse as she cantered down the road.

"Thank you again, Rainee. I shudder to think what would have happened to my son if you hadn't shown up when you did."

They both stood, and Katherine hugged her. A hug so like her own mother's that Rainee had to cast aside the melancholy that tried to force its way inside her.

Rainee helped hitch the horse and buggy and watched as Katherine, too, headed down the road to check on an elderly neighbor. She headed back to the porch and sat down, waiting and watching for Haydon to return from taking Ben in to town, which was silly because he said it would be late.

Tired of sitting, she paced the length of the porch, pondering what to do to make the time go by faster. It was then that she remembered the letter, tucked in her pocket, waiting for the chance to be read. After the events of the afternoon, Rainee was not at all sure she could even read its contents, and yet, she knew she must.

She slipped the envelope out and with shaking fingers tore it open. The letter was handwritten and only two sentences long:

> *Dear Miss Devonwood, It is with my sincerest regret that I must inform you I am no longer searching for a bride...*

That was all she read. The rest scattered into the joy of knowing it meant she was to be with Haydon. She refolded the letter and tucked it once again into her pocket. Life suddenly felt immensely livable again.

After pulling in a long breath of relief, she contemplated what to do next. It was too early to start preparations for the evening meal, and with everyone gone and all the chores finished, Rainee decided to go for a walk. She left a note on Abby's slate again in case anyone wondered where she had gone.

She made her way through the pine and cottonwood trees and up the rocky soil. She stopped to admire a cluster of flowers growing amid the craggy rocks. Tiny white flowers with pink centers surrounded a darker pink center. The dark green leaves with white tips reminded her of the shape of pine cones.

After a long stroll, she walked toward the road so she

could watch for Haydon. She wondered how she would tell him the news and if he would think it as wonderful as she did.

Billowing dust clouds on the road caught her attention. She stepped over a felled tree and hastened toward the road, anxious to see Haydon again. But as she got closer, she realized the dust was not from Haydon but from two men on horseback.

She ducked behind a large cottonwood tree and strained to see if she recognized the men. The branches made it difficult to get a clear picture of them. Wanting to see better but not wanting to give her position away, she rose on her toes and shifted right, then left, but she still could not tell who they were.

Something about them, though, filled her spirit with dread.

Rainee dropped to the ground and crawled to some bushes nearer the road. Pine needles pricked her hands and knees, but she kept going. She had to see who those men were because even at a distance, there was something vaguely familiar about them.

At the base of the bush, she spread the branches far enough to peer through them while keeping her position hidden. Her gaze zeroed in on the riders until she could finally make out their features. She released the branches. They fell back into place with a slap. *Dear God. No. No. This cannot be happening. Not now.* Rainee struggled to draw a breath. "Not him. Please, not him."

Getting them back into view, on her hands and knees Rainee crept backward until her back collided with a tree. She hurried around the base of it and stood. With her palms flattened against the trunk, she forced air into her lungs. The giant black dots dancing before her eyes faded, and she could once again see clearly.

Running through the woods with a dress would make getting away in a hurry difficult. She reached down and pulled the back of her skirt through her legs, tucked it into her waistband and darted into the thick wooded area, running as fast as her short legs would carry her.

Several yards into the forest, she stopped and glanced behind her to make sure no one was following her. Through a haze of sheer fright, shadows danced behind her in the shape of men. She whirled and fled as if her life depended on it because if her brother caught her, it would.

Panting from exertion and fear, Rainee continued running, fighting branches and dodging rocks as she darted her way through the trees and bushes.

The toe of her shoe hooked on something. She plunged toward the hard ground. Her hand shot out to break her fall, but it slipped on the floor of pine needles. Her face collided with a large tree root, sending a surge of pain through her cheek.

Although dazed, Rainee managed to scramble into a sitting position. She plucked the pine needles out of her hand, arm and knees—the pain from each one battling with the fear for her attention. When she finished, she touched the tender spot on her face and looked at her hand.

Blood stained her white lacey gloves. Her stomach churned, and the black spots returned, but there was no time to dwell on that now. Once again she pulled in large gulps of air until the spots slipped away.

She had to escape. Pushing to her feet, her first few steps were shaky, but before long she took off running again. She pushed her body to its limits. Because she would rather die in the wilderness or be eaten by a wild animal than have them find her.

* * *

Having dropped Ben off at the sheriff's in Paradise Haven, Haydon knew home was only minutes away. He couldn't wait to see Rainee. He pictured her holding a gun on Ben and chuckled. *That woman has spunk, Lord, and she's gutsier than any female I ever encountered.*

He nudged Rebel into a canter and reined his horse around the row of trees and into the ranch yard.

Abby ran toward him. "Haydon!"

Before Rebel came to a stop, Haydon swung his leg over the saddle and planted his feet on the ground. "What's wrong, Squirt?" He squatted eye level with Abby.

"She's gone."

"Who's gone?"

"Rainee." Abby sniffed and ran the back of her sleeve across her wet nose.

"What do you mean, Rainee's gone?" He scooped Abby into his arms and carried her toward the house. Dread plunged into his gut as all sorts of scenarios ran through his mind.

He ran up the porch steps and flung the screen door open. When he stepped inside, his instincts went on full alert. Inside the kitchen were two well-dressed strangers sitting at his mother's table.

Haydon's gaze flew from the two men to his mother. Her skin was pale. She was wringing her hands, and his mother never did that.

He whispered in Abby's ear as he let her down slowly. "Go find Jess and tell him to come here right away."

Abby glanced at the two strangers and nodded. She bolted from the house, letting the screen door slam behind her.

Thank God he had grabbed his gun and strapped it around his waist before he had taken Ben to the sheriff. Knowing it was within reach, Haydon strode toward the men. "Afternoon, gentlemen." He extended his hand toward the elderly man, who in return gave him a limp handshake. He stuck his hand out toward the younger man, who kept his hand at his side and looked Haydon up and down. Dark features perfectly matched the black hair and mustache.

Haydon refused to be intimidated by the rude man. "What can I do for you?" He looked the younger man directly in the eye.

"You have something that belongs to us." The bitterness in the man's tone snaked around Haydon's spine.

Haydon squared his shoulders against the man in the expensive black suit. "And what would that be?" He never took his eyes off of the stranger.

The man stepped closer to Haydon, a sneer on his lips. "Do not play games with me. You know exactly what I am talking about." The man had a good four inches on him, but Haydon was acutely aware that what he lacked in height he had always made up for in strength and agility.

Haydon took a step closer and put his hands on his hips. "I don't have a clue what you're talking about. Now, if you want to tell me just what it is you think I have of yours, I'll be happy to return it."

"Stop playing ignorant. The name is Ferrin Xavier Devonwood. And we—" he glanced at the older potbellied gentleman with disdain and then back at Haydon "—came to take my sister Rainelle back home in time for her wedding."

His sister?

Her wedding?

Fury and frustration slid down over his spirit. Rainee was engaged? Haydon's lungs ceased to draw air, but he refused to let the man see just how hard his words struck him. How could he have been so stupid to trust another woman? A woman betrothed to another. A woman he had gone and fallen in love with.

He should've learned this lesson the first time around with Melanie. A trip to the woodshed to beat himself black and blue for giving his heart to yet another deceptive woman was in order. But first things first. If these men wanted her, they could have her. And he would help them find her.

Rainee forced her body through the woods. Her muscles rebelled, her stomach ached from hunger and her cotton mouth begged for water. She glanced around, trying to get her bearings. The trails Haydon had shown her were nowhere in sight. She had probably long since passed them. Her heart fell to the rocky soil. She was lost. Lost without food and without water. The sun was dipping low into the western sky. Night would be here in no time.

Out of hope and mind-numbingly tired, she dropped to her knees, raised her head toward the color-tinted sky and cried out, "Lord, I am so frightened. I do not know where I am. Please, Lord, if You would be so kind, show me the way to the Palouse River. Keep me safe and give me the grace and strength I need to keep going, for I cannot go back home, Lord. I cannot." She placed her face in her hands and wept.

Rainee thought about her parents and the secure life she had when they were alive. "Oh, Mother. I need you." She sniffed and wiped her eyes. "I wish you were here. You and Father. Everything is falling apart around me, and I do not know what to do." Craving the love and security her parents had provided for her, she wrapped her arms around herself, longing to feel her parents' arms around her, telling her everything would be okay.

Again she was reminded that those things were long gone. They had been replaced with a life of uncertainty and worry, and not even the Bowens could help her now. Her arm crunched against something in her pocket. The letter. Even that possibility for escape had been closed. Tears burned the backs of her eyes, but she refused to cry.

She had to face the fact she was on her own. She willed her fighting spirit to rise to the occasion. Glancing toward the heavens, Rainee let out a hard breath, raised her voice, and declared, "I might be exhausted, and I might be alone. But I shall never give up. Never." Although it took great effort, she rose and forced one trembling foot in front of the other, stumbling her way deeper into the trees.

Minutes turned to hours as Rainee searched for anything familiar. Every tree and every spot looked the same as the last. "Lord, You said You would never leave me nor forsake me. I am in great distress here and in need of guidance. Where are You, God?" She stopped at a tree and listened, but the only sounds she heard were the whispering breeze rustling through the tree branches and the twittering of birds as they sang their happy melodies.

If only she had wings like those birds. She would fly far away. Someplace where no one could ever find her. Someplace safe and warm. Haydon's arms came to mind. She felt secure and safe in his embrace. But they would never offer her comfort or security because she would never see him again.

Rainee sat on a felled log and removed her shoes. Angry red blisters covered the heels of her feet. She gently rubbed at the soreness, trying to soothe them, but nothing helped.

She rolled her neck in a circle. Her muscles cried out with want of rest. But she had to force her body farther. She rose, wincing with pain.

Each step she took was pure torment, but she knew she had to keep going, to put as much distance between her and the Bowen's ranch as possible.

Where she would go, she did not know. All she knew was she had to keep going—even though she knew beyond any doubt there was no place out of Ferrin's reach. He had proved that.

Chapter Eighteen

Still dealing with the shock of Rainee's betrothal and betrayal, Haydon gathered his wits about him and turned to his mother. "Did Rainee say where she was going?"

"She—she left a note saying she was going for a walk, and I haven't seen her since." With dread-filled eyes, Mother looked at him, then at the two men.

"Are you trying to pull a fast one on us?" The one who'd said he was Rainee's brother, Ferrin, glared at Haydon's mother.

Her face turned a blotchy white.

How dare these men come into his mother's home and frighten her. Haydon placed himself between her and the men. "No one is trying to pull anything. You heard my mother. Rainee went for a walk and hasn't gotten back yet." He passed a warning glare at each of the two men.

"Liar!" Ferrin flicked a small derringer out of his pocket, cocked it and aimed it at Haydon.

The door swung open.

Jesse, Smokey and Michael barreled into the room, guns aimed at the two men.

Ferrin whirled. His gun fired.

Michael clutched his arm, and his pistol clambered onto the floor.

Seeing an opportunity, Haydon rammed Ferrin with his body, sending them both crashing to the ground. Ferrin's gun flew from his hand and slid across the floor. The older man rushed toward the derringer and stooped to pick it up.

"Touch that gun and you're a dead man." Smokey's voice held the authority of one who meant what he said.

The man froze, then rose slowly with his hands raised in front of him.

With Smokey's gun aimed at the older man and Jesse's aimed at Ferrin, Haydon jumped up, plucked Ferrin to his feet and twisted the man's arms behind his back.

A quick glance at Michael told Haydon he was okay.

Ferrin yanked one arm free.

Haydon snatched the man's arm back and tightened his hold. "I suggest you stand still if you want to live to see another day," he ground out before reverting his attention to his youngest brother. "Michael, you okay?"

"I'm fine." Michael lifted his hand off of his arm. A large patch of blood soiled his shirt sleeve.

Their mother scurried over to Michael's side. She ripped open his sleeve and examined his wound.

Knowing Michael was in good hands, Haydon aimed his attention back onto the two men. He shoved Ferrin forward and pushed him onto a nearby kitchen chair. "Move and you're dead." Haydon turned to do the same to the older man, but before he got a chance to say anything, the wide-eyed man plopped his portly frame down.

"Look, I didn't come here to cause any trouble. Only to get what is rightfully mine." The gray-haired man's trembling words drew out slow and long.

"What do you mean 'what's rightfully yours'?" Haydon asked, his eyes narrowing on the man.

"Rainelle. I own her. Paid Ferrin a handsome price for her, too. She's mine."

Disgust roiled through Haydon's gut. He couldn't believe what he was hearing. Did this man just say he had bought and paid for Rainee as if she were some animal sold at a livestock shipyard? He bore down on his teeth as anger pressed in on him. He turned and glared at Ferrin.

Ferrin smugly crossed his arms over his chest, and a smirk of satisfaction covered his face.

Haydon wanted to beat that haughty grin right off of his face. What kind of brute was this man anyway?

No wonder Rainee had placed an advertisement looking for a husband. Realization kicked him in the head as the full weight of the situation came rushing in on him. Rainee was running away from this no-good scoundrel of a brother. Haydon wondered what else she had suffered at this gutter rat's hands. He had to find her. To do whatever he could to protect her and keep her safe from these two lowlifes.

Haydon grabbed a length of rope from a peg by the kitchen door, cut it in four pieces and tied the men up. He stopped by his mother. "How is he?" He kept his voice low.

"The bullet just grazed the skin," Mother whispered. "We'll bandage it up. He'll be okay." The color had returned to her cheeks and the wrinkles around her eyes disappeared. Having cleaned the flesh wound already, she tore strips of cloth to bandage Michael's injury.

Haydon looked at Michael, then at Jesse. They could handle these two men. The two of them were each as strong as a draft horse.

"Michael?"

"Yeah?"

"Do you think you and Jesse can take these two to Sheriff Klokk and tell him what's going on while Smokey and I go look for Rainee?"

Michael skimmed his gaze over his arm, then turned a scathing glare toward the two men. "You bet we can." At that moment, Michael no longer looked like a sixteen-year-old boy but a mature man. It was one more step on his path. If only their father could see him now. He would be so proud. Haydon sure was.

He squeezed Michael's shoulder, then strode across the room to Jesse, who kept his gun trained on the two men.

"Jesse, you up for taking these two to the sheriff?"

Jess gave a quick nod, never taking his eyes or his gun off the two men.

Haydon turned. "Smokey, I want you to come with me. If anyone can find Rainee, you can."

"Yes, sir, boss." Smokey handed his gun off to Michael.

Haydon shook his head at Smokey, but now was not the time to correct the older man about calling him boss. They had to find Rainee. And fast.

When she had finally found the river, Rainee followed it until the sun dipped behind the mountain and an evening chill replaced it. Her stomach ached with hunger, and every inch of her body cried out from fatigue. She walked to the edge of the river and dropped down on her knees. Cupping her hands, she scooped the cool water up and drank freely before sitting back on her feet and perusing the area.

Moonlight reflected in the ripples in the water along with the shadows of trees and rocks that seemed to come to life in the slow current. An eeriness settled in around her. Rainee kept looking over her shoulders, even when she sat down to rest.

Her body trembled at the thought of being alone in a strange place, in the dark, without food or warm clothing or anything else. Except wild beasts. Both animal and human. Farther travel at this late hour was not wise. All that remained now was to wait until morning came and hope and pray that no one found her in the meantime.

Exposed by the openness of the riverbank, one could find her easily. That thought terrified her. Not only did she fear Ferrin, but there were other dangers lurking in the darkened wilderness. Were there wild savages nearby? She had heard tell of them from travelers back home. Fear squeezed the breath from her lungs. She hopped up, stumbling and fumbling as she scurried back into the safety of the trees.

With only the moonlight to guide her, Rainee searched for a spot where no one would see her. Each step she took made her legs threaten to dump her to the hard ground.

"God, help me find a spot." No sooner had the words left her mouth than her gaze snagged on a small opening between a boulder and bush. She dropped to her hands and knees and burrowed herself into it.

She wrapped her arms around her knees, hugged them tight against her chest and rocked herself gently.

Her thoughts placed her in another time and another

place—a situation similar to the one she now found herself in.

Shortly after her parents had died, when the beatings had started, Rainee found she could no longer tolerate the painful abuse so she had run away, but she had not gotten far before Ferrin and his men had found her. Her brother threw her into the woodshed with no food and very little water for three days.

If it had not been for Jenetta slipping her tiny scraps of food through the knothole, she did not know what would have become of her. Jenetta had also sneaked out during the night and slept outside the shed, singing Rainee to sleep. Many times, the poor woman tried to break the lock so she could provide Rainee with adequate food and water, but she was unable to do much more than make noise.

Spiders and bugs had crawled on Rainee's arms and legs until Rainee thought she would go mad. The sensation that insects were crawling on her even now felt so real Rainee swiped at her arms and legs, brushing away the invisible bugs.

Jenetta's words drifted through her mind. "Honey, child, don't you be frettin' nun. Jist think of dem bugs as God's creatures. Dey won't bodder you none. Besides, ole Jenetta, she done threatened dem and dey knows better den ta hurt you." If only Jenetta were here now. If only her mother were here now.

Rainee had never felt so alone or so frightened in her life. She looked over her right shoulder and then her left. She looked behind her, beside her and in front of her. With each turn her fear escalated. Did snakes or any other unwanted creatures share her tiny quarters? The very idea made her tremble. The thought of the bears

Haydon had mentioned drifted into her mind and held there.

Rainee hugged her knees again, only tighter. She rocked harder, fighting the tears coated with fear, but she could not beat them. They slipped over her eyelashes and ran down her cheeks, stinging the open scratches on her face. She blotted the moisture away as best as she could, but it did not take the sting away. Mother used to wipe Rainee's tears and fears away. "Oh, Mother. I wish you were here." She sniffed. "I need you so desperately."

As if her mother were right there, her words drifted through Rainee's mind. "Anytime something causes you to be afraid, all you have to do is call on the name of the Lord and He will help you. He will never leave you nor forsake you. He lives inside you and is only a whisper away."

If she ever needed the Lord, now was that time. She closed her eyes and bowed her head. "God, I am so very frightened. Mother always said You would comfort me and give me peace. And she was right. You always have. Thank You for reminding me that I can come to You when I need help. Wrap Your loving arms around me and hold me close." A clear image of a painting she had in her bedroom back in Arkansas popped into her mind.

The little blonde girl in the picture was sitting on Jesus's lap. His large hand held the girl's head against his chest, and his other arm encircled her. It was a picture of serenity, of the Lord's protection. Of His comfort. Of the safety of His arms. A measure of peace enveloped her like a comforting hug. "Thank you. I needed that."

Dampness seeped through her dress, sending chills

rushing through her body. She rubbed her arms, trying to warm them and trying desperately to ignore the hunger pains gnawing at her stomach.

Somewhere, not very far away, a twig snapped.

Rainee's attention whirled toward the sound. Her body cemented statue-still.

God, please do not let it be them. I cannot go back there.

Only with her eyes did she search for the source of the noise. Through the distorted shadows of the trees an outline of an animal appeared.

Rainee pressed her teeth into her hand to stifle her scream. Pain sliced through her thumb. Her wide eyes followed the animal heading toward her.

A pig stepped into view.

Rainee did not know whether to be relieved or more frightened until she remembered Kitty and how gentle and loving the little beast was and how Haydon had said a pig would not bother her.

When it neared, her breath caught.

The swine stuck her head in between the gap of the bush and the rock. "Kitty?" she whispered, recognizing the chunk missing from the bottom of the sow's left ear. Rainee let out a long whoosh, and the fear went with it. "I never thought I would say this, but am I glad to see you." Who would have thought that she, Rainelle Victoria Devonwood, would be relieved upon seeing a pig?

With her nose in the air, Kitty sniffed and pushed her way into the thick brush. The small space had just gotten smaller. But Rainee did not mind. She would gladly share her space with Kitty.

Kitty sat on her rump in front of her. Rainee patted her head and rubbed her behind the ears. Pig odor filled the small space, but Rainee did not care. She felt somewhat more secure with the creature here. With each rub, the tightness in Rainee's muscles loosened, and she found herself relaxing little by little, until her body shook with another chill. Rainee stopped scratching Kitty behind the ears and curled into a ball, hoping to get warm.

Her stomach cramped. At this moment, even bark sounded good. Thoughts of wild strawberries made it ache worse. But she did not see any along the way, so she would have to suffer through the pangs.

The dankness soaked into her bones. Her whole body trembled. Kitty flopped on her side in front of her. Heat drifted from the sow and seeped into Rainee's body.

The warmer Rainee got, the heavier her eyelids became until she could no longer hold them open.

Through the haze of slumber, Rainee heard a noise. Her eyes darted open.

Darkness surrounded her.

She tilted her head, straining to listen. Her ears honed in on muffled voices somewhere in the distance.

She flounced into a sitting position, kicking Kitty in the process.

Kitty squealed and bolted upright, sniffing the air. Squeezing her rotund body through the opening, the pig waddled away until Rainee could no longer make out her shadow as Kitty disappeared into the darkness.

The voices neared.

Rainee pressed her back against the rock, wishing it would crack open and ingest her into its crevice.

Her overwhelming fear and shallow breaths strangled her.

She prayed Kitty's squeal had not captured the attention of whoever was out there and that she was far enough in the thick bushes that whoever was there could not see her.

Without Kitty's body heat, she started shivering again. She longed to rub her arms in hopes of getting her circulation going, but she did not, for fear the movement would draw attention to her whereabouts.

A horse snorted.

Rainee froze.

Leather creaked.

Male voices echoed through the trees, but she could not make out what they were saying. She had a sick feeling those voices belonged to her brother and Mr. Gruff. *Dear God, please do not let my brother find me.*

Time crawled at a turtle's pace.

Again leather creaked, but this time the sound was closer.

Pine needles crunched under the weight of someone's boots as they neared.

Kitty and two pairs of legs stopped in front of her hiding spot.

Rainee swallowed the cry welling up inside her.

Then a man knelt in front of the opening.

Rainee scarcely drew breath and remained stock still.

The bushes parted. Leaves rustled and branches crunched. The urge to bolt shot through her like the blast of a cannon, but her body would not move, and there was nowhere to go.

On hands and knees, the man crawled through the small opening.

Rainee screamed, but she would not give up without a fight. A strength she never knew she had visited her at that moment. She raised her legs and kicked wildly at the intruder. Strong hands clasped her feet, rendering her powerless.

Her hands took up the battle.

In vain she struggled to free herself, but no matter how hard she tried, she could not break his hold on her. "Let go of me, Ferrin. I would rather die than go back with you. I will not marry him and you cannot make me. I refuse to be sold off like a piece of merchandise."

"Rainee. Rainee, it's okay. It's me, Haydon."

Rainee stopped struggling. "Haydon?" Through moisture-filled eyes she saw the blurred image of him hovering before her in the darkness. "Is—is it really you?"

"Yes, it's really me." He released her legs.

Rainee lunged forward, throwing herself against Haydon. His arms wrapped around her and pulled her against him.

Pools of tears pocketed her eyes and sobs tore from her.

Haydon rubbed her back. "It's okay. You're safe now."

Rainee wrenched away and shook her head venomously. "No! It is not okay. It will never be okay again," she cried before melting into the haven of his sturdy arms. Ferrin had found her. She would have to leave the man she loved. Because his life was now in danger, too. Ferrin would stop at nothing to get his way.

Haydon held Rainee's trembling form close to him. He needed the connection to her. Almost losing her had frightened him half to death. When he had first discovered she was betrothed, he had been angry until he learned the truth. Now, Haydon refused to let those infidels take her. "Come on. Let's get you out of here and get you warm."

She nodded against his chest and slid from his arms. He crawled out and held the bushes back while she climbed out.

"It's too late to try to get back to the house. We'll have to camp out here."

Her chin shot upward. "I—I cannot sleep out here alone with you. It—it is not proper," she said through chattering teeth as she wrapped her arms around herself. That was one rule of propriety she would never break.

Haydon removed his jacket and held it out as she slipped her arms through the sleeves. She wrapped her arms around herself and closed her eyes as if relishing the heat his jacket provided.

"We're not alone, Rainee."

She glanced at Kitty and looked up at him like he had slipped a few knots.

He smiled. "Smokey's here, too."

Smokey stepped out of the shadows. "Miss." He gave a quick nod.

"Smokey, why don't you…"

"Get some wood for a fire. I'm already on it, boss."

"And quit calling me boss," he spoke to Smokey's retreating shadow.

Haydon placed his arm around Rainee's shoulder and led her to an opening near the river. Reluctantly he let her go to roll a log over for her to sit on.

She clutched his jacket tighter. In the light of the moon, her lost, sad eyes pecked at his heart. Haydon wanted to pull her into his arms again and make her forget all of her troubles.

"Sit down. I'll be right back."

"Where—where you going?"

He wrapped his arms around her and pulled her

close. His lips pressed against her hair and he kissed her there. "It's okay, sweetheart, I'm not leaving. I need to get a blanket from my horse. I'll be right back."

A moment and she nodded her head against his chest.

He didn't want to let her go, but he helped her sit down and then walked over to his horse. After securing Rebel to a tree branch near the river, he untied the blanket from his saddle and reached inside the saddle-bag and pulled out the sack his mother had given him before he'd headed out the door.

Smokey was arranging the wood he had gathered into a pile.

Haydon unrolled the blanket and draped it over Rainee's legs, then sat next to her.

The small fire started to crack and pop. Within minutes it grew stronger and warmer, filling the air with smoke, pine and heat.

"I'm going to gather more firewood."

Haydon nodded at Smokey, then reverted his attention back to Rainee. Shadows from the fire danced across her face.

"Here." Haydon handed her the bag of food. "You need to get something in your belly."

Rainee took the sack from him and wrenched it open. She dove her hand into the bag. Her actions reminded him of Abby at Christmastime. His little sister couldn't wait to open her Christmas stocking. When Abby finally received permission, she dove into it and yanked the items out as fast as her little hands would let her.

That's what Rainee was doing now. Only this wasn't a happy occasion like Christmas.

She yanked out the sandwich and removed the cloth around it. In one bite, a huge portion of the sandwich disappeared. Rainee's cheeks swelled like a chipmunk's.

She tore off another large portion and then another until the sandwich disappeared.

Haydon watched her devour the sandwich like a starving animal, and the sight tore at his heart.

Without saying a word, she rammed her hand into the sack again and plucked out an apple. She opened her mouth wide and bit into it, closing her eyes as she chewed. Within minutes it too vanished.

All of a sudden, she froze and turned wide eyes up at him. "Merciful heavens," she spoke through the last bite of apple. "Where are my manners?" She quickly turned away.

Haydon reached over and gently pulled her chin toward him. Yellow-orange, fiery shadows pranced across her face. Her eyes refused to look up at him. "Rainee." He tilted her chin up. "It's okay. I won't tell anyone." Humor threaded his voice.

Her gaze flew to his, and he smiled. After a single moment, her lips tilted upward as well. Haydon stared at her lips, and then his eyes traveled to hers.

She blinked, and her gaze dropped to his mouth.

Haydon leaned slowly toward her and gently nudged her chin closer to him. Her soft skin under his fingers was intoxicating.

Her eyes slid shut, and their lips connected. Rainee's parted lips tasted like sweet apples. His mouth caressed hers and she returned his kiss with a sweet, innocent passion.

All the popping and cracking coming from the fire didn't even come close to all the sizzling and popping going on inside him.

Suddenly she pulled back and scooted away from him.

Why did that always feel like such a rip to his soul? "What's the matter?"

"I am sorry, but I cannot do this. As much as I want to, I just cannot." She shook her head.

"Do what? Kiss me?" He searched her eyes as if they held the answer, but all he saw was fear and pain. He reached for her hand, noticing the lacey gloves she always had on. The question of why she always wore them drifted over him. Another time he would ask. Right now he wanted, no needed, the connection to her again. He reached for her hands, but she tucked them under the blanket. Disappointment drifted over him like the smoke from the fire.

"There is something you need to know. And once you hear it, you will be sorry you ever kissed me."

Chapter Nineteen

Her heart had never hurt this badly before. Rainee stared into Haydon's bewildered face. He deserved to know the truth. And once he heard it, she feared he would no longer want anything to do with her.

"Haydon, I—I…" She drew in a long breath for courage and shifted her body toward his. "Remember when I first came here, and I told you to trust me that I had no choice but to place an advertisement? You need to know the real reason why I left and the truth about my family."

"I know what you're going to tell me, Rainee."

"You—you do?" She swallowed hard and stared at him. How could he possibly know?

"Yes. You placed the advertisement looking for a husband so you wouldn't have to marry that old man your brother sold you to like some worthless animal." His words spewed bitterness.

Rainee sucked in a sharp breath and slammed her hand against her chest. *Dear God, no. Ferrin must be at Haydon's ranch.* She swallowed the lock of air lodged in her throat. "Where—where is Ferrin now?" Her heart slowed to a crawl while she waited for his answer.

"He's in jail. Right where he should be."

Ferrin? In jail? She gulped. All sorts of scenarios dashed through her mind about what Ferrin must have done to land in jail. Each idea increased the dread inside her. "What happened?"

Haydon relayed what had transpired and how Ferrin had pulled a gun on them. Knowing what evil her brother was capable of, relief rained over her that no one had been seriously hurt. Or worse, killed.

"I am so sorry, Haydon." Her eyes met his. "I never meant for your family to get involved in my family's problems. I thought I had done a secure job of covering all my tracks so that he would never find me. I should have known better. When Ferrin sets his mind to something, he will do whatever it takes to achieve it. And right now, he is determined I shall marry Mr. Alexander." She shuddered at the very idea.

Haydon took her hands in his.

She stared down at their hands, relishing the strength and feel of his even through her lacey gloves. Her heart ached for what could never be.

"Rainee, you don't have to marry him. He can't make you."

"Yes, he can, Mr. Bowen. For he is cruel to his very soul, and he will stop at nothing to get his way. And there is nothing you, nor I nor anyone else can do about it." Her body had the scars to prove it.

So it was back to being called Mr. Bowen again. That didn't bode well.

She removed her hand from his.

He wanted to snatch it back, but he controlled the urge.

What did she mean there wasn't anything anyone

could do about it? The Civil War had ended the sale of one human being to another. "Of course you have a choice." His gaze sought hers. "You can stay and marry me."

Her eyes widened. "Marry you? But I thought you did not want to marry again."

"I didn't. Then I met you."

She faced the fire. The light from the flames danced across her lovely face, accentuating the glistening trail of tears trickling down her cheeks. Haydon slid his arm around her shoulders. He tucked her under his arm and pressed her head against his chest.

Smokey tossed a few more logs onto the fire. A look of compassion passed between the two men. Smokey jerked his head toward the bushes, a signal that he would give them some privacy. Haydon mouthed his thank you and Smokey slipped into the thick brush.

He positioned Rainee so he could see her face. Her eyes were downcast.

Haydon thumbed the tears from each cheek, then lifted her chin toward him.

With her eyes still closed, Haydon lowered his head, inching his lips toward hers. When their mouths touched, Rainee clutched a fistful of his shirt with one hand. They clung to each other. Their hearts beat as one as their kiss deepened. Salty tears trickled over his lips. Whether they were hers or his, he didn't know.

He wanted to pull her close, but the way they were seated made that impossible. Instead, he allowed his lips alone to get closer to her.

When his need to show her how much he loved her increased, he released her mouth and once again snuggled the side of her face against his chest. "Rainee. What would I do without you?" He struggled to calm his erratic breathing and noticed she was doing the same. They held each other tight for a long time.

Smokey slipped from the shadows, carrying a bed-roll.

He tossed several more logs onto the fire. Haydon shifted Rainee until he could see her face. A yellow-and-orange glow danced across her lovely features. Her eyes searched his with a yearning he could not describe. He wanted to kiss her again. To hold her forever. To shield her from the beast that waited to take her from him.

He pressed his lips against her forehead, lingering for several moments before he reluctantly withdrew his arms from around her. It was time to get some rest. "We'll talk more in the morning."

After helping her get situated by the fire, he lay opposite to her and watched her until she fell asleep.

As he drifted off to sleep, he determined that no matter how long it took, he would find a way to stop her brother from marrying her off to that old man. He had to. His heart depended on it.

Hours later, daylight filtered through Haydon's eyelids. He slowly opened his eyes to greet another sunny day. He scratched his neck and yawned, then looked toward Rainee.

The blanket she had used lay neatly folded on the ground.

Haydon sat up and scanned the area.

Smokey stepped into the clearing and headed toward him. "Miss Devonwood is gone again, boss."

He closed his eyes, then slipped his boots on and stood. "Where'd she go?"

"Her tracks lead that way." Smokey pointed down

the river. "I'm sorry I didn't hear her leave. I must have been more tired than I thought."

"Well, I did. I heard her moving about earlier, but I thought she was just going to relieve herself." Haydon snatched his hat up and plopped it on his head. "Listen, I don't want Mother worrying about us, so will you head back to the ranch and tell her what's happened? I'll go look for Rainee."

"Yes, sir, boss." Smokey bent down and hoisted his saddle over his shoulder.

"Smokey."

The older man faced him. "Yes, boss."

"Please stop calling me boss and sir. You're family, remember?"

Smokey just smiled and then proceeded to saddle his horse.

After Haydon snuffed out the fire, he hauled his saddle over his shoulder and saddled his horse. "God, please help me find Rainee, and keep her safe until I do." A sigh squeezed out of his heart and past his lips.

"Amen," Smokey added.

Rainee glanced over her shoulder before she stopped and leaned her back against a tree to catch her breath. Having traveled so far and so fast yesterday, every muscle in her body ached, and the blisters on her feet screamed with pain. She had no idea where she was or how far she had gone.

Last night, her fears of what Ferrin might do to the Bowens if she did not leave them had kept her from a good night's sleep. After all, he had already shot one of them. Worse was the understanding her brother had found her even though she and Jenetta had been so careful. On her journey here, she had even disguised herself as an old woman and had worn several other disguises to keep Ferrin off of her trail. Only at the last stage stop had she changed into her own clothing because she did not want to meet Haydon looking like a haggard old woman.

She still could not believe he had actually mentioned marrying her. It was the one thing she had wanted to hear since her arrival. But she knew that marrying him would put his life into jeopardy, and she could not stand to be the one putting a target on his back. He didn't understand what Ferrin was capable of. She pressed her lips together and sniffed. Choppy, short breaths were all she could manage as she silently cried, stumbling through the underbrush.

She had to keep going. The idea of being at her brother and Mr. Alexander's mercy was all the incentive she needed to force her body into submission.

Broken tree limbs crunched under her feet and the sound of water rolling over the river rocks echoed in her ears.

Coming around a bend in the river, Rainee stopped. In the distance, Indian men, women and children milled about. Knots of terror twisted in Rainee's stomach. She had heard stories about the savage Indians out West and how they brutally murdered and scalped white people. She touched her blond hair and fingered a loose strand. The spotted mule deer jerky she had eaten before her escape churned in her stomach. She pressed her hand against her mouth, gulping down her fear.

On unstable legs, Rainee backed up, then whirled, smacking hard into a wall of flesh. The pulse in her neck matched the rapid drumbeat coming from the Indians' campsite. She opened her mouth to scream but stopped when her trail of vision landed on Haydon.

"Rainee, why did you leave?"

She pressed her hand against her heart, willing it to calm down. Ignoring his question, she asked, "What—what are you doing here?"

"I came to take you home."

Rainee swung her head back and forth. "No! It is too great of a risk." She pointed toward the Indians. "I would rather be taken captive by those—those savages than go back and be forced into marrying that ogre."

Haydon threw his head back and laughed.

Rainee frowned. When he continued laughing, she slammed her hands on her waist and glared up at him. "And, pray tell, just what is so funny about that?"

"Those savages, as you call them, Rainee, are Nez Perce Indians. They're friendly."

"Well then, all the better for me. I shall go live with them."

"And just how will you communicate with them? Do you speak their language?" Humor waltzed through his eyes.

Glad he was finding this whole situation so funny, she planted her hands on her hips. The idea of going back and being forced to marry a man she did not love…a man old enough to be her grandfather…a man who was every bit as cruel as her brother was, there was nothing funny in that.

She whirled, placing her back to him. She did not know any Indian language. That fact caused her spirit to deflate. Now what would she do? Every time she ran, Haydon followed her, determined to take her back. She could not let that happen. Not with the threat of Ferrin nearby. No jail cell would hold him. That she was certain of.

"Rainee." Haydon's hands rested on her shoulders.

He circled her until she faced him. He clasped her hands in his. "Trust me. I meant what I said last night about you marrying me. And I promise I won't let him harm you or force you into marrying that man. Let's go back to the ranch and—"

"No!" Rainee ripped her hands from his, and one of her lacey gloves came off in the process. Her eyes widened in horror. She slammed her gloved hand on top of her naked one to cover the hideous scars.

Horrified by what he had seen in that one, short flash, Haydon gawked at the raised scars trailing up and down Rainee's hand and wrist, which he could still see although she tried mightily to cover them. Concern and compassion drove through him as he gently raised her hand off the one she covered. His stomach churned at the sight of the raised scars marring her small hand.

She yanked her hand back, and with shaky fingers she snatched the glove from him and rammed her hand into it.

"Rainee." He wanted to see her, but she turned from him. Red flooded her cheeks, and she slid her hands behind her back. "How did you get those scars?"

Rainee chewed on her lip.

Haydon waited for her to answer, but anger at the one who had done that to her boiled within him.

Finally, she whispered something, but he didn't hear what she'd said. "What did you say?"

"Ferrin." This time she spoke a little louder.

His fist clenched at his side and his blood ran hot. That man was even worse than Haydon had imagined. If Ferrin thought Haydon would let him anywhere near Rainee, the thug was sorely mistaken.

In that second, he made up his mind to marry her

as soon as possible. She may have come here to marry him out of convenience, but someday he hoped that convenience would turn to love. One thing was for sure, he vowed he would not fail her like he had Melanie. Haydon extended his hand toward her. "Come on." Contempt for her brother spewed through his voice.

Rainee jerked her head up and looked at him. "I am so sorry, Haydon. I know my hands are hideous," she blurted. "I never meant for you or anyone else to see them. But you jerked my hand so quickly the glove came off, and I could not get them hidden fast enough. I know they are grotesque. The ones on my back are even worse."

She was talking so fast Haydon had a hard time keeping up with her.

"My Aunt Lena was right. She said no one would ever want me because of them, but I—" Tears glistened in her eyes, and her shoulders rose and fell as the words died away.

Haydon stood there speechless. She actually thought he was offended by the scars and that no one would want her? And what did she mean by the ones on her back? Just how many beatings had she endured? He reached for her, but she stepped backward and bumped into a tree.

"I am so sorry. I should have never come here." Faster than a bolt of lightning, she shifted past him and took off running.

"Rainee, wait!" He bolted after her, barely dodging the branches. When he caught up to her, he captured her by the elbow and turned her toward him.

Tears streamed down her cheeks. "Let me go," she said through gasps of air. She tried to jerk free, but

Haydon clutched her forearms. "You are better off if I leave."

At that moment he could only be ashamed of his previous behavior toward her. All he had thought about was himself and what he wanted. He never once cared about why she had written the advertisement. Or why Jesse had responded to it.

Wanting to shield her from everything she had ever been through, he wrapped her in his arms, pressed her head against his chest and her body against his and cradled her.

Moisture from her eyes seeped through his shirt.

"Rainee, I'm so sorry."

Her body trembled and sobs racked her small frame.

"I'm not offended by your scars. I'm angry at Ferrin for doing this to you." Enraged was more like it. Any man who would hurt a woman like that, let alone his own sister, deserved to hang from the nearest tree.

"Then—then they do not bother you?" She pulled back enough to look into his face. The pain he saw there, mixed with a smudge of relief tore at his soul.

"No, sweetheart, they don't." He reached for her hands and tugged on her gloves, pulling them off.

Rainee blinked several times as she watched him remove her gloves. With the lightest touch, he ran his thumbs over the raised scars that covered her hands and wrists. His heart was weeping hard for her and what she had endured.

Rainee's eyelids dropped. She stood there like a frightened fawn ready to bolt but knowing there was no place to run.

Haydon struggled to keep back the tears burning the back of his eyes. He raised her hands and gently pressed his lips on them, kissing them. His tears dropped onto her marred flesh. "I'm so sorry, Rainee." His voice quavered. He kissed her hands again and again. "I'm so sorry for what you've had to endure." With each touch of his lips against her hands another tear fell. He pressed her tear-covered hands against his wet cheeks and cradled them there.

He heard her short intakes of breath and her silent cries. He tilted her chin upward and gazed down at her. His heart ached with the desire to comfort her, to hold her, to kiss away the uncertainty in her eyes. Haydon cupped her face with his hands and allowed the love and compassion he had for her to rain through his eyes without shame or restraint. He leaned his head down, and tenderly touched his lips to hers.

He raised his head and locked gazes with her. "I promise you, Rainee, that man will never hurt you again. You and I are getting married. Today."

Chapter Twenty

Still dazed at Haydon's second mention of them getting married, Rainee brightened but dimmed just as quickly. Her gaze fell along with her heart. She had never met a more tender, loving man in her life. "We need to talk." The huskiness in her voice matched Haydon's. She led him over to a large tree stump. She sat down, and Haydon lowered his bulky frame beside her and faced her.

Wishing she could blot away the confusion from his face, Rainee drew in a long breath to settle the words inside her. What she had to say was breaking her heart, but she wanted to do right by Haydon, so she reached down and pulled out the words buried inside her. "When I first came here, I was in desperate need to get away from Ferrin. No, let me back up a bit. I had already written to you—to Jesse—because of the severe beatings, but then I overheard Ferrin telling Mr. Alexander he had just bought himself a wife and how he would have his hands full with me. I quickly found Jenetta and told her. She and I packed a few things in the dead of the night, and I left. I stayed with a friend in Chicago until plans were made for my trip out here.

"But when I got here and discovered it was not you who had sent for me and that you did not wish to marry me, I panicked. I was so afraid Ferrin would somehow find me before we married that all I thought about was trying to figure out a way to get you to marry me." Her eyes snagged on his. "But since then, I have gotten to know you, and you are a very kind, caring person, Haydon Bowen."

He smiled.

"And that is why I cannot marry you."

His smile faded and his forehead wrinkled. "I don't understand."

"I cannot in good conscience marry you just to relieve myself of my family's burdens. Nor can I marry you knowing you never wanted to wed again, let alone marry someone you do not love. I cannot. No. I will not do that to you."

"You wouldn't be doing anything *to* me. You'd be doing it *for* me."

She tilted her head sideways. "Excuse me?"

Haydon reached for her hands. "I meant what I said last night. I *want* to marry you, Rainee. Not because I feel like I have to. Actually, my motive is a rather selfish one. Because you see, I do love you. And I can only hope that in time you can come to love me, too."

Hope ignited within her as she searched his eyes for the truth. Tenderness and love mirrored through his eyes and into hers. "Oh, Haydon. I already love you. I have for a long time. You are everything I want in a man. And much much more. But before I answer you, I do have one more thing that concerns me. It is the reason why I fled this morning."

Puzzlement darted across his face and landed in his eyes. "What's that?"

"I fear my staying here will...*has* already put your family in danger. You have seen what my brother is capable of. He does not like to lose. He and Mr. Alexander are very powerful and controlling men who will stop at nothing to eliminate anything or anyone who gets in their way. If Ferrin struck a bargain with Mr. Alexander, neither will stop until they get what they came for."

"You," Haydon interjected.

Rainee nodded.

"Well, sweetheart, if that's all that's stopping you from saying yes, then we have a wedding to plan. I have dealt with worse men than your brother. My brothers and I, and Smokey, are more than able to protect ourselves and our families from the likes of Ferrin. We've done it before, and we'll do it again. I won't lose you. And I know Mother and my family will agree. There is no way any of us will let you go. We all love you too much. So what do you say? Will you marry me?"

Rainee searched his eyes, seeing he meant every word he said. She dipped her head coyly and responded the only way she properly could. "Why, Mister Bowen," she drawled, "I thought you would never ask a third time...." She laughed, then frowned. "But are you sure that is what you want?"

In one swift motion, Haydon rose, pulled her into his arms and kissed her. When their lips parted, he whispered, "Does that answer your question?"

His lips found hers again. The intensity and love behind his kiss melted any remaining doubts Rainee had about his love for her.

With her heart racing like the wind, she pulled back and slowly stepped out of his arms. "So, now what?" she asked, her voice rasped with love.

He gathered her hand in his and led her toward Rebel.

"We have a wedding to plan. So let's head back to the ranch."

As they mounted the horse, sitting in front of Haydon, Rainee silently prayed, *God, please work everything out for Haydon and I to wed before Ferrin can stop us.*

Haydon reached around her, pulling her against his chest. She loved the feel of his arms around her. Loved the security they offered. She sighed. She may as well enjoy it while it lasted. For as soon as they reached the ranch, she was certain it would all come to an end. Ferrin would find a way to get to her before they could wed.

"Rainee." Haydon's breath tickled her ear. "You said the scars on your back are worse. What happened? Whatever possessed him to treat his own sister like that?"

Rainee licked her lips and swallowed. "Ferrin said I was in need of discipline because I was spoiled. Said I needed to be taught a lesson. So he put me to work. When something was not done to his satisfaction, I was punished. Ferrin would whip my hands for each watermark I left on the dishes or silver.

"I also had to haul wood to the firebox. It was back-breaking work, and we had servants to do it, but he informed me I was no longer a member of *his* household but a paid slave whose wages were a roof over my head and food.

"He forced the servants to pile wood in my arms until it reached my nose. If I dropped any on the way to the house, Ferrin would rip the back of my dress open and give me a lash for every piece I dropped." The memory of his beatings tore at her heart and mind, reopening cavernous wounds like the leather strip that had torn her flesh. She felt the pain of those beatings as if they had happened yesterday instead of months ago, but she refused to shed any more tears over them.

"Several times the beatings were so severe, I blacked out. It was as if he were punishing me for something more than watermarks and dropped wood. Ferrin said it was for my own good. That he needed to break my wild spirit. But as you have daily proof, you can see he did not break my spirit." She chuckled, but no humor accompanied it.

"If I ever get my hands on that man, I'll—" Haydon's chest vibrated with his throaty groan.

"If you put your hands to him that would make you like him. And you are nothing like him."

"It still makes me livid to think about what he did to you."

"It makes me sad." She shifted in the saddle. "I do not wish to talk about this anymore."

"I didn't think about how difficult it would be for you to relive what he did. I'm sorry. I should have never asked."

She laid her hand on his arm and patted it. "You have nothing to be sorry for." She tilted her head up at him, and he kissed her cheek.

They dismounted near the river to fill their canteens and to allow Rebel to get a drink.

"Rainee." Haydon took her hands in his. "I've been thinking. You've shared your past with me. Before we get married, it's only fair that I tell you something as well. And after hearing it, I can only hope and pray you'll still want to marry me."

"Nothing you could tell me would make me not marry you."

"I hope so."

He prayed God would help him to tell her all, no matter how ugly the truth was. "In Jesse's letter, did he tell you I was married before and that it's my fault my wife died?"

"No. He did not. But I cannot imagine it is your fault that she is dead."

"It is. Even though Melanie was warned ahead of time what it would be like and how hard it would be out here, she still agreed to move. And was even looking forward to it. When the reality of this land hit her, she ended up hating it and resenting me for bringing her here. I should have noticed all the signs sooner. But I didn't. I failed my wife, Rainee. I failed her in every way. And because of that failure, she ended up having an affair."

He turned, not able to bear looking at her, as he told her the awful truth, and he debated whether to take her back now and forget about marrying her or to continue. He decided he had to take the risk. He loved her too much. Plus she may as well hear all of the ugly, sordid details.

He faced her.

"The night she died, we got into a big argument. She said she wanted to go back East. I promised her that as soon as traveling weather permitted I would take her back. She said she wouldn't wait. She would leave right away with or without me. I forbade her to go, ordered her to wait. I should have never done that, knowing that as soon as I told Melanie she couldn't do something, she would do it out of pure spite."

He rubbed the back of his neck. "She left during the night on foot and I found her body the next morning at the base of a hill wrapped around a tree. I could see the trail of broken branches down the hill where she'd fallen." He shook his head. "I should have guarded my words more carefully."

Rainee laid her hand on his arm. "There is no way you could have foreseen her leaving, Haydon. What woman in her right mind would leave in the middle of the night out in this wilderness territory?"

He wanted to mention that she had, but he didn't. She was right. Most women wouldn't. And yet...

"If I hadn't gotten so angry and hadn't slept in the barn that night, I could have prevented her death. I would have heard her leave. I knew better. It's as if I killed her myself. I drove her away by being such a lousy husband. I'm so afraid I'll do the same to you. I failed her and I've already failed you. Last night I didn't even know you'd left. You could have fallen or been attacked by a wild animal." As if a rain cloud had burst open, tears poured from his eyes and drizzled down his face.

Instantly, Rainee's arms were around him, pulling him close and cradling him. He clung to her, pulling the love she offered into his soul.

"You are no more to blame for Melanie's death than I. Do you not see she made a choice to leave? As did I. Haydon, my love, you cannot stop people from making wrong choices. It is impossible for you to be with someone every second of the day and night. We all make choices every day. And we have to live with the consequences of those choices whether they be good or bad. Sometimes the consequences of our actions hurt the ones we love. Melanie's spitefulness and poor choice caused her death—you didn't."

Her words poured warm honey over his soul. She was right. Melanie did have a choice. For the first time since his wife's death, he found a glimpse of forgiveness for himself, knowing eventually Melanie would have left whether or not he was there.

He pulled back and looked into Rainee's eyes. "Thank you, Rainee. I've carried this guilt around for so long. The Lord told me I needed to forgive myself and to tear down the wall I'd built around my heart, to be open to love again. I'm not sure I could have done that without you, but now I'm so glad I did. I love you, Rainee." His lips parted and covered hers in one of the sweetest kisses he'd ever given and received. The weight of the past disappeared with his sigh of contentment.

When their lips parted, Rainee's eyes were shining. "There is just one more little thing." She reached into her pocket and brought out a yellowed piece of parchment.

Haydon's heart hitched when he saw the name scrawled there. Bettes. He looked at her, willing her not to say what he was afraid she might.

Her gaze stayed on the letter. "Jesse gave this to me yesterday. I do not know how long he had it in his possession." She laughed. "You never know with Jesse."

The center of Haydon's heart began to pang painfully. He saw nothing funny in this news.

Then her eyes captured his again, and there was mirth in them. "It appears in my absence Mr. Bettes found himself another bride. He said he has no use for my services."

The relief came out in a whoop as Haydon scooped her up and twirled her around. "Rainelle Victoria Devonwood, I do believe that's the best news I've heard in years."

She smiled as she lowered her lips to his. "I was hoping you would say that."

* * *

The closer they got to the ranch, the more a nervous fluttering filled Rainee's stomach. Thoughts of seeing either of the two men still sent chills of dread up and down her spine. She tucked herself farther into Haydon's chest, wanting to disappear into him.

As she and Haydon rounded the trees heading to the ranch, Rainee started trembling.

Haydon tightened his hold. "You have nothing to be afraid of, Rainee. I'll take care of you."

Rainee wanted to believe him, wanted it to be so regardless of the fantasy she had allowed to take root in her heart, but knowing her brother's determination, along with his uncanny knack of twisting things and making people believe the worst of lies, it would not surprise her if he and Mr. Alexander were at the ranch waiting.

The house came into view. Rainee expected to see Ferrin's horse along with the sheriff's. Instead, she saw Katherine leap from the porch swing and race toward them.

Haydon slid from his horse and reached up to help Rainee down.

The moment Rainee's feet touched the ground Katherine grabbed her and threw her arms around her. "Rainee, I'm so glad you're okay." She pulled back. "I've been so worried about you." She hugged Rainee again.

"I am so sorry I caused you concern, but I just had—"

"There's no need to explain. None at all." Katherine jerked back and clasped Rainee by the elbows. "You're here now. And there is no way that you are *ever* going back to that—that man again."

"That's right, Mother. Because—" Haydon joined his hands with Rainee's and flashed a luminescent smile her direction "—Rainee and I are getting married."

Katherine's gaze whipped to Haydon, then back at Rainee. She grabbed Rainee in an exuberant hug. "I knew God was in this." His mother released her and turned to collect Haydon in her arms. "Congratulations, son. I'm so happy, I could just cry." She pulled back. Squaring her shoulders, she ran her hands over her skirt and patted her hair. "Yes, well. It looks like we have a wedding to plan, now don't we?"

"We sure do." Haydon faced Rainee. "I'll need to send someone to get the reverend so we can get married right away. We can have a proper reception later on. Would that be all right with you?"

Before she had a chance to respond, Katherine blurted, "Surely we have time to make Rainee a dress and invite all our friends and neighbors, don't we?" Disbelief and disappointment flitted across Katherine's face.

"No, Mother. We don't want to take any chances."

"Katherine, I am sorry it has to be this way, but if we make haste and get married, then Ferrin will have to accept that I am legally wed to another. If we do not, I fear he will do something drastic, and I cannot marry that evil man, for he is far worse than my brother."

"Worse than your brother? In what way?" Katherine asked.

She raised her hands and showed them to Haydon and Katherine. "These are nothing compared to what Mr. Alexander did to his wife. At least I am still alive. I cannot say the same for the first Mrs. Alexander."

"Mrs. Alexander? What about her?" Haydon frowned.

"She died two years ago at her husband's hands. No one ever proved it, but Mother believed it to be so because Mrs. Alexander had confided to her the brutality of her husband. Mother offered her sanctuary in our home, but Mrs. Alexander feared what would happen to us if she accepted, so she refused Mother's help. Shortly after Mrs. Alexander shared her fears with Mother, the poor woman was found at the bottom of her stairs with a broken neck and bruises on her body."

Katherine gasped. "Oh, how awful."

"Mr. Alexander claimed her shoe had caught the hem of her dress. Mother wanted to tell the sheriff of her beliefs, but Father said they had no proof, so she needed to remain silent and that God would vindicate Mrs. Alexander's death. As you see, the man my brother sold me to has likely gotten away with murder."

"It's even worse than I imagined." Katherine looked up at Haydon with concern and determination.

Just thinking about her brother gave Rainee a case of the nerves. She scanned the area.

"What are you looking for?" Haydon asked.

She gazed up at him. "Ferrin."

"Ferrin? He's in jail."

"He very well may be, but you do not know my brother and what he is capable of." Rainee closed her eyes and swallowed the lump of dread before she captured Haydon's eyes again.

"There's no way I'm letting that man take you anywhere." Haydon spoke confidently, but Rainee knew even his confidence would not keep her safe if Ferrin was released from jail.

Rainee's breath hitched when Michael came around the corner. Before she saw his face, for a moment she feared it might be Ferrin.

Haydon put his arm securely around her shoulders. "Michael. I need you to run an errand for me."

"Sure. What do you need?"

"Rainee and I are getting married."

Michael's eyes brightened. "That's great. Congratulations."

"I need you to fetch Reverend James for me."

"Now?"

"Yes, now."

"Why the rush?"

"It's a long story, Michael. I don't have time to explain it. Will you run and get him for me?"

"Well, I would, but he's not here."

"What do you mean he's not here?"

Rainee's heart hitched in her throat. She wanted to know the answer to that question, too.

"When I went to town the other day, I ran into Reverend James. He said he had some business to attend to, something about a close relative who passed away and left everything to him. Anyway, he said he'd probably be back for our next gathering here in two weeks. I'm sorry, I forgot to tell you."

Rainee's stomach plummeted. Exhausted from running and all the emotional ups and downs of the day bore down on her. She needed to sit. She walked over to a handmade bench near the barn door and plopped down. The shade gave her a nice reprieve from the hot August sun.

Katherine joined her on the bench.

"Now what?" Rainee asked.

"Don't worry." Katherine patted her knee. "Haydon will think of something."

Rainee stared at Haydon as he talked with Michael.

Moment after moment slipped by, and to Rainee, each moment felt like an eternity.

Michael nodded then headed back around the barn and out of sight.

"What if you, Leah and Rainee hid out for two weeks?" Katherine suggested when Haydon walked up to them. "You could head over to The Eye of the Needle at *Coeur d'Alene*. There's a lot of narrow passages in those mountains where you could hide out. It would take weeks for Ferrin to find her there."

"That's a good idea, Mother, but I don't know how long Ferrin will be in jail, and from what Rainee said about her brother, I won't risk leaving you for two weeks and risk him coming back and hurting you."

"Smokey and Jesse will be here."

"They won't be near the house. They have to get the wheat in and take care of the hogs. No, I think it best if I send Smokey into town. I sent Michael to tell him to run in and talk to Sheriff Klokk to see how long Ferrin will be in jail and what can be done. After all, he did shoot Michael. That's attempted murder. Charges could be brought against him."

If only they *could* leave until Reverend James arrived, but Rainee knew Haydon was right. Leaving his mother and sisters unguarded would not be safe or wise. Nor would she ask him to do such a thing. Ferrin was too crafty a man. He could talk or manipulate his way out of any kind of trouble. She had seen him do it often enough. To keep this family from any further danger, there was only one solution. "Perhaps it would be best for everyone if I just took my leave."

In the blink of an eye, Haydon squatted in front of her and laid his hand on her arm. "No, it would not be best for everyone, and I know it would not be best for me."

"Or me," Katherine added.

"I love you, Rainee. And I will not lose you. Please don't do anything foolish and run off again. Promise me you won't." His eyes frantically searched hers.

Rainee knew he was remembering his wife and what happened to her when she had fled. As badly as she wanted to protect them all, she would not do that to him. She had been foolish enough to try it before. "I promise."

Relief pressed through his eyes. "Good." He stood and gazed down at her. "You look exhausted, sweetheart. Why don't you go inside now and get some rest?"

She nodded. "Yes. I am quite done in for, actually, and a nap sounds lovely. Thank you." She only hoped and prayed she would be able to sleep.

Haydon extended his hand to help her up. Before letting her go, his gaze bore into her. "Remember, you promised."

She held his gaze. "Yes, I did. So, please, do not make yourself anxious. I will not do anything foolish. I gave you my word, and I shall keep to it."

He nodded and gave her a quick peck on her cheek. "I need to go take care of Rebel. But I'll be back."

"Come on, Rainee." Katherine stood and looped arms with her. "I'll walk with you."

At the house, Katherine opened the door, and Rainee stepped inside the kitchen.

Leah turned from stirring a pot at the stove. "Rainee!" Leah wiped her hands on her apron and ran toward her, throwing her arms around her friend. "I'm so glad you're safe. I was so worried about you."

"Rainee!" A sleep-rumpled Abby barreled into her, nearly knocking her and Leah over. "I'm so glad those bad men didn't finded you."

Rainee knelt down, scooped Abby into her arms and hugged her. Soon, if everything worked out, this little girl would be her sister.

The next morning, Rainee woke up refreshed. Realizing the lateness of the hour, she made haste in getting dressed and heading downstairs. Haydon was the only one sitting at the table, and he had a coffee cup in front of him.

He stood when she entered, and she could not help but notice the relief on his face. He probably feared in spite of her promise that she would run away again. She did not blame him because she had not given him reason to trust her in that area yet.

He rose and gave her a kiss on her cheek. "Morning, sweetheart. Sleep well?"

"I did. Thank you. Where is everyone?"

"Michael and Jesse are out in the field. Smokey's finishing up a few chores before he heads in to talk to Sheriff Klokk, and Mother, Leah and Abby are out seeing the new baby kittens."

"Kittens?"

"Miss Piggy had kittens last night."

She did not even know the cat was expecting little ones. "I want to see them. Will you take me to them?"

"Mother left you a plate of food in the oven. Don't you want to eat first?"

"No. I want to see the babies first."

Haydon stood, chuckling. "You're as bad as Abby. She couldn't wait to see them either."

Rainee grinned. "No, I am as good as Abby."

He shook his head. "I give up."

They stepped out onto the porch. As they headed out to the barn, a chill settled over her.

She stopped, shivering in the warm morning sun. "Can you wait a moment? I need my wrap." She whirled, gathered her skirt and ran toward the house.

Near the back door of the house, she found her wrap hanging on a hook. When she reached for it, something covered her head and a hand slammed against her mouth, preventing her from screaming. She was suddenly yanked backward and her body slammed against a solid form.

Smothered by fear and the lack of air, Rainee jolted right and left. Her legs shot out, trying to connect with her kidnapper's legs. Someone grabbed her ankles in a strong grip, and she was powerless to move them. She twisted with all the strength she possessed, trying to break free, but the lack of air pressed the darkness in around her.

Chapter Twenty-One

Haydon walked into the barn. His mother and sisters were huddled over the kittens making a big to-do over them. "Well, is Miss Piggy letting you see them?"

Katherine stood and Leah and Abby squatted closer together. His mother looked around him. "Where's Rainee?"

"She ran back to the house to get her wrap. She should be along any minute now." He walked over to where Miss Piggy was and leaned over to count the kittens. Two white, three gray-and-white, and one black.

He stood and glanced toward the barn door. It shouldn't be taking her that long to get her wrap. His gut told him something wasn't right. "I'll be right back."

Dashing out of the barn, he scanned the area all the way until he ran up the porch stairs and into the house. "Rainee." He glanced around. When she didn't answer, he headed to the back porch where she kept her wrap. The door was standing wide open, and Rainee's wrap was lying half-inside and half-outside.

Haydon quickly stepped out of view of the door and went to the closest window. Careful to stay out of sight, he peered out.

His breath snagged. Two men were carrying Rainee between them. A sack covered her head, and she was twisting, squirming and kicking. Haydon immediately recognized Ferrin's expensive suit.

He needed to do something and fast. Neither man appeared to have a weapon on them. And Haydon didn't see any on their saddles either.

He ran to the front door, grabbed the rifle hanging above the door and headed toward the back porch, loading the gun along the way.

He made sure neither of the men were looking before he slipped out the back door and hurried behind the woodshed. He peered around the building, and his breathing stopped. Rainee was no longer moving; her body hung limp as a rope.

Time was running out.

Their backs were turned to him as they prepared to load her onto one of the horses.

Now was his chance.

Haydon stepped out from behind the outbuilding and cocked his rifle. "Put her down now, or I'll shoot!"

The old man dropped her legs and threw his hands in the air.

Ferrin yanked Rainee up against his chest. Her arms and legs flopped around like those of a rag doll.

Rainee's brother faced Haydon, his face filled with arrogance and spite. "Go ahead and shoot. But before you do, I'll snap her neck in two." He wrapped one arm around her neck.

"I wouldn't do that if I was you."

Haydon's gaze swung toward the sound of the voice.

Sheriff Klokk and five men stepped out of the trees with their rifles aimed at the two men.

Crazed fear flashed through Ferrin's eyes.

Sheriff Klokk pressed the tip of the rifle into Ferrin's back. "Let her go now, or you're a dead man."

Ferrin closed his eyes, then slung Rainee away from him, slamming her body onto the hard earth.

Anger blurred Haydon's vision. He rushed to Rainee and dropped to his knees beside her. He untied the knot holding the sack in place over her head and gently removed it. He placed his hands under her arm and back and pulled her into a sitting position. Her head swayed, hair going in all directions, and her arms hung wilted at her sides. "Come on, sweetheart, stay with me. Breathe."

Rainee moaned and coughed. Her hazy eyes rolled open. "Haydon?" she rasped. "What—what happened?"

"Your brother's what happened."

"What do you mean?"

"He tried to kidnap you."

Rainee stirred and glanced toward Ferrin. Never had Haydon seen such hatred and evil in a man's face.

"Is she all right?" the sheriff asked.

Haydon nodded.

Sheriff Klokk yanked Ferrin by the arm and handed him over to his deputy several yards away, then he strode toward Haydon.

"How did they get away?" Haydon glanced up at the sheriff.

Klokk raised his hat and swiped his sleeve across the moisture on his forehead. "I reckon when they realized they wouldn't be getting out of jail until the circuit judge came through, they hit my deputy over the head. When he came to, he told me what had happened. I knew just where to look for them because of Ben."

"Ben?" Haydon stopped. "What does he have to do with this?"

"Well, the way Ben tells it is, Devonwood here—" he yanked his chin once toward Ferrin "—heard about Ben's run-in with his sister in Prosperity Mountain. Ben's buddy told him where they could find him. Devonwood paid the guy to take him to Ben and then he hired Ben to find Miss Devonwood and bring her to him. Apparently Ben ran into you first and he figured he'd get even with you for getting him tossed out of town. But then Miss Devonwood rescued you, and, well, I guess you know the rest. Ben was so mad he didn't get paid that he spilled the beans on these two and told me where they were headed. Looks like it's a good thing we got here when we did."

With Haydon's aid, Rainee stood on shaking legs and looked her brother in the eye. "I do not understand, Ferrin. Why do you, my own brother, hate me so much?"

"I am *not* your brother." He spat on the ground.

"What—what do you mean?"

"I mean," he sneered, "you and I are related in name only. I was adopted."

Rainee could not believe what she was hearing. Never had she even suspected such a thing. "That—that cannot be true."

He snorted. "Well, it is. I overhead Father and Mother talking about how after years of trying to have a baby, how blessed they were to have adopted me from the orphanage. And how shortly afterward Mother discovered she was with child. That child was you."

A million centipede legs crawled up and down her spine as Ferrin stared at her with scorn and hate.

"Father favored you even in the end."

"That is not true. Mother and Father treated us equally."

"For once, you are quite right." He snorted. "Even in death they treated us equally." He laughed a laugh of the devil, and a mocking look of derision covered his face.

Nothing he said was making any sense. In fact, the more he talked the more confused she became. "I do not understand."

"Of course you do not. Do you want to know the real reason why I despise you?"

Did she? Could she handle the truth? She searched her heart for the answer and decided it would be better knowing than always wondering. She braced herself for the truth. "Yes, I want to know."

"The day Mr. Pennay came to the house to draw up Father's will, I snuck through the secret passageway and listened to their conversation. Most fathers leave everything to their son, but not ours. No. He could not leave out his precious Rainee." He said her name with such spite, it slithered over her ears like a slimy serpent. "The more I listened to him, the madder I became. Father stipulated that upon their death half of Father's estate went to you, and you would have equal say in running it. That meant everything I did I would have to come to you for your approval. Whoever heard of a man having to get a woman's approval? He showed his favoritism of you right up to the end."

"I had no idea."

"Of course you did not. Why do you think I encouraged you to stay home from the reading of the will? I am no dunce."

"I thought you were protecting me. I trusted you.

You made me believe Father had left nothing to me. Not even a dowry." She pressed her eyes shut as the pain of his lies and vicious beatings sliced her heart and soul in slow painful shreds. If only she would have thought to ask Mr. Pennay to reveal everything in her father's will when she contacted him about whether or not Ferrin was her legal guardian. But she had not. Her mind was too filled with fear and thoughts of running away. "To think I stayed there and bore your constant abuse when I could have taken my leave at any time."

"Pretty clever of me, don't you think?"

Rainee's heart crushed under the weight of his words. For it was all true. She had not imagined it. He really did hate her that much. "It all makes sense now. When we were younger, you were nice to me and then all of a sudden you started doing things to bring me harm. I now understand why you beat me. Why you ran off every suitor. You knew if I got married I would discover the truth about my inheritance. It had nothing to do with watermarks or dropping wood. You wished me dead." She leaned into Haydon as the truth of her words sunk in.

Ferrin sneered at her. "You are not as ignorant as I thought. And you are a whole lot tougher than I gave you credit for. That was my first mistake. My second was coming after you. But then again, I could not risk you coming back for your inheritance, now could I?" There was no remorse in his voice. Nothing but coldness. A coldness that chilled Rainee to the bone.

"You were finally rid of me, Ferrin. So why did you bother to come looking for me?"

"If it were not for old man Alexander here, I would not have bothered. I would have told the lawyer you were dead and then your part of the inheritance would have been mine. But Alexander threatened to kill me if I did not give him what was rightfully his."

"I paid you a small fortune, Devonwood," Mr. Alexander butted in. "I just knew you were pulling a fast one on me when you told me Rainelle was gone. Threatening you was the only way I could think of to get you to give me what was rightfully mine. I would have never followed through with my threat." Mr. Alexander's jowls wiggled with the fast movement of his head as his gaze darted between Ferrin and the sheriff.

"Do you expect me to believe that?" Ferrin looked at Rainee. "We both know the old man is capable of murder, do we not?" Ferrin sneered the look of Satan himself first at her and then at Mr. Alexander, who said nothing to deny it.

"I've heard enough," Sheriff Klokk interjected.

"As have I." She looked Ferrin in the eye. "I am sorry for you, Ferrin. But no matter what you have done to me, you will always be my brother and I shall always love you."

For a brief moment, his face softened, then just as quickly it turned to stone. "As far as I am concerned, I do not have a sister. I am still an orphan. I have no one in the world but myself." Hatred filled every word. He diverted his attention away from her.

Having scarce drawn breath the whole time, she filled her lungs and slowly exhaled. "I am so sorry you feel that way, Ferrin." She turned away from her brother and faced the sheriff. "What will happen to him?"

"Well, after the judge gets here, I reckon he'll hold a trial. I can almost guarantee he'll send these two away for quite some time."

Rainee nodded her ascent.

The lawmen handcuffed the two men and none-too-gently hoisted them onto the horses.

Haydon wrapped his arm around her. "Come on. Let's get you out of here." He led her toward the house.

Leah, Abby and Katherine were standing in front of the window, their anxious faces peering through the glass.

They disappeared and within seconds all three of them darted out the back door and took turns hugging Rainee and telling her how much they loved her. Their love warmed her.

Rainee looked back at her brother. The cold look he sent her saddened her.

As they led him and Mr. Alexander away, she faced Haydon, who looked down at her with concern.

He brushed at her hair, which had come down in all the ruckus. She did not bother to straighten it. Even her mother would understand why. His hands slid down her shoulders to her arms. "I'm so sorry, Rainee." He pressed her head into his chest. His lips covered hers, smothering her with even more warmth.

When the kiss ended, Rainee drew back and looked Haydon in the eye. "Haydon, I must go away."

He jerked back. Rainee staggered but his strong arms steadied her. "What do you mean you have to leave?"

Abby threw her little arms around Rainee's legs and hugged her tight. "I don't want you ta go."

"Me either," Leah and Katherine said in unison.

Rainee picked Abby up and held her. "No, no, it is not what y'all think. You are not getting rid of me that easily." She looked at their shocked faces and smiled. "I shall only be gone a short time."

"Yay!" Abby gave Rainee's neck a tight squeeze, then squirmed until Rainee set her down. Off the little girl scampered, disappearing around the corner of the house.

"We need to follow Abby's example and leave you two alone." Katherine smiled, hooked her arm through Leah's, and the two of them walked away.

"You're not going back to…" Haydon frowned. "Just where are you from, anyway?"

She smiled. "Little Rock, Arkansas."

"Well, you're not going back there without me."

She tilted her chin sideways and frowned. "How did you know where I was going?"

"Well, I figured with Ferrin in jail, you would want to go back to make sure your parents' place is being taken care of."

Stunned by his perception, she only nodded.

"Why don't we get married first and we'll both go? I'd love to see where you grew up."

"What a delightful idea. I would love to show you my family's plantation. It is quite lovely." They smiled into each other's eyes.

Haydon bent and his mouth covered hers in a long lingering kiss, melting her heart into a liquid pool of love. With his lips still against hers, he whispered, "Rainelle Victoria Devonwood, you'd better get busy planning that wedding. And the sooner the better."

Rainee giggled under the light pressure of his lips and silently agreed.

Epilogue

Before Rainee had left Little Rock, she and Jenetta had hidden her mother's beautiful silk wedding gown, long white gloves, single-strand necklace with matching earrings and one other precious treasure in her trunk, her mother's wedding ring. Soon to be hers.

Mother would not be here today to witness her marriage, but wearing her dress would help Rainee feel as if she were.

Sitting in front of Leah's bedroom mirror, Rainee watched Katherine remove the last cloth strip from her hair.

"Oh, Rainee, you look so beautiful." With her hands on Rainee's arms Katherine locked gazes with her in the mirror. "My dear, I know I can never take the place of your mother. No one can. But I want you to know I love you like a daughter, and I would be honored if you would call me Mother."

"You mean that?" Rainee swallowed the tears clogging her throat.

"Of course I do."

Rainee's heart could scarcely contain one more exciting thing. But contain it, it must. For she had something even more exciting awaiting her—a compassionate, loving, handsome mail-order groom.

* * *

After a bath and a shave, Haydon dressed. The formal black jacket and pants looked out of place in the rugged Idaho Territory, but he wanted Rainee to have the wedding she deserved. Although she cared nothing about the high-society frippery, he knew this one time she would appreciate it.

On the way to the backyard where the guests were already gathering, he met Jesse.

His brother whistled. "Don't you look nice?" Jess fell in step with him.

"So do you." Haydon glanced at Jesse's scar. Even though he'd asked Jess's forgiveness, every time he saw it remorse and shame for his stubborn selfishness knifed his spirit. He turned, stopping them both.

"Something wrong?"

"Nothing's wrong. I just wanted to thank you for sending for Rainee. If you hadn't, I wouldn't be getting married today. Thanks, Jess." He grabbed his brother in a bear hug.

"You're welcome. Now let me go. I have a special job to perform, and I don't want to be late. I'm giving the bride away, remember?"

Rainee slowly descended the stairs like a proper young lady, knowing her mother would be so proud.

At the bottom step, Jesse reached for her hand and looped her arm through his. "You ready?"

She nodded. "Jess. Thank you for answering my advertisement. If you had not, I would have never met Haydon."

Jesse chuckled. "I heard those same words from Haydon a few minutes ago." He patted her hand. "You're welcome."

She looked at her mother's long white gloves and marveled at how they covered her hideous scars. Scars that were a sign of what God's great mercy had delivered her from.

"Now, let's go get you two hitched," Jesse said.

Outside, Rainee's gaze locked on Haydon already standing by the preacher.

She and Jesse strolled down the aisle between the rows of benches, smiling. Her smile grew as she gazed on Katherine, Leah, Abby, Hannah and her newborn baby Tomas, Michael and Smokey. When they reached Haydon, Jesse handed her over to him and with a wink whispered, "Here's your order."

"Best one I ever got too," Haydon whispered for her ears only.

Her heart and lips grinned.

"Dearly Beloved, we are gathered together to join this man and this woman in the bonds of holy matrimony. If there be any just cause why these two should not be joined, speak now or forever hold your peace."

A loud grunt came from the barn area. Rainee's gaze swung that way. A hearty laugh rose from her. Good thing Mother was not here to witness it. But then again, even Mother might laugh at the sight before Rainee.

Ears flapping like an upset hen, Kitty headed straight for them at a fast trot.

Michael and Smokey leapt up and tried heading her off, but Kitty dodged them, racing around the festivities until the sweet little beast ended up at Rainee's side. Without touching Rainee's gown, Kitty sat, ooooing with contentment.

Laughter filled the ranch yard.

Rainee looked at Haydon and laughed.

His mouth hung open, his eyes were fixed on the pig and he was shaking his head.

He looked at Rainee. "Sorry about that, sweetheart."

Her shrug was accompanied by another laugh. "Do not be sorry. Kitty is family, and now she is an honorary bridesmaid." She winked at Haydon, then faced the preacher. "Please continue, Pastor James. Kitty has no objections and neither do I."

* * * * *

Dear Reader,

I hope you enjoyed reading *The Unexpected Bride* as much as I enjoyed writing it. When I discovered there was literally a place informally called Hog Heaven, I had to write a story about it. I've always enjoyed pigs and their cute, loveable, inquisitive personalities. Also, because I'm a huge Jane Austen fan and a lover of Southern culture, I wondered what it would be like to combine the two. The result was Rainee—a woman who prayed and followed the Holy Spirit's guidance and did not allow her faith to waver even in the midst of adverse, questionable circumstances. Haydon, however, had his own agenda and wasn't open to what God was trying to do in his life. I think of how many times I, too, have done that and missed out on a blessing because of it. My hope is that all of us will see the importance of seeking the Holy Spirit's guidance and that we'll trust Him even when it's the hardest thing to do, and even when things make no sense, we'll trust Him anyway. I love hearing from my readers. You can write me at christianromancewriter@gmail.com or you can visit my website at www.DebraUllrick.com.
God bless you and yours.

Debra Ullrick

QUESTIONS FOR DISCUSSION

1. When faced with life's challenges, what is the first thing you do?

2. Rainee prayed and earnestly sought the Lord about her decision to place an advertisement and whose response she should accept. Yet, when she arrived at her destination and nothing went as planned, it appeared she hadn't heard from the Lord. Have you ever had this happen? Did you continue to trust God in spite of the circumstances?

3. Haydon blamed himself for Melanie's death and used that as a shield from ever falling in love again. So when love came to him, he turned it away. Have you ever blamed yourself and carried the guilt of another's actions? If so, how did you overcome it?

4. Was Haydon wrong to carry the guilt of Melanie's poor choices? What should he have done instead?

5. Holding on to unforgiveness, even against ourselves, keeps us from moving forward. Can you think of an example of this in your own life? Explain.

6. The Bible says that man looks on the outward appearance, but God looks at the heart. Rainee was taught a lot of rigid rules based mostly on outward appearances, and she rebelled against them. Do you think she was wrong? Why or why not?

7. Haydon judged Rainee based on her outward appearance, her apparel, and compared her to Melanie because of it. He almost let the love of a sweet, generous-spirited woman slip away because of it. Have you ever avoided getting to know someone because of their outward appearance? What was the result?

8. Rainee risks her life to save a fellow human being. Would you? Why or why not?

9. Rainee is told that no one would want her because of her scars. Do you know anyone who feels this way either from physical or emotional scars? What would you tell them?

10. Jesse prayed about answering Rainee's advertisement. He sent for her without Haydon's knowledge. Do you think he should have consulted Haydon first? Or was Jesse right to go ahead with his plan even though he knew it would make his brother angry? Explain.

11. Have you ever had to do something you knew the Lord was asking you to do, knowing it would probably stir up a hornet's nest? What was the result?

12. Ferrin held bitterness and jealousy in his heart against Rainee for years. Who do you think suffered the most, Rainee or Ferrin? Why?

13. Was Rainee right to forgive Ferrin and continue to love him even though he abused her and showed

no remorse for his actions? What would you do if you were Rainee, and why?

14. Haydon's acceptance of Rainee's scars helped her to heal. Do you know anyone who has inward or outward scars that are in need of healing? What would you say to them if you got the chance?

15. What lesson did you take away the most from this story and why?

INSPIRATIONAL

Inspirational romances to warm your heart & soul.

Love Inspired.

HISTORICAL

TITLES AVAILABLE NEXT MONTH

Available June 14, 2011

GOLD RUSH BABY
Alaskan Brides
Dorothy Clark

MARRYING THE PREACHER'S DAUGHTER
Cheryl St.John

THE WEDDING SEASON
Deborah Hale & Louise M. Gouge

THE IRRESISTIBLE EARL
Regina Scott

REQUEST YOUR FREE BOOKS!

2 FREE INSPIRATIONAL NOVELS
PLUS 2
FREE
MYSTERY GIFTS

Love Inspired.

HISTORICAL
INSPIRATIONAL HISTORICAL ROMANCE

YES! Please send me 2 FREE Love Inspired® Historical novels and my 2 FREE mystery gifts (gifts are worth about $10). After receiving them, if I don't wish to receive any more books, I can return the shipping statement marked "cancel". If I don't cancel, I will receive 4 brand-new novels every month and be billed just $4.24 per book in the U.S. or $4.74 per book in Canada. That's a saving of at least 23% off the cover price. It's quite a bargain! Shipping and handling is just 50¢ per book in the U.S. and 75¢ per book in Canada.* I understand that accepting the 2 free books and gifts places me under no obligation to buy anything. I can always return a shipment and cancel at any time. Even if I never buy another book, the two free books and gifts are mine to keep forever.

102/302 IDN FDCH

Name	(PLEASE PRINT)

Address	Apt. #

City	State/Prov.	Zip/Postal Code

Signature (if under 18, a parent or guardian must sign)

Mail to the **Reader Service:**
IN U.S.A.: P.O. Box 1867, Buffalo, NY 14240-1867
IN CANADA: P.O. Box 609, Fort Erie, Ontario L2A 5X3
Not valid for current subscribers to Love Inspired Historical books.

Want to try two free books from another series?
Call 1-800-873-8635 or visit www.ReaderService.com.

* Terms and prices subject to change without notice. Prices do not include applicable taxes. Sales tax applicable in N.Y. Canadian residents will be charged applicable taxes. Offer not valid in Quebec. This offer is limited to one order per household. All orders subject to credit approval. Credit or debit balances in a customer's account(s) may be offset by any other outstanding balance owed by or to the customer. Please allow 4 to 6 weeks for delivery. Offer available while quantities last.

Your Privacy—The Reader Service is committed to protecting your privacy. Our Privacy Policy is available online at www.ReaderService.com or upon request from the Reader Service.

We make a portion of our mailing list available to reputable third parties that offer products we believe may interest you. If you prefer that we not exchange your name with third parties, or if you wish to clarify or modify your communication preferences, please visit us at www.ReaderService.com/consumerschoice or write to us at Reader Service Preference Service, P.O. Box 9062, Buffalo, NY 14269. Include your complete name and address.

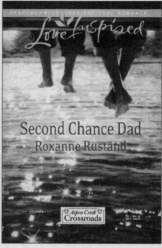
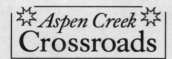